MIMESIS

Eric Sipple

Cover art by Kring Demetrio

ISBN: 0-9898136-2-2
ISBN-13: 978-0-9898136-2-4

This one's for Gino
the first writer I knew

Act One

Just Out Of Sight

Chapter One

SAMANTHA LIVED FOR the sound of the starting pistol. She was meant for that moment, to leave her mark and feel the soft, artificial track give way beneath her. The race was where she belonged. Not waiting, motionless, at the last leg of a relay. Not trapped while her teammates fell behind, fumbled the baton, lost the battle before she could join it. Samantha wasn't born to stand still. Stillness was death.

Ferris Ashley, third leg, rounded the final turn. Her grip on the baton was weak and slipping, and the other runners were pulling ahead. Samantha's opponents sprang forward and caught their passes. As Ferris approached and Samantha went into motion, what came before ceased to exist. The feel of the aluminum baton, warm and a little slick with Ferris' sweat, wasn't as satisfying as the starting pistol, but it meant the same thing. Win if you can.

When Samantha ran, there was nothing but the *push*. It was always there, just over her shoulder. She'd felt its pressure for as long as she could remember. It had been with her since the day she first ran, ready for her to stumble, to slow, to falter. The push was fast. Faster than the other runners. Faster than everyone but the girl who'd spent her life keeping ahead of it. Samantha didn't race her opponents. She didn't run for her coach, or for scholarships, or the thrill of victory. She ran not to be caught.

Two of Samantha's opponents fell behind before they knew what was happening. She passed the leader with ten meters to spare and crossed the finish line alone. The push would have to settle for the losers.

If there had been a crowd, it might have gone wild.

The field house at Sheffield High had been built in the 1950s, renovated in the 70s, left untouched through the 90s, and given a thorough repainting during Samantha's sophomore year. The plumbing barely leaked and the lockers closed if you slammed them hard enough. It had charm. Most days, it even had hot water.

Samantha changed into a pair of jeans and a faded team t-shirt faster than most of the others could get their shoes off. There was no time to waste. She walked halfway to the door before realizing she'd thrown her track clothes in her locker. They'd never get washed before her next meet if she left them. Samantha sighed and darted back, head down to deter anyone from talking to her. She snatched her clothes out of the locker and stuffed them into a red Hello Kitty duffle (a gift from her mom, who didn't realize Samantha was both too old *and* too young for it) and waved to Ferris on her way out. The sound of the metal door closing behind Samantha should have been a relief. Would have been, too, if there wasn't someone waiting for her outside.

"What's the rush, slut?"

Krista Shaw — 5 feet, 8 inches, and 140 pounds of unfiltered disdain for humanity — leaned against the field house wall with a cigarette in her right hand and a half-empty bottle of water in her left. Two smoldering butts lay at her feet. She'd been here a while. Samantha set the duffle on the ground and gave Krista a quick hug.

"You're smoking again," Samantha said.

"Hey, I promised Evan I'd quit," Krista said, and dropped the cigarette beside the others.

Krista's boyfriend Evan ran for Blackhawk, one of the other schools at the meet. Krista hated sports, yet she always ended up dating athletes who'd drag her into the bleachers to cheer them on. Samantha wished she'd make things easier on herself and date musicians.

"Want to walk me to my car?" Samantha asked.

Krista waited for Samantha to pick up her bag before stepping into the grass beside her. The white cement-block field house sat at the opposite end of the football field from the parking lot. There was no path away from the field house, but the grass between it and the field was well kept. They headed in the direction of the mostly empty bleachers.

"You and Evan doing something today?"

"Nope. He's taking the bus back to Blackhawk and going to paintball. Ferris wants to hit up some vintage shops. You coming?"

Samantha shook her head. "I have plans."

Krista grabbed Samantha's arm and pulled her to a stop. "What plans?"

Samantha didn't need this. She was already late, and way too tired to be evasive. Direct but vague would have to do. "I'm picking Danica up from camp."

"For real? You're blowing us off for her? Ferris'll love that."

Samantha pulled her arm away. "Krista."

"What is it today, bug photography?"

Samantha couldn't afford to get defensive. Annoyed was fine, but angry? Angry would mean questions. Questions bad. Questions very bad. "Yes, Krista. Bug photography and haiku."

Krista rolled her eyes. Something in the bleachers caught Samantha's attention. No, not something. Someone. A guy. A maybe possibly cute guy who was definitely looking *right at her*. Samantha turned away as soon as she noticed.

"What was that? What happened?" asked Krista.

"Is someone looking at me?"

"Someone? Who?" Krista looked over Samantha's shoulder, narrowed her eyes, and smiled. "Oh, he's not just looking, girl."

"What? What?"

Samantha chanced another look. Whoever-he-was cute guy was walking towards her. This was not happening. Samantha turned back to Krista, hoping he wouldn't bother her if she looked busy with her friend. Except Krista wasn't there. She was gone, headed to the parking lot, too far to catch without running. *Oh, the bitch*!

"Hey," cute guy said from behind her.

Samantha turned, hoping to see something off-putting — a cocky smile, a previously unseen hairy mole — to make this easy. No luck. He had dark, thick hair that covered the top of his ears, olive skin, and a sort of sweet, lopsided smile. He looked a little nervous, but only a little.

"Hi," Samantha said.

"Hey. I mean, I'm Alex."

"Samantha."

"I know," Alex said, then quickly added, "I saw you race. And we're in class together."

"Right." Samantha tried to place Alex's face. He looked familiar, but she had no idea what class they shared. She almost pretended to recognize him, but worried it might send the wrong signal.

"I'm sorry, you've probably got to get going, right?" Alex asked after a long silence.

"Yeah, you know. Things to do."

Alex looked in the direction of the parking lot. Cautious, he asked, "Plans with your friends?"

"Yep, with friends," Samantha lied. It would have been kinder to tell him the truth, that it didn't matter if he was cute or sweet. There was someone waiting for her. Samantha couldn't afford that kindness. The best thing for both of them was to chase him off. "So, was there something you wanted? I really need to get going."

Alex didn't respond right away. He stood there, eyes on Samantha, like he wanted to say something and couldn't decide what. Finally, he shook his head. "Nah, it's cool. I just wanted to say hi. Good to meet you."

"Thanks."

Alex didn't say goodbye. He spun on one foot and marched back to the bleachers. Samantha frowned. He *was* sort of cute. There were only so many times she could turn away the cute ones before someone asked why.

Samantha ran for her car before anyone else could stop her. Danica was waiting.

~

If not for the late afternoon clouds, it would've been a perfect day. Not warm, but just sunny enough to lose the hoodie. Danica was sick of hoodies, sweatshirts, and jackets. It was March. Was a warm day too much to ask for? Still, the second weekend as counselor for the United Presbyterian Church of Sheffield's Super-Awesome Jesus Fun Camp (Danica could never remember its official name) was going better than the first. No nosebleeds, no allergy attacks, and only one sobbing fit over a dropped popsicle. There were worse things than needing to put on

Eric Sipple

the hoodie, even if it hadn't been washed in months and reeked of her mom's cigarettes.

Camp had ended a half hour before, and all but three people were gone. Pastor Fresh, who was still cleaning up. Craig, whose mother hadn't showed up on time to anything in years and was even later than usual. And Danica, who really needed Fresh and Craig to get the hell out before Samantha arrived.

"Have fun today, Craig?" Danica asked.

Craig nodded.

"What did you like best?"

"Lots of things," he said. Craig was ten years old and never had much to say. At least, not to Danica.

"Okay," she said. "My favorite part was the swimming."

"You didn't swim."

"Nope. I napped while the rest of you did."

Craig stared at her for a moment, then nodded in approval.

"Danny boy!" Pastor Fresh shouted. He was carrying the last of the plastic tubs out to his Explorer one-handed. The tub swung into his leg with every step. "You're still here?"

"I'm waiting with Craig."

Fresh set the tub on the table. "Where's your mom, buddy?"

"Late again," Craig said.

"Later than usual. She needs a watch or something."

"She has a cell phone."

"You want me to call her?" Fresh asked.

"I mean it has a clock. She doesn't need a watch."

Danica turned her head to hide her smile when Fresh forced out one of his fake laughs. The fake ones were *really* fake.

"Good one, dude. Good one. Okay, so, Danica, you

8

want to get out of here while I wait with Craig?"

"I can wait with him."

"I don't know," Fresh said, rubbing his chin. It was one of those pretending-to-think gestures he used when he'd already made up his mind. It probably worked great on preschoolers.

The sound of tires crunching on gravel cut Fresh off. Danica put her hands on her thighs and squeezed so hard her fingernails almost broke skin. This could be a disaster if that was Samantha's Accord. Or, at best, definitely, absolutely weird and awkward.

It wasn't the Accord. It was Craig's mom in her pickup truck. Craig slid off the bench without a goodbye and ran to the car. Fresh waited until Craig closed the door to lift the plastic tub back off the table.

"You need a ride, Danny boy?"

"Nope."

"Want me to wait until yours shows up?"

One reliable thing about Fresh: he didn't want to stay unless his job demanded it.

"No, I'm good," Danica said.

Fresh nodded and threw the bin into the back of the Explorer. Danica waited on the park bench until his truck was out of earshot, then slipped back into the cabin to get changed.

Unlike Craig's mother, Danica didn't have a cell phone. What she had was a yellow Swatch that Mom had given her for Christmas. When Samantha's Accord finally rounded the corner into the parking lot, Danica had been staring at the watch's exposed, multicolored gears for twenty-one and a half minutes.

Danica slid off of the picnic table before remembering she was wearing nothing but a bathing suit and a hoodie. She pulled the hoodie down as far as she could. Why hadn't she put her pants back on?

Samantha grabbed a duffle out of the car and shut the door and waved with her free hand. "Hey!"

"Hey," Danica replied.

"I need to get changed. The bathroom's in the kitchen, right?" As she spoke, Samantha looked Danica up and down.

Danica nodded and yanked hard on the bottom of her hoodie. She knew it was stupid to feel so exposed. What did she expect when she agreed to go swimming? Samantha met Danica's eyes again and smiled, then sprinted into the camp's main building. That was it. No, "Sorry for being late," or even, "Nice legs." Just, "Hey, I need to get changed," and a once over.

Samantha re-emerged from the cabin in a teal two-piece bathing suit with black trim. Long, sandy hair ran down her shoulders to her mid-back. Samantha's arms and legs were a shade darker than the pale skin of her stomach after weeks of track. She was tall and thin, with stupidly long, muscular legs and a flat stomach that made Danica want to leave her hoodie on for the rest of her life. Danica felt her own one-piece suit riding up, a reminder that it *barely* fit.

"So? Are we going?" Samantha asked.

"That's it?"

"What do you mean, 'That's it?'"

"You barely said hi," Danica said, "and you were really late. I thought you were blowing me off."

Samantha dropped the towel on the seat of the picnic table, squared up to Danica and stepped very, very close. Danica was at least five inches shorter than Sam, but with the slight slope of the ground they were nearly eye to eye.

"How late was I?"

"Almost an hour," Danica said, her voice low.

"That's a lot."

Danica nodded.

"I should have apologized, huh?"

Again, Danica nodded.

Samantha leaned forward and pressed her lips against Danica's. It took Danica an awkward second to realize she was being kissed. When they finally pulled apart, Samantha touched Danica on the cheek.

"Sorry, Danny."

"It's fine," Danica said, this time so quietly she wondered if she'd done more than move her lips.

"The meet ran late, then some guy made a pass at me."

"Some guy?"

"Alex, I think. Do you know him? Anyway, he chased Krista off before she could ask what we were up to, so it wasn't all bad."

There were only two rules when it came to their relationship. Avoiding questions was rule number two. Questions were dangerous. It was too easy to get caught in a lie. Better not to give anyone the chance to ask in the first place.

Rule one was more direct. Don't get caught. For the love of God, do not ever get caught.

Samantha smiled and pulled on the zipper of Danica's hoodie. "Are you going to take that off so we can swim, or what?"

Danica took a step away and turned her back. Wearing a bathing suit was bad enough without seeing the disappointment on Sam's face at how very *not* flat her stomach looked in it. Samantha leaned over Danica's shoulder as the hoodie came off and whispered, "You look amazing. Stop being weird."

No one had ever told Danica she looked amazing. Why would they? There was nothing *amazing* about Danica, especially not how she looked. Yet with

Samantha's breath on her neck and hands on her hips it almost felt real. She leaned into Samantha and wished she'd still feel that way tomorrow, knew she wouldn't, didn't care.

Samantha grabbed Danica's hand and pulled her through the grass to where a small pier jutted out into the cool water of Sheffield Lake. The park was a large bowl with the lake at the center. The only break in the steep hills surrounding them was the narrow valley of the creek that flowed out of the park. Between camps and youth group gatherings, Danica knew every trail here by heart and had seen the park from every angle. The view from the pier still hadn't gotten old.

At the end of the dock, Sam kissed Danica again, hard this time. "Ready to swim?"

"The kids said the water's pretty cold today. We don't have to."

Sam put a hand on Danica's chest and shoved. Shoved her, Danica, backwards into the bracing water. No, bracing was an understatement. The water was *cold cold cold*. Danica went in butt first. The lake was deep and calm. There was no danger of hitting a rock (despite the dire looking **No Diving** signs, complete with head-on-rock iconography) or being dragged away by an undertow. Still: *cold!* Danica shouted obscenities into the water that rose to surface in bubbles of air. Samantha pushed her in! *She pushed her into the water!* Danica *hated* swimming! She was only doing this for Sam, and the jerk *pushed her into the water!*

A hand closed on Danica's. Smooth, delicate fingers slid between her own. The hand was warm, the grip strong. It pulled Danica gently upward. Danica's head broke the surface and she felt a final squeeze before the hand released her. Samantha could be sweet for such a jerk. Danica whipped her hair back and wiped the water out of her eyes.

"I can't believe you did that!"

Samantha laughed — but not from beside her. From the pier. She was still on the pier. Totally dry. Sam wasn't, and hadn't, been in the water. Danica spun left, then right. Nothing. No one else. She was alone.

"What's wrong?" Samantha asked.

Danica kicked her legs out, expecting her foot to strike something or someone. Again, nothing. "That wasn't funny."

Samantha jumped into the water. Other than a single sharp scream when she broke the surface, she didn't complain about the cold. Samantha waded to Danica and pulled her close. The warmth of Samantha's body against hers was a welcome relief from the lake's chill. Samantha met Danica's eyes and said, very seriously, "It was a little funny."

Danica would have laughed if Samantha hadn't chosen that moment to kiss her. Their hands touched, and Danica knew without a doubt that Samantha was not who'd pulled her to the surface. There was no one else it could be, either. No way someone could stay underwater that long. She had to have imagined it. There had been no hand. They were alone. Alone was the only way Samantha and Danica worked.

Real or not, the sensation of the touch lingered. Its warmth had been more than physical. For a moment, Danica had felt something she hadn't with anyone, not even Samantha. She felt needed.

Danica imagined the hand finding hers again as she kissed Samantha in the cold, cold water.

Chapter Two

ALEX PASSED SAMANTHA'S locker every morning. They shared a class — 4th period trigonometry — and sat three tables apart at lunch. Yet, for months, Samantha might as well have been invisible to him. It was nothing personal. Alex hadn't been himself in a long time. Not since the funeral he couldn't think about, and the long drive to his father's house in Sheffield that followed. He'd spent half of junior year drifting through hallways and classrooms, handing in assignments he couldn't recall, seeing the same blank faces on all of his classmates. Alex went to school because it was expected. He joined the baseball team because it was easier than explaining why he'd rather stay home. Habit and routine were all Alex had. It didn't matter who was in his class, whose locker he passed, who ate lunch three tables away.

And then, one morning before baseball practice, Alex saw Samantha run.

He'd arrived an hour early, as usual. Alex needed the time alone to survive a day with the team. The sun was dull and red in the sky, the lawn covered by a cool shimmer of dew. He walked circuits of the school through the lawn and left dark patches of crushed blades in his wake. On his tenth lap (counting helped, kept him focused), Alex realized he was no longer alone. Shouts echoed up from the football field below. Confused, curious, he followed the sidewalk to the edge of the hill.

There were at least two dozen people on the field. Some were laying out equipment: javelins, shot puts, and discuses. Others stretched themselves into painful-looking shapes. Alex sat as a cluster of runners in shorts and bright yellow sneakers finished a slow warm-up lap around the field. Years ago, before baseball coaxed him onto the pitcher's mound, Alex had thrown shot put and run a feeble 1600m dash. He missed it a little.

The track cleared. Four girls took their marks at the starting line. Alex noticed her as soon as she went into motion. The others ran. She moved like something was pushing her forward, her feet struggling to keep up as her body rushed ahead. Though he'd never noticed her (or at least never *noticed* noticing her), Alex somehow knew her name was Samantha Rowland. Quiet in class but always ready with the answer if called upon, rarely without a crowd surrounding her like guards on castle walls, never smiling unless she knew someone was looking. Alex knew all of this as soon as he saw her run. The details, locked away behind the fog of the last year, were dragged out by whatever force pushed Samantha down the track.

Alex felt himself breathe. Heard his heart beat. He smelled wet grass and warmed under the rising sun. Alex returned to the world, and through Samantha Rowland, the world welcomed him back with open arms.

Things went wrong before homeroom and got worse from there. He passed Samantha's locker like always. Avoiding his normal route would've been safer, but Alex hoped a casual hello could set right the awkward mess he'd caused at Saturday's meet. She was there as he approached, trading out her jacket for a stack of books.

Alex stopped. Froze, actually. He'd had a plan, hadn't he? What was it? Samantha turned and saw him standing in the middle of the hall, staring right at her. Her expression hung between an annoyed frown and a full-on scowl. Whatever the plan was, this wasn't it. Alex managed a feeble wave in her direction before slipping into the stairwell. Too late. The damage was done.

During trig, Samantha caught Alex every time he so much as glanced in her direction. He tried not to, but eventually he'd see movement out of the corner of his eye and instinct would take over. What the hell was he doing? Alex wasn't used to freezing up. He wasn't shy, wasn't awkward, and wasn't the kind of person to make a fool out of himself saying hello to a girl. This was new, and it sucked.

He decided to try again when the bell rang. *Hello. How are you? How was your weekend?* Something to cover for the lonely, desperate gazes. But the wall between his mind and his mouth went up once again. He sat silently while Samantha picked up her books and walked out of the classroom.

Was this who Alex was now? Were shame and guilt all he had left? No. Absolutely not.

Alex bolted out of his seat and into the hall so fast he almost dropped his books. Samantha was already halfway to the stairwell. Before he could decide whether shouting or running after her was the less embarrassing option, a huge hand came down on Alex's shoulder. There was only one person Alex knew with hands that big. Sheffield's second baseman, Nick Sarris.

"Alex, hey! Hold up!"

Nick wasn't really a friend, but it was hard not to hang out with teammates. He'd always made Alex a little uncomfortable. Little things, like how his smile wasn't exactly a smile. Just a single upturned corner of his mouth that was his way of saying, "Yeah, man, I got the joke. Cool."

"Nick. Hey. What's up?" Alex chanced a look over his shoulder. Samantha had stopped at someone's locker to say hi.

"You're free this Saturday, right?"

"Free for what?"

"If you're free, you're free," Nick said. "It doesn't matter what for. Are you or aren't you?"

Nick was the master at bullying people into plans. Alex could hold out until he gave up, but it would take time. Alex looked back at Samantha. Time he did not have.

Alex said, "I'm free. No plans."

"Then you're coming to my bonfire party."

"What party?"

"The one I'm having on Saturday. It's at my field," Nick said.

"Sure." Alex chanced one more glance at Samantha. She was headed for the stairs. "I'll be there. What time?"

"Who were you looking at?"

"No one."

The right corner of Nick's mouth raised. "Come on. Don't try to play me. You looked at someone like a dozen times. Samantha, right? Crazy legs on that girl."

"That isn't—"

Nick raised a hand to cut him off. "Say no more. I've got you covered."

"What does that mean?"

"It means I've got your back." The half smile went from the right to the left side of Nick's face. "You're coming on Saturday. Guaranteed. Right?"

Alex nodded slowly.

"So will she. Ask her out then. Seriously, dude, trying to pick her up in the hall? You should know better."

He slapped Alex on the arm and walked off, but Samantha was long gone. Maybe Nick was right. If Samantha came, the party might be his best chance to salvage things. As Alex walked to class, he felt the flutter of something in his stomach. Another emotion buried beneath the debris of the last year. It took Alex until the bell rang to realize what he was feeling was fear.

~

It didn't matter that 7th period health was on the opposite side of the school from 8th period graphic arts. Sure, the walk took every second of the time between bells, but Danica was never, ever late for 8th period. She didn't stop for anything, not even her friend Leslie, who sprinted out of the gym to catch up. Leslie was short — so short that it was a miracle no one picked on her for it. Then again, when the last person tried (a moment Danica fondly remembered as the Oompa Loompa Incident) they learned not to taunt someone with that clear a shot to their balls.

"Are you limping?" Danica asked as Leslie matched stride with her. She was favoring her right leg.

"I twisted my ankle doing dishes," Leslie said. "Yeah, I know. Pure Leslie."

"Ow."

"Whatever. At least I got to skip gym. How did the weekend with High-tops go?"

They headed up the wide, short staircase out of the lobby and into the main hallway. With so few classes on this side of the building the crowd was thin. Even so, even talking in code, Danica was careful. Rule number one: don't get caught.

"Weird. Good. I don't know," Danica said.

"So the swimming happened?" Leslie was watching

Danica so closely she almost knocked the books out of someone's hands as they passed. A freshman, thankfully.

Danica nodded, "There was swimming."

"You're killing me. Details. Now. You went swimming with High-tops and…?"

Danica didn't want to talk about this in the hallway, so she used the approaching crowd as an excuse to shake her head before Leslie could ask again. The code talking — High-tops for Samantha, He for She — was fun when things were just a crush and an inexplicable friendship. *High-tops messaged me! High-tops looks hot in those jean shorts!* Now all it did was remind Danica that she *had* to talk in code. If Leslie hadn't spent the weekend with her grandparents, if they could've met at the elementary school's empty playground like usual, Danica would've happily spilled her guts. Not here, though. Not now.

Still, she'd have to give Leslie something. "We swam. It was cold. Then it wasn't cold anymore. Okay?"

Leslie grinned. "Come over after dinner and tell me more."

"I have to take care of Jake."

"Fine. Then you'd better call me. I want all the dirty High-tops details," Leslie said. She was still smiling.

Danica rolled her eyes. Leslie was the only person Danica could talk to. Of course she was going to call.

Four proof sheets were spread out on the oversized desk between Danica and Samantha. Danica ran her finger across the smooth photo paper, tracing the bottom edges of tiny, rectangular photographs. On each sheet was a grid of photos, six across and four down. The images on Samantha's were perfectly spaced and even. Danica's… weren't. Placing strips of film negative on the paper without bumping the table or shaking the exposure box was too much for Danica to handle. Even in photography, Samantha was out of Danica's league. Was there anything she couldn't do perfectly?

Danica and Samantha had been granted temporary ownership of the school's single aging 35mm camera. A reward for the only two students in class for more than an easy A. Each had been given two precious rolls of black and white film and access to a tiny darkroom that somehow survived the school's renovation. Danica reviewed Samantha's proof sheets while Samantha looked over Danica's. They were supposed to have chosen which photos to print over the weekend. That was their cover for Saturday's meet-up, but then they'd gone and lost track of time in the lake.

"Did we shoot the same picture?" Samantha asked. She lifted a finger from one of the black and white squares on her proof and dropped it onto Danica's. "That one. Same bridge, right?"

Danica leaned over to get a better look. Both were shots of graffiti on the side of a squat cement bridge near Danica's home. Someone had drawn three sunflowers in pastels. She'd been struck by the way the morning's brief rain left lines of brown and black bleeding into the bright yellow of the flowers' petals. Danica wondered who had put so much time into something so fleeting and impermanent. She'd had to balance herself between the shore and a crooked rock poking through the surface of the water to get the photo. Samantha, it seemed, had done exactly the same, only she'd found the drawing while it was still pristine.

"It reminded me of the sunflowers we saw. The ones by the well," Samantha said.

"They were growing through the rocks," Danica replied. "You wouldn't let me pick one."

They couldn't talk about the rest of that Saturday

afternoon. Not here. It was their first time meeting after camp. Danica had led Samantha along one of the winding trails into the hills, where they'd found the decaying remains of a long-abandoned house. There was a stone well in the center of the yard, surrounded by four tall sunflowers. Samantha took Danica's hand when she tried to pick one. *There shouldn't be sunflowers this early. We should let them grow while they can.* She pulled Danica away gently, not letting go until they were back on the path, the house out of sight.

Danica said, "I was going to make a print for you, but yours is better."

Samantha smiled at Danica and looked down. Her smile faded. Danica followed Samantha's eyes and saw their hands were side by side on the desk. Danica's index finger was pressed against the side of Samantha's pinky.

Out of nowhere, a pair of hands slammed onto the desk. Nick's. He liked his arms to make an entrance. He put a lot of time into them.

Nick shouted, "Sammy!"

Danica flinched and regretted it immediately. *No one will think anything is going on unless you act like something is going on,* Samantha had told her over and over. Danica was sure she'd hear it again the next time they were alone.

"What the hell do you want?" Samantha asked. She looked at him sideways without turning her head.

"Ouch," Nick said. He glanced at Danica like he hadn't noticed she was there until now, then turned back to Sam. "You have a second?"

That meant *do you have a second away from this other girl and by the way who is she because I haven't been paying attention for the three months we've been in class together.* Danica knew all the subtle and nuanced ways people had for saying, "Go away, loser." She was also used to ignoring them. Danica sat down and returned her attention to the proof sheet. It was as close to playing it cool as she could manage.

Nick gave up on getting Samantha alone and asked, "What are you doing Saturday?"

"Something. Why?"

"Get out of it and come to my bonfire."

Samantha finally looked up. "Who's coming?"

"Everyone I invite. Bring Krista and Ferris. I'll have drinks and fire. What else do you want on a Saturday?"

"Sounds like you've got a full house without me."

Nick shook his head. "Dude, you're a superstar. People will show up just to sit and stare at you in, like, awe and appreciation."

"You're so full of shit," Samantha said.

"And you're coming to the bonfire."

"Fine. I'm coming to your bonfire. Can I get back to work?"

Danica held back a sigh. The only reason Samantha would have given in was sitting across the desk from her. The longer it took to get Nick away…

"Behind on homework? I get it," Nick said. "And, hey, you can bring a date if you want."

Danica stared down at the desk, the proof sheets, the floor. Anything that wasn't Samantha's face.

"I don't have one. Will and I broke up at one of *your* parties, remember?" Samantha kept her voice so controlled and level that if Danica didn't know Samantha was freaking out, she'd never have been able to tell.

"Right. Single. Maybe you'll meet someone there," Nick said with a lopsided grin. He walked back to his desk, slumped into his chair, and laid his head down to take a nap. His default classroom pose.

Samantha didn't look at Danica for the rest of class. She stared down at the proofs and marked the ones she liked with a small black plus sign. They each chose five of the other's photos without saying another word. The only thing that mattered had already been said. *Single*. Even after all the Saturday afternoons at camp and after-school make out sessions in Danica's bedroom, they were both still *single*. Danica wondered if the day come when she could be Samantha's date. Maybe not to a party, but to a movie, or shopping, or even coffee. What if it never did? Could Danica live with that?

Class ended, and the two parted silently. When Danica got to her bus, she noticed a folded up piece of paper in her pocket that wasn't there before class. She didn't dare open it until she got off the bus and crouched behind a row of dying shrubs at the edge of her yard.

Party is at night. Afternoon still free. See you after camp? Please?

That was all it took for Danica to forget 8th period had ever happened.

Chapter Three

SAMANTHA HAD LEARNED a word in physics that didn't make sense until she met Danica: *discrete*. Something that existed separately, unrelated to what came before or after. Her feelings for Danica were like that. Discrete. Distinct. They weren't a phase, weren't temporary or fleeting. Not at all. Danica felt right, righter than anything ever had, but *right* didn't have a place in Samantha's life. The only way Danica was safe from the things that would take her away was if Samantha kept her discrete.

It wasn't easy. For the second week in a row, Samantha woke up, ran track, ran to Danica, ran home to change, and was about to run out with friends. It was a clear, straight line from one side of her life to the other with Danica directly at the center. Indiscrete. Interconnected. It was easier when things weren't so close to each other, when Samantha and Danica stood alone.

Keeping Danica separate took a combination of luck and timing. Samantha's parents had afternoon plans with friends, which meant both that her father couldn't attend the meet, and that he wouldn't get home until late. An opening to meet someone, swim in a very cold lake, and arrive home with wet hair and a used bathing suit without raising suspicions. By the time Samantha heard the garage door motor through her bedroom floor, her now-dry bathing suit was in her dresser. The circle around her afternoon with Danica closed, leaving evidence only of a track meet in the morning and a party in the evening.

All that remained was to finish her makeup. Samantha screwed the applicator back into the eyeliner bottle and reviewed her work. Flecks of glitter in her eyeshadow caught the light as she turned her head from side to side. Things looked good. A little lip gloss and she'd be ready to go. Samantha was playing the part of a single girl and needed to look it. She'd gone to a concert last weekend without trying hard enough and the questions started before they were out of the driveway. Her favorite was from Krista.

"Are you depressed or something? Jesus, did you even wash your hair?"

Samantha heard the door between the kitchen and garage slam. Her dad was talking, but she couldn't catch the words. When he paused, Samantha imagined her mother responding in a low whisper, the voice she used when she feared her daughter would overhear. Samantha wished she could grab a book and wait them out on her bed. She couldn't risk things getting worse before Krista arrived, though. If Samantha was going to interrupt, it would have to be now.

She stopped with her hand on the doorknob when her father's voice raised. He was saying something about being embarrassed. The bed — safe, quiet bed — was right behind her. All she had to do was lie down. They'd never know she was here. She was ready to retreat when her dad's volume dropped. Now or never. Samantha swung the door open.

"Hey! You got home just in time to say goodbye." Samantha knew cheerful and oblivious was the only way to act. She spoke before she was down the steps, before she walked into the kitchen and was in sight of either of them. Walking in unannounced during a fight was a terrible idea. Samantha learned that lesson too many times.

The kitchen was like being inside of a granite and stainless steel monolith. LED track lights illuminated every surface, contrasting the dark wood of the cabinets against the gleam of silver appliances. Her father stood at the island, his hands on the brown and black granite. Samantha's mother was pressed against the only wall clear of countertops, trying (and failing) to look unconcerned by her daughter's intrusion.

"Hey, Sammy, how's it going?" her father asked, like she hadn't walked in on an argument. It was better than the alternative.

"Good. Ferris is taking us to that party at Nick's."

"Party?" her mom asked.

"Nick's?" her dad added, eyes narrowed.

Samantha and her mother were both tall and thin, though Samantha thought her mother looked frail in comparison. Her father, on the other hand, was 6'1", broad shouldered, and fit. He had a gym membership at an expensive club, the kind with a bar and fancy restaurant in the same building, and worked out there every day. There was never a question of which parent Samantha answered first. It was always Dad.

"Nick. He's on the team with me. You met him. Don't worry, his parents are home." She didn't mention that they'd be a quarter mile away from said home, in a field, out of sight and mind of his parents.

Her father nodded once. "How was the meet?"

"No surprises." That was how you told someone that you'd won in the Rowland household. No surprises.

Silence fell. Samantha's mother took a step forward

with an eye on Dad, unsure if the fight was over or deferred. The doorbell's merciful electronic chime sounded before she could find out.

"That's them!"

Samantha ran down the hardwood floor of the hallway to their front door. It was Krista. Ferris waited in the idling car parked in Samantha's driveway. Krista wore a tight, short skirt, the purple knee-high tights Samantha lent her for homecoming, and a scoop necked t-shirt with some kind of angel-fairy-thing on the front that she'd bought for when she felt like "goth-slumming it."

"Isn't it a little cold for that?" Samantha asked.

"Evan skipped. I'll put jeans on after you post some pics of me in this. I want him to see what he's missing."

Samantha's smile cut off. It was completely silent in the kitchen. The fight was on hold. After all, there was someone at the door. She imagined them standing in the kitchen, Dad's eyes locked on Mom, Mom's eyes everywhere but on him. Samantha gave Krista a gentle shove backwards and slammed the door behind them.

~

Someone handed Alex a beer. He held the plastic cup by its rim and let it hang beside his leg as people said hello, punched his arm, bumped fists, high-fived, and asked over and over if he was ready for Monday's game. Alex did his best to pretend that the first game of the season mattered, though it was the last thing on his mind. He had a really, truly awkward week to turn around. Try to turn around, anyway. Alex's chances weren't good.

Nick's parents owned the field a quarter mile from their house, plus everything else in a ten mile radius. The field was surrounded on all sides by shrubs that had grown out of control for years, and oak, pine, and maple trees that looked just as wild. No one — not in Nick's house, not on the road — could see what was happening in the field. The bonfire was at the far end, near the keg they'd hidden amongst the trees. Other than the people in line for a drink, everyone was crammed into the fire's small circle of heat and light. Alex spiraled through the crowd, moving from group to group, looking for Samantha.

Her found her near the fire, flanked by friends. Ferris sat on one side with a water bottle held between her knees, legs stretched out in front of her. On the other was Krista, who'd dressed for far warmer weather. She hunched forward, forearms across her bare thighs, face as close to the flames as she could risk. A weathered log, the bark long washed or scraped off, served as their bench. The fire needed wood, and the glow of it on Samantha's face was as dim and red as the sun the day he'd noticed her. Samantha never seemed relaxed. Even here, at a party, with friends, tension lurked behind her laughter. If Samantha ever owned a gun, she'd probably sleep with it under her pillow.

"She's taken," said a voice Alex didn't recognize.

Alex turned. The speaker pulled a hand rolled cigarette out of his mouth and smiled. He wore a shirt patterned with alternating light and dark brown stripes, its cuffs purposefully and carefully frayed. His brown hair was styled into a perfect mess and streaked with blond highlights. Blue eyes studied Alex closely, searching for a reaction.

"What did you say?" Alex asked.

He took a drag on the cigarette, blew smoke out of the corner of his mouth, and dropped the unsmoked half of it on the ground. "The tights are sexy as hell, but she's not single. I already took a shot. Don't waste your time."

"Oh," Alex said with a glance back to the girls. "You

mean Krista."

"Oh," Highlights echoed, "you don't."

"Do I know you?" asked Alex.

He shook his head. "Nope. And I don't know you. I'm Conn."

"Conn?"

"Yeah. Two Ns. Never went to jail. What about you?"

"Alex."

Conn nodded and held out an open hand. He wanted to shake. *Who is this guy?* Alex reached out, unprepared for how strong Conn's grip was.

"Is Conn short for something?"

"Sort of," Conn said, and returned his attention to the girls. "So if it isn't tights, who is it? Crazy tight sweater? No, you were looking past her. That leaves the Amazon."

Alex listened to Conn talk and couldn't help but think he'd known exactly who Alex was watching. That should have put Alex on guard, but there was something about Conn that felt trustworthy. Safe.

"Her name's Samantha."

"Samantha."

"Samantha Rowland," Alex said.

Conn nodded and glanced down to the full beer in Alex's hand. Without asking, he took the cup from him and swallowed a third of the glass in one go. Then he handed Alex back the plastic cup and smiled.

"Have at it, man. Into the breach or whatever."

Alex turned again to Samantha, who had an arm around the now-shivering Krista. Now wasn't the time.

Conn noticed Alex's hesitation. "Hey, let's get a beer and have a cigarette and you can tell me all about her while you think of what to say."

"I don't drink." Alex lifted the cup of beer and

extended it to Conn as proof that that he really, honest to God, didn't drink.

"You don't drink."

"Even if I did, why would I want to talk to someone I don't know?"

Conn laughed. He took the beer from Alex and finished it, then dropped the cup beside his discarded cigarette. "I'm being pushy as hell, aren't I? Sorry. I don't know anyone here and I'm bored and I hate making friends and you looked like you could use one. I didn't mean to be up your ass. I'll see you around."

Conn turned and headed back into the crowd. Alex had the feeling that once Conn was out of sight, he'd never see him again. He was strangely certain of it. Though he couldn't explain why, Alex was just as certain he'd regret it.

"Conn," Alex shouted, "I could go for a cigarette."

~

Samantha trudged across the field, thankful for curfews. Nick's parties were notorious (celebrated? beloved?) for going until morning, the fire still smoldering as the sun climbed above the tops of the surrounding trees. The last thing Samantha wanted was to be here with whomever was desperate, lonely, and drunk enough to spend the waning hours of the night in a cold, dewy field with an empty keg and a dying fire. In another hour or two she could drag Krista to the car and leave. In the meantime, Samantha needed to keep Krista happy enough not to throw a fit when the time came to make their exit. That meant, at minimum, getting her beer.

The chill hit Samantha as soon as she left the warmth of the bonfire. Why had she broken down and given away her jacket? It was Krista's fault for wearing that idiotic outfit in the first place. Now she was fetching beer like she was Krista's shivering, miserable waitress. Samantha thought of the last time she was cold, floating in the brisk lake at Sheffield Park. She thought of what, of who, had kept her warm, and slammed the door on the memory. She couldn't afford to drift off to thoughts of Danica tonight. The cold, the fire, the beer, and the fake smiles were all to keep up appearances. Keeping up appearances was going to get her killed.

There was a line for the keg. Of course. Samantha shifted her weight from leg to leg, hoping movement would keep her warm. The ground, still wet from yesterday's storm, squished beneath her feet. One of the guys in front of her turned and smiled. Samantha would have smiled back (appearances!) if his eyes were on her face instead of... lower. By the time he looked back up, Samantha didn't care enough to play along. She looked down at the empty plastic cup in her hands, and he returned his attention to the backside of the girl in front of him. Just before it was his turn at the keg, he'd forgotten he already made eyes at Samantha's boobs and gave it another shot. This time Samantha didn't look away until she was sure he saw her middle finger.

Samantha grabbed the tap from the top of the keg, aimed it at Krista's cup, and depressed the lever. A sputter of white foam dripped into the cup. She cursed and tried again. Not even foam this time. Only air.

"Hey, hold on, let me try something," a guy with blonde highlights said as he grabbed the tap out of Samantha's hand. He shook the tap violently, like someone trying to get ketchup out of a new bottle. He looked back up at her and smiled. "Conn. I'm Conn. Nice to meet you."

"Conn. Hi. I think it's empty."

Conn kicked the keg once. Then again. Then went

back to shaking the hose. "Kegs are never empty for me. Here, give me your cup. I'll do this. Go talk to my friend."

"Friend?" Samantha asked. She followed Conn's line of sight. A few yards back from the keg stood Alex. He'd seemed nice when he introduced himself, but a week of awkward, yearning stares had edged him into creeper territory. Samantha wanted to march back to Krista, tell her the keg was empty, and drag her home.

Alex sighed when he realized he'd been spotted and walked over. He said, "Hey."

"This is getting a little weird," Samantha said.

"'Yeah," Alex said with a laugh. "It's been awkward. Well, I've been awkward."

"You think?"

"Awkward is kind of new to me. I'm not good at it, am I?" He was back to smiling. The smile Samantha had liked when they first met.

Samantha returned the smile. "No, dude. You suck at it."

"Yeah, I crashed and burned at the meet and it was all downhill from there. Sorry about that. And, you know, about this," he said, gesturing at Conn.

"See if I help you again," Conn said, still shaking the keg hose. The line behind him was getting increasingly impatient. He didn't seem to mind.

"You didn't crash and burn at the meet," Samantha said.

"Really?"

"No. That didn't happen until you walked past my locker and stared at me without saying hi."

Alex laughed and looked down. "Right. That."

Conn shouted triumphantly. He pushed a full cup of beer into Samantha's hand. "Never empty for me. What did I say?"

"Oh. Thanks, I guess."

Conn slapped Alex on the arm, then turned and headed for the bonfire. Samantha had no idea who Conn was. Did he go to Sheffield? Maybe he was new. New was possible.

"There's no way I could get a do over, is there?" Alex asked.

He was smiling again. Two competing responses raced from brain to mouth. *What did you have in mind? And Why bother? I'm taken.* The second thing was *so* the wrong thing to say that the first was out of her mouth before she could stop herself.

"Well," Alex replied, "it's been a while since I went bowling. Bowling is pretty awkward. I've got to seem normal compared to that."

Samantha stifled a laugh. "Would that be a date type of thing?"

"That's the plan, yeah."

There was a fine line between keeping up appearances and going out on a date. That wasn't a line Samantha had been asked to cross since things with Danica got real. She could say no. A week of weird stares was all the ammunition the rejection gun needed.

"Where's my beer, bitch?" Krista shouted. She pushed through the line and reached clumsily for the cup in Samantha's hand. Samantha pulled it out of reach before Krista could spill it.

"I had to wait in line."

"That's no excuse, you..." Krista noticed Alex. "Oh, hey there. What's your name?"

Samantha tried not to roll her eyes. Hitting on the guy Samantha was already with was so very Krista. Jealousy took over before Samantha realized what she was saying. "He's Alex, and he just asked me out."

"Oh. Awesome. Say yes and give me my beer

already."

Samantha was trapped. Say no and she'd never hear the end of it. Say yes, and… *no, it's not cheating*. This wasn't a betrayal. It was protection. Samantha and Danica both knew they'd have to lie to make this work. She handed the beer to Krista, turned to Alex, and said, "Fine. Bowling. Pick a day and talk to me in trig."

"Really?" Alex asked, like someone who'd imagined this conversation a million times and was shot down in every one.

"You're back to being weird. Yes, really. Talk to me in trig." She turned to Krista. "Come on. Finish your beer so we can go. My dad will kill me if I miss curfew."

Krista giggled into her beer and stumbled back to the bonfire. Samantha couldn't understand how things had spun out of her control so quickly. If she'd said yes to someone else, like eyes-on-boobs guy from the keg line, it would have been tactical. Anyone else, anyone Samantha didn't have a shred of interest in, would have been the kind of sacrifice she was ready to make. This, though. This was a lie. There were only two ways out. Back out, tell Alex to screw off, and hope there weren't any horrible, probing, revealing questions. Or tell Danica and pray this wasn't one hurt too many.

That was when Krista threw up on Samantha's shoes. She almost appreciated the distraction.

Chapter Four

ALEX WOKE WITH cotton balls stuffed in his brain and his throat rubbed raw by sandpaper. Something in the field had kicked him right in his allergies. Too miserable to fall back asleep, Alex pushed himself upright. He'd fallen asleep in his jeans again. At least he'd taken his shirt off this time.

He heard footsteps on the uncarpeted hallway floor. His father. He stopped at the closed door of Alex's bedroom and, in a thin, timid voice, said, "Alex, your friend is here."

Friend? What friend? He looked at the red LED numbers of his alarm clock: 9:32. Everyone Alex knew was at the field last night. No way they'd be up yet, not with how hard they were drinking. He hunted for a shirt in the pile of clothes on his floor. The laundry situation was getting critical. Last night's shirt was his least terrible option. Alex stretched it out a few times (as if that would take the wrinkles out), pulled it over his head, and opened the door.

"Your friend is here," Alex's father repeated. His nearly black hair was a sterling example of unkempt bed head. His mustache, flecked with grey, badly needed trimmed. A white t-shirt clung to his expanding pot belly.

Whoever was waiting for Alex had gotten more than they bargained for when his father answered the door.

"Who?" Alex asked.

His father shrugged, embarrassed. Alex was sick of the man's constant, apologetic shame. The things he was sorry about weren't going to be said. They were best filed away, not worn on his face like an open invitation for a Really Deep Talk. Alex pushed past his father and headed down the short hallway to the living room. His guest waited on the other side of the screen door, scuffing the soles of his feet impatiently on the cement porch.

"Conn?" Alex asked, shuffling through memories of last night. Had they made plans for today? How was he up already with how much he'd had to drink?

"Hey," Conn said. "Did I wake you up? Sorry if I did."

"Kind of."

Conn smiled. "Ouch. My bad."

Alex's father joined them. "Are you going to introduce me to your friend, Alex?"

"This is Conn. Conn, this is my dad," Alex said, then quickly added, "Let's go for a walk."

Conn waved as Alex joined him on the porch. "Nice to meet you, Mr. Ribeiro."

Alex ignored his father's shouted goodbyes and led Conn down the slope of the front yard. They headed down the road to a small dairy. Behind it was a path into the woods — Alex's escape route from his father's guilt. Conn pulled a cigarette out of the pack in his pocket and lit it with a cheap yellow lighter.

"Did we have plans or something?" Alex asked.

"Nah," Conn replied. "I just wanted to stop by. You ever notice how when you meet people at parties, half the time you don't see them again until the next one?"

"I guess."

"I hate that. I had a good time last night, and since I don't actually have any friends here…"

Alex shook his head, but smiled. Conn passed Alex the cigarette. The truth was, Alex didn't have any friends, either. The guys on the team were just that. Teammates. Alex hadn't realized he *missed* friends.

"Hey, follow me. I want to show you something," Alex said.

The path dipped down the hill. Conn talked as Alex guided him through the trees. Twice, he brought up Samantha. Once to goad Alex into admitting he owed Conn for the opening to ask Samantha out. The second, to figure out what Alex saw in her.

"Just the running?" Conn asked when Alex told him about the day at the track.

"Not just the running. More like what I saw when she ran, you know?"

Conn nodded and said nothing else. Alex couldn't tell if he understood or was doing a great job of pretending. They said nothing else until they finished their shared cigarette.

"Your dad seems all right," Conn said.

"I guess."

"You guess? My dad's a serious dick. Yours is okay."

"How do you mean?" Alex asked.

"Long story," Conn said flatly. "At least yours gives a shit. Well, mine too, but not the kind of shit you want someone to give, you know?"

Alex didn't, but he nodded anyway.

"So what's wrong with yours?"

"Nothing, I guess. Things used to be worse."

Conn let the silence stretch out before continuing. "It's just you and your dad, right?"

"Can you drop it?" Alex asked, harsher than he intended.

"Sorry." Conn kept looking at Alex, though, like he expected Alex to go on anyway.

Not this time. Instead, Alex said, "We're almost there."

The path cut past a row of old oaks, then leveled out and narrowed. Alex glanced over his shoulder and saw that Conn had stopped a few yards back. There was a look on his face that Alex couldn't read. Was he worried about something? Unsure of how to ask, Alex continued on, only to be stopped by Conn's hand on his arm.

"Where are we going?" Conn asked, a tightness in his voice that matched his expression.

"There's a view you've got to see. The reservoir is back there and you can see the whole thing. It's awesome."

For a moment Conn said nothing, just stared past Alex. The noise of the forest seemed to fade, leaving only the distant sound of flowing water. Not of the reservoir lapping against the shore, but of a swollen river racing downhill. It sounded close, like it was rushing in from behind him, but when Alex turned the sound was gone, replaced by the rustle of leaves and the chirping of birds. It happened so quickly Alex was sure he'd imagined it.

When Alex turned back, he saw Conn shaking his head, creeping backwards onto the hill. Conn said, "I don't know, man. Heights, you know? Can we turn around?"

Alex knew what a panic attack looked like. He'd seen enough of his mom's to recognize them. The dilated pupils. The labored inhales and exhales, the shaking hands. Alex brushed off the memory and focused on Conn.

"No problem. We can go back. I didn't know."

Conn calmed. He turned to Alex and smiled, the glimmer of perspiration on his forehead the only sign there'd been anything wrong. "Yeah. Let's get out of here. Sorry."

Neither spoke until they cleared the woods and returned to the paved road beyond the dairy. When they did, Conn lit a cigarette. Alex noticed a tremor in Conn's hand as he struggled with the lighter's thumbwheel.

"Guess I should've slept in," Conn said. "I'm going to head home. Catch up with you later?"

"Yeah. You sure you're okay?"

Conn nodded and waved over his shoulder. Alex watched him go before returning to the woods, still confused. Was he really that afraid of heights? They couldn't even see the reservoir from where they'd stopped.

The path ended in a sudden drop; a viciously steep, rocky hill that plunged into the reservoir below. Alex sat and hung his feet over the edge. He'd found this place over a year ago, the day he'd arrived. Another day Alex didn't want to remember. He stared into the water and tried to think of nothing at all. When that didn't work, he retreated into memories of the previous night. Of Samantha, of a date to come, of anything but his father, his mother, and the days before today.

~

Danica sat cross-legged on the tile floor of the rectangular kitchen while her brother crashed toy hotrods into her. He'd grab one clumsily, roll it backwards to wind the spring, then aim it at his sister before letting it go. When he'd gotten them for Christmas, Jake didn't realize he could race them without crawling alongside, hand constantly pushing them forward. Now that he had it figured out, he couldn't get enough of revving them up and driving them into Danica's knee. Over and over and over again. He laughed when they hit at the right angle and flipped over. Even car wrecks were hilarious to four-year-old boys.

Jake and his oldest brother Pete were under Danica's care until Mom got home from work. Since her shift at the hospital ended at midnight, Danica was babysitting until bedtime. Mom's boyfriend Ian was in charge, if it was possible to be in charge of something while snoring on the living room couch. Ian was a security guard at a copper plant. His shift, he complained whenever awakened from his couchy slumber, really sucked. He'd stumbled in at noon, just in time to drag Mom back to their bedroom before she left for work. He was asleep by the time her car was out of sight and stayed that way all afternoon. Now, Pete was out back practicing with his soccer ball, Steve was at a friend's, and Jake and Danica were playing in the kitchen.

Danica was used to taking care of her brothers. She'd done it most of her life, since her father took Mom's third pregnancy as an excuse to make his escape. She hadn't seen him since. Danica didn't remember enough about him to miss him. Steve and Pete had been Danica's responsibility for so long that they treated her with as much respect as they did Mom. It wasn't much, but it was more than Ian got. Not that Ian cared. The only reason he felt obligated to return every afternoon to sleep on their couch was Jake, Danica's half-brother. Ian's only son. Danica didn't mind it so much. The little munchkin was worth a thousand Ians.

Still, this was one of those nights when Danica would've given anything to be alone. Because of the call she'd received. From Samantha.

"Is it okay if I come over?" she'd asked. That was new. Samantha always told Danica she was coming. She never asked like she expected to be turned down.

That was an hour ago. The drive from Samantha's

house in the heart of New Sheffield to the boondocks where Danica lived wasn't short. An hour, though? Did it usually take Samantha that long?

Finally: the growl of a car engine, followed by a slammed car door, followed by Pete's muffled voice saying hello. That had to be Samantha. Danica let Jake crash the hot rod one last time, then ran to the back door. Samantha opened the screen door without knocking, a strained smile on her face. She wore jean shorts and a tight black t-shirt printed with a faded, once-sparkly rose. And high-tops. *The* high-tops. The blue Chucks that Samantha had on the day Danica admitted her crush to Leslie. Samantha put her arms around Danica and gave her a hug, crushing Danica against the washer/dryer that took up most of the tiny room. It was long hug, more than they typically risked with others nearby.

"Everything okay?" Danica asked.

"Yeah," Samantha said. "I just wanted to come by. Can we work in your room?"

Work. Homework. The always reliable excuse. "Yeah," Danica said, leading Samantha into the kitchen. "Jake, hey, Sam and I need to do some homework. Are you okay out here?"

"What homework?" Jake asked.

Danica looked down at Samantha's very empty hands. She hadn't brought a textbook. She always brought a textbook. A nearly public hug and a blown homework cover? What was going on? Danica spoke quickly, as if their entire relationship hinged on fooling a four year-old. "We need to choose photos to print. They're in my room."

Jake went back to his cars. They snuck down the hallway to Danica's bedroom, careful not to trip over the scattered toys, shoes, and pieces of Ian's guard uniform. Waking Ian would ruin any chance for privacy.

Danica's room was a horrifying collage of every era of her life: fuzzy bunny plushes from her childhood, magazine pull-outs of Disney Channel original movies from her humiliating tween years, and a recent scattering of high school art assignments. Danica could never bring herself throw any of it out, which she regretted every time Samantha came over. The first time, back when doing homework was still the real reason they saw each other, Samantha ran her finger down the edge of Danica's giant *Hairspray* poster and said, "I liked the dancing in this."

Samantha half-closed the door before joining Danica on the unmade bed. Danica swore at herself for failing to spend two minutes of the hour she waited straightening up. She kicked the comforter and sheet off the bed (at least the mess was on the floor) while Samantha leaned against the chipped wooden headboard. Danica scooted herself towards Samantha, close enough for their legs to casually touch. Close enough to lean in if the moment arose.

"You sure you're okay?" Danica asked. She glanced out of the bedroom door to be sure they were alone before putting a hand on Samantha's bare knee. Samantha set her own hand over Danica's and bent forward. Their lips met midway. Samantha moved her hand to the place on Danica's neck just below her ear, one thumb on Danica's cheek.

Danica's memories of their first time on this bed were hazy and muddled. All they did was homework, but the closeness and the fleeting moments of accidental contact made it impossible to concentrate. A week later, when Samantha visited again, Danica complained that looking down at their textbooks was killing her neck. Without a word, Samantha slid behind her and rubbed her shoulders, pressing hard into the knots. When Samantha stopped, Danica turned, intending to say thank you but finding Samantha's face so very, very close. Without a thought, Danica kissed Samantha twice on the cheek. They both froze, eyes locked, Danica's heart pounding with certainty that Samantha would flee and tell everyone that Danica the Dyke was actually and truly a lesbian. That didn't happen. Samantha didn't run. She touched Danica on the neck, just where her hand was now, and returned the kiss.

It didn't last. Not then, and not this time. It never did. There was always the threat. Of interruption. Of discovery. Always an eye out the door. Samantha leaned back against the headboard but left her legs against Danica's.

"Do you want to talk about something?" Danica asked. "Did something happen last night?"

Samantha broke eye contact. "It was just a stupid party, like always. Stupid and loud and a waste of time. And Krista got drunk and puked on my shoes."

"Which shoes?"

"The purple Clarks," Samantha said, still not looking up.

"I liked those. But those are sandals. Krista straight-up puked on your feet."

Samantha laughed; the short, soft laugh of someone too caught off guard not to. Her smile faded as quickly as her laughter. "I hate what I do to you."

"What do you mean?" Danica asked, sliding a hand down Samantha's calf. "I kind of like what you do to me."

The flirt was a mistake. Samantha pulled her leg under her body, away from Danica. "I get invited to parties that I can't take you to and then you have to listen to me tell you all the things you missed. It's not fair."

"I don't mind. I don't care."

"You should care. Why don't you care?"

"Fine, I do," Danica said, "but it's worth it. Don't you think it's worth it?"

When Samantha didn't answer, Danica felt a familiar weight crush her chest. She'd been dumped before. Twice. Memories flipped past, a stack of photos tossed before her eyes and searched for some proof that today was different. She welcomed the paralysis that crept into her arms and legs. A statue would be safer than fleshy, weak Danica.

Samantha might have said *yes* before diving onto her, but it didn't matter. The pushing Danica onto her back, the sliding her arm around Danica's waist, the forceful kiss; it was the only answer Danica needed. They wrestled each other on the narrow bed, rolling over each other twice without falling off — a skill learned after a lot of trial and error. Danica let Samantha lead, let go of worry, forgot that there had been fear at all.

"What are you doing?"

Jake. God, Jake! Samantha pushed herself up, arms straight, hair spilling down onto Danica's chest. Danica's head hung over the edge of the bed. Her brother was frozen with his hand on the doorknob. More confused than horrified, Danica hoped.

"Samantha's being a jerk," Danica said, too out of breath, too flushed, to think clearly. "About homework."

"Why?" Jake asked.

"Because Danica won't do it for me," Samantha answered. Danica looked up, expecting to see cold, restrained horror in Samantha's eyes. It wasn't there. Samantha was smiling.

"Oh. Can I go outside with Pete?"

Danica nodded. Jake turned and pulled the door shut behind him. When the door's latch clicked shut, Samantha collapsed onto Danica, laughing. Danica laughed with her. She put her arms around Samantha, half-expecting to be brushed off. Samantha kept laughing.

"That was close," Danica said, to test the waters.

"*So* close."

"You aren't freaking out?"

Samantha pushed herself up again. Smiled. "No. I'm good."

"You're good." Danica didn't think she could fit so much *are you kidding me?* into two words.

"Yeah. Nothing to be afraid of. I'm always safe here." Samantha gently lowered herself. Danica felt lips brush her neck. Then kiss. Then kiss again. Samantha whispered, "Only place I'm safe."

There was very little said after that.

Chapter Five

LESLIE'S BEDROOM WAS barely big enough for the four of them. Danica and Will Pope on Leslie's bed, Leslie half-hanging off the edge of her dresser, and Texas on the floor, back against the sliding closet door, feet pressed against the side of the bed. Texas had the joint. Texas always had the joint. If anyone else had it, they did their business and passed it to the next person. When it ended up in Texas' hands, he talked, waved it around, took tiny hits ("That wasn't a real one, hold on!") and didn't let it go without a ton of nagging. They'd given up for now. With how little was left, Texas was more likely to burn his fingers than anyone was to get another hit.

"You looking at porn again?" Will asked Danica. He reached for the laptop on Danica's legs so suddenly she barely had time to alt-tab to the other browser. *To* the one with less-than-clothed women. "Degenerate. Good taste in girls, though."

Danica spun Leslie's laptop back around and switched to the browser with the open chat window. When it came to guys, there were few better covers for deceit than porn. Will's eyes stayed on Danica. When they first met (through Leslie), Will had fallen hard for her. Finding out she was gay hadn't ended Will's crush so much as mutated his feelings into the platonic ideal of unfulfillable attraction. Danica wondered if he'd be her type if she *were* into guys. She did love his smooth, dark brown skin and how his voice sounded so much deeper when he laughed.

"I want to swing," Texas said. "Anyone else want to swing?"

Leslie shrugged. She was busy scraping her index fingers against her thumbnails. Fidgeting was Leslie's go-to activity after smoking a joint. Texas turned to Danica and gave her the *help me out here* look. If Danica went for a swing at the playground, Leslie would follow. Texas always felt better when Leslie was around. The two of them were close. Not dating close, but pretty tight. Danica didn't think Texas was even into girls, though she couldn't think of any reason he'd hide being gay from her. Then again, he'd only been at Sheffield for few months and Danica didn't know much of anything about him. His real name was Mike. Like most military brats (Texas' dad was Air Force), he'd burned through four schools since junior high. Leslie gave him the nickname when she heard his dad's last posting was Laughlin Air Force Base in the Lone Star State.

"I don't want to swing," Danica said.

Will stood up. "I need to get out of this room. It smells like sweaty stoned people. Let's go."

A message box opened on the screen. **Save me. Ferris drooling over Stinky Vince again.** Danica was definitely not going to the playground. "Have fun," she said.

The boys closed the door behind them. Leslie looked up from her fingernails. "So?"

"She's on!"

Leslie slid off the dresser and crashed onto the bed next to Danica. "What's she saying?"

Danica was glad to have the boys out of the room.

Sure, they knew she was gay. The only reason that wasn't common knowledge was the school's stunning lack of interest in Danica Perlich. Samantha, though, was Top Secret, This Message Will Self Destruct In Five Seconds. It didn't matter whether she could trust the boys or not. In fact, as secret-keepers went, Danica knew no one more reliable than Will. If Leslie hadn't been a part of things from the beginning, Danica wouldn't have told her, either. There was just too much at risk.

"Bitching about Ferris," Danica said.

"Yawn. Ask her what underwear she's wearing or something."

Danica smirked and went back to typing. **I'm home alone tonight. Whole family is gone. Until late.** She paused before hitting enter on that one. They flirted a lot, sure (Samantha got the messages on her phone, and *no one* touched Samantha's phone), but their meet-ups were carefully planned. Spur of the moment wasn't their thing.

"Oh," Leslie said, reading. "Something awesome, then."

"Shut up."

"I want to know what kind of underwear someone's wearing." Leslie saw the look on Danica's face and punched her arm. "Texas doesn't count. Dude needs to pull up his damn pants."

Samantha's reply appeared on the screen: **Love to. Can't. Dad wants me home for dinner.**

Danica bit her lip and said nothing.

Leslie touched Danica's hand. "Hey, she's just busy. No big deal."

"I guess."

"That's crap. You asked your girl over to make out. She *is* your girlfriend, right?"

Danica shrugged.

"That's crap, too. You were supposed to say *hell yes.*

Let's try again. Is she your girlfriend?"

Danica hated putting a name to it. It felt like she was begging to be proven wrong. Like as soon as she let herself believe Samantha was her girlfriend, she'd find out how wrong she was. Danica forced herself to nod.

"Better. Now tell her how bummed you are and that you want to see her bethonged butt in your room as soon as possible." Leslie grinned.

Danica laughed despite herself. "Perv."

Leslie fell back onto the bed and laid her legs across Danica's. She said, "Shut up and type. I'm taking a nap."

Danica rolled her eyes, set the laptop on top of Leslie's shins, and typed.

~

There were many, many reasons Ferris drove Samantha insane. Nearly losing races. Actually losing races. That picking what shoes to wear to go shopping for a new pair of shoes could take an hour. That buying said pair of shoes could take three. Her voice. The stares she got whenever they were out. The stares Samantha *didn't* get if she stood next to Ferris. Time with Ferris on a good day wase a chore. Time with Ferris when she had Stinky Vince on her mind was unbearable.

"He was so sad," Ferris said. "You could see how sad he was. He doesn't like to say it but you can tell. He stares at you and you know he *needs* you to be there with him, you know?"

Samantha let Ferris talk. She had her own problems. Alex had been at Samantha's desk as soon as trig was over to confirm their date. Saturday night. Bowling. 8 p.m. Now she needed something to wear. She flipped through hanger after hanger, looking for the grey jeans she'd found in a smaller size. Nothing was ever where it was supposed to be. She could buy something else, sure, but if she was going to bother with this date she was going to do it right. Anyway, the jeans could be her payment to herself. A bribe to ease the guilt. Samantha hated guilt. She should have told Danica about Alex no matter how much it would've have hurt.

"And he was so, so tense when I got my hands on his shoulders. You know how tense he gets when he's upset. Like rock."

Stinky Vince was Samantha's nickname for the worthless object of Ferris' unrequited affection. They'd never dated, Ferris and Vince. He took Ferris to Homecoming in October, made out with her in his father's GTO, stopped somewhere between second and third base, then only returned Ferris' calls after he'd gained, then lost, a girlfriend. Janice something. Samantha could never remember her last name. It was the same story every time. Vince would get dumped and show up at Ferris' house for attention. She'd give it (along with a back rub), get her hopes up, and act shocked when he crawled back to Janice. Vince, everyone but Ferris agreed, was a grade-A douche. A grade-A douche soaked in discount cologne. Stinky Vince.

The phone in Samantha's pocket buzzed. A message from Danica, and an escape from Stinky Vince and her own fruitless quest for jeans that fit. Samantha unlocked the phone and smiled. Danica, so hesitant and shy in person, was a hell of a flirt over text. She couldn't bring herself to flirt back, though. Not when she was shopping for her pseudo-date with Alex. Samantha stared at the phone so long that Ferris — in-her-own-world-when-on-a-rant Ferris Ashley — noticed.

"Are you even listening to me?" she asked.

Samantha locked her phone and nodded. "Yeah. Yeah, totally. You were saying...Vince's shoulders?"

"Yeah, that was so convincing." Ferris' eyes fell on Samantha's phone. "Who's so important, anyway? Is it Alex?"

"No," Samantha replied, returning her phone to her pocket. "Just a friend."

"What friend?" She was back to annoyed.

Samantha sighed. "You don't want to know."

"That's what I thought. Thanks for ignoring me for your psycho charity case. You know I love that."

"I'm sorry. I spaced out. I'm listening, I promise." There'd been no way to hide her time with Danica without admitting something to her friends. Ferris was the only one who seemed to mind. For some reason, Ferris hated Danica. Samantha had never seen Ferris hate anyone. Well, anyone other than Janice.

"Whatever. If she's more important than me, go back to texting."

"No, let's keep talking about Vince. How long did it take him to get back with Janice last time? I can't remember."

"Why are you such a bitch? I only came shopping with you to talk. Like I need another skirt." Ferris hung up the skirt in her hand with all the fury she could manage. The rack shook. A little.

Samantha was running out of room for guilt. Lying to Danica, lying to Alex to hide Danica, and now treating Ferris like crap over it all. Things were supposed to be *discrete*. How had everything gotten so damn connected? Everything she did made something else worse. She needed an out. It was too late to break off her date with Alex, but maybe...

"We should do something stupid Saturday. You know, blow off steam." Samantha said as the idea came together.

Surprising Ferris always calmed her down. She

couldn't juggle anger *and* confusion. "Stupid would be awesome. But isn't Saturday your date?"

"Yeah, but it's just bowling." Samantha felt the pieces fall into place. If it was a party, then it wasn't *really* a date anymore. "Why don't we *all* go bowling? There'll be other people there anyway. Come on. We need a night for us."

"Yeah. We do," Ferris agreed. "So who should we invite?"

"Everyone. Let's take the place over."

Ferris' phone was already in her hand. Samantha lifted her own. Breaking this to Alex the right way could back him off. Maybe even keep it from being a date at all. She just had to choose her words carefully.

~

Alex wasn't looking forward to a whole week of this. It wasn't a losing streak, not yet, but a 0-2 season was cause enough for a grueling Monday practice. The losses weren't even his fault. They were in the lead when the coach pulled Alex to give their freshman relief pitcher some experience, and Alex spent the second game on the bench, resting his arm. Alex took it without complaint; the sprints, the repetitive batting drills, the endless line drives at the mound. This was baseball. This was what Alex signed up for.

Nick caught up with Alex as they stumbled into the field house, dragging their catcher Logan behind him. Logan's sweaty, shaved head glowed under the afternoon sun. He was breathing heavily, barely keeping up with Nick. No one had it worse in a brutal practice than Logan. His stocky body wasn't built for long runs. Nick, on the other hand, didn't look tired at all. The guy worked out for fun and played every sport but hockey.

Nick pushed Alex through the field house door and into their corner of the locker room. Alex slapped Nick's hand off of his back. "What the hell?"

"Logan told me what happened at the party," Nick said.

Logan nodded.

"Okay, what happened at the party?"

"Nothing, dude," Nick said.

"Nothing," Logan added.

"Okay, so nothing happened."

"With Samantha, dude. Nothing happened with Samantha." Nick shook his head disapprovingly.

Alex grabbed his phone out of his locker while deciding how to respond. Four new texts. The most recent from his father. Alex looked up before going through the other texts. "How do you know what happened with Samantha?"

Logan had his own phone out. "Party with the track team. Sweet."

"I just do," Nick said, ignoring Logan, "and I didn't get her there so you could say hi and go home. If you needed help you could have asked."

"I didn't need help."

"Dude," Logan interrupted. "Did you get this, too? You going?"

Nick looked at his phone while continuing to harass Alex. "So what happened? Did you make *any* progress?"

"Does a date Saturday count?" He didn't want to be goaded into locker room bragging by Nick. Didn't need to. Still was.

"Hell yes it does!" Nick turned to Logan. "Hey, yeah, I got the text. Huh. Weird, but why not?"

"You in, Alex?" Logan asked.

Nick slapped Logan on the arm. "He's on a date, idiot. I'm getting a shower. Tell me all about this Saturday thing later, A."

Alex changed as quickly as he could. He wanted to be out of here before they got back. It was so barely a date, Alex felt stupid calling it one. He'd backed Samantha into a corner with Conn's help and begged for a chance to get to know her. Was Samantha curious or letting Alex get his one date out of his system? Better to avoid Nick and his questions as much as possible. Alex pocketed his phone and slipped out of the field house.

Alex replayed the conversation he had with Samantha after trig. He'd hopped out of his chair, too eager (way, way too eager) and caught her before she could stand. At least he tried to laugh it off. "It's been a long weekend," he said. "I might have had this conversation with myself a few times."

It worked. Samantha smiled. "But just a few."

"Enough times not to forget my lines."

"Lay it on me," Samantha said as she stood.

"If we're going to do a maybe-date, we should go for it and do it Saturday. If I can't make a Saturday date work, you should stop giving me chances."

It did the trick. She didn't pretend to forget about their plans *(Bowling? You thought I'd go bowling?)*, and she didn't push for a less date-ish night like Wednesday (a sure sign of rejection). Everything was good except for the look that crossed her face before she agreed. It was like she was wrestling with whether she should say yes. He told himself he was being oversensitive, but Alex couldn't get it out of his head.

Alex ascended the steps beside the bleachers and spotted Conn laying on the top bench. A cigarette dangled from his right hand as he stared up at the cloudy sky. He wore factory-stressed jeans and a ratty t-shirt. His hair was the same planned mess as always. Conn was showing up everywhere. He wasn't kidding about wanting a friend.

"You don't want to get caught smoking on the bleachers," Alex said.

"Why not?" Conn sat up. He took a drag from his cigarette and spoke as he exhaled, the words coming out in smoke. "You ready to get going?"

"I have to wait for my dad. If you need a ride he can probably drive you."

Conn said, "That's why I came. I kind of bolted Sunday and felt bad. Figured I'd make it up and give you a ride home. Oh, how'd it go with Samantha?"

"Ride home? You've got a car?" Alex asked.

"Sort of." Conn walked up the cement steps ahead of Alex. He waited until Alex caught up, his cigarette pointed at a rust and white Ford Festiva without a front bumper or a passenger window. "It runs on gas and it usually turns on. Car might be a stretch."

"Is it older than we are?" Alex laughed.

"It's probably older than both of us combined. Treat it nice or it'll kill us both. Get in and tell me how it went."

Alex threw his bag in the back seat (surprisingly clean for such a beater of car) and closed the door. He felt around for a seatbelt and found only the rough, frayed remains of what was left of the strap. "Seriously?"

Conn put the key in the ignition. The car coughed, hacked, and shuddered to life. "Don't ask me. The car came that way. Samantha, man. Come on. What happened?"

As Conn pulled onto the road, Alex related his conversation with Samantha. Conn nodded through the whole story, except when Alex told him Samantha agreed to the date. Then he punched Alex in the arm.

"That's what I wanted to hear. You've got to *start* with the good part. I hate being on the edge of my seat."

"I'm going out with Samantha on Saturday. There.

Happy?"

Conn grinned. "I'm pleased. I'd be happy if you got me a date with Krista."

"Not a miracle worker, man."

"Screw you," Conn said, laughing. "And I was about to ask if you wanted to shoot some pool."

"Pool sounds great."

"I said I *was* going to ask you."

"Now *I'm* asking. Let's go shoot some pool. Practice sucked and I don't want to go home. I'll tell my dad I'll be late." Alex pulled out his phone. Still three new texts. He'd completely forgotten.

"Fine, if you're twisting my arm, I'll think about it."

Alex flipped through the first two texts. One from his aunt back in Boston asking how he was. The second was an update on his phone plan from his provider. The third stopped him. Stopped him right there and killed everything good about the day.

Conn asked, "What's wrong?"

"Samantha invited me to a track team bowling party."

"That girl loves her some bowling."

Alex shook his head. "The party's on Saturday. *During* our date."

Conn punched the steering wheel of his car and swore. Alex didn't understand why Conn was so angry. Didn't really care. A wound reopened, brought on the throbbing hurt he now felt when things spiraled out of his control. There was only one thing Alex could do with that pain. He punched the car, too.

Chapter Six

SAMANTHA KICKED HER shoes off and let them fall onto the wooden slats of her deck. The air still held a bit of spring chill, but the sky was clear and the sun wouldn't set for another hour. She leaned back in the reclining chair, intent on making the most of her only evening off this week. She stared down from the second story deck onto their backyard, eyes following the slope to where a small creek marked the end of their property. She'd never been allowed to play in the creek, only dangle her feet in on hot days. Even that had stopped years ago, after the storm that flooded their yard and basement. The damage drove her dad into a rage beyond any she'd seen before or since. So bad that her mom threatened to move out with Samantha until he calmed down. That was the only time she'd seen his gun, the black piece of metal clutched in his hand, his voice so loud her ears rang when it was finally done. Now, the closest she got to the creek — and the memories of that flood — was the recliner on the deck.

"Ready for lunch?" Samantha's mom asked through the open kitchen window.

Samantha answered without turning. "Sure. I'll be right there."

"No, stay! I'll bring it out."

One of the signs Dad wasn't home was Mom's voice. He'd been gone less than an hour and she was already unwound, relaxed, almost cheerful. The sliding glass door opened, then closed. Mom sat in the chair beside her and set a plate on the table between them. Grilled cheese on rye. Mom's way of apologizing for what had happened before Dad left. Another fight. Something about his job, the new development he was building. Everything was worse at the start of projects, and this one wasn't going smoothly. At least he'd stormed out before things got past shouting.

"You doing all right?"

Samantha looked up. How long had she been staring at the sandwich, playing out the fight, imagining how much worse it could have been? She replied, "Yeah. I'm fine. Why?"

"Eat." Mom pointed at the plate. Samantha took a bite, chewed, swallowed. Then Mom continued. "You've seemed stressed. Is it school?"

"School's fine. Track's fine." Samantha continued to eat, hopeful her mom would accept her answer and move on.

"It's okay if you don't want to talk about it."

"Well," Samantha began, but immediately cut herself off. Saying anything would lead to questions. "It's nothing. Forget it."

"I understand. I never wanted to talk to my mother either."

"Mom, come on. That's not it." Samantha didn't need to talk. She needed a vent in her heart that she could open, to let the pressure out as tears before it burst through her chest, but she couldn't allow herself to cry. Wasn't even sure she remembered how.

"I know things have been hard lately," Mom said, looking away as she did. She paused before continuing.

"Talk to your friends. Anyone. It doesn't have to be me."

There wasn't anyone she could talk to, not about any real problems, but telling Mom that wouldn't help. So she lied. "I do. And I'm fine. I promise."

"Speaking of friends, how's your new one doing? The girl. Danica, right? She hasn't been over in a while."

"Danica?" Samantha asked. Her mom remembered Danica? Samantha brought her over a few times, back when it was just a friendship that felt a little *too* intense. She'd kept Danica away from her parents since, hoping they'd forget about her.

"Wasn't that her name?"

Samantha nodded, stalling, unsure how to answer. The wrong response could be as bad as saying nothing. She was saved by something worse: the door to the garage opening. Mom was on her feet before the door closed, and back in the kitchen in time to meet Dad. Samantha sunk low into her chair, listening without turning.

"How did it go?" Mom asked.

"I need to go to Charlotte to meet with the investors. They're skittish." The refrigerator door opened then slammed. Her dad getting a bottle of water, probably. After a moment of silence, her father asked, "What?"

Samantha couldn't hear her mother's response, which meant she was trying to escape the question.

"Where are you going? Come back here and tell me what that look was for." Dad wasn't yelling yet, but he was close.

"I'm worried. That's all."

"That again? You don't think I can do this?"

Mom's voice was small and quiet. "It's just... the house."

"Because that faggot accountant you hired told you we could lose it? We needed to put it up to— Where the hell are you going?"

The fight moved to the bedroom and the noise of it faded enough to be tuned out. She realized she'd been holding her breath, hands clenching the armrests, certain she'd be trapped on the deck as things got ugly. Why couldn't Mom let him have his way? Samantha knew when to back down, to hide. She learned that lesson every time her mom poured gas on the fire as if *this time* she wouldn't get burned.

Something moved at the edge of the creek. Samantha crept across the deck and leaned over the railing. A figure stood in the calf-deep water of the creek, hands at its sides, face turned toward Samantha. It was a woman with long hair and a sodden grey dress that floated on the surface of the creek. There was something familiar about her that Samantha couldn't place. The distance played tricks on Samantha's eyes; for a second, she was sure the woman's hair was floating through the air above her head. Fear washed over her, so strong she nearly fled inside despite what waited there.

A door slammed. Samantha spun, ready to be discovered and accused of spying on the fight. She pressed herself against the railing, trapped between the fury of her father and the fall to the yard below. Her father stormed past the window without a glance outside. A moment later, she heard the roar of his car as it sped down the street. Samantha turned back to the creek, heart pounding, but saw nothing. No woman, and no sign she'd ever been there. Samantha backed away until her legs touched the table. She grabbed the plate with her half-eaten sandwich, and ran through the door. Her hands trembled as she threw away the remains of her lunch. There'd been something so familiar about the woman. Her eyes, Samantha thought. They reminded her of Danica's. That was impossible, though. She'd been too far away to make out the woman's features. Just her imagination, then. Stress (fear? guilt?) making her see things that weren't there.

Samantha crept down the hall to her room. As she passed her parents' bedroom door she thought she heard her mother crying and hoped it, too, was just in her head.

~

Four boys in t-shirts and gym shorts unstacked chairs and slid them across waxed linoleum toward the far end of Pepto Bismol Hall. Two girls, hair in matching pony tails, caught the chairs and pushed them into semicircular rows. Youth Group setup was a team effort. Danica walked in through the metal double doors, past the girls' careful chair placement to the small kitchen beside the boys and their diminishing stacks of chairs. The hall was a long rectangle split into three pieces by support posts. The pale pink walls glowed hideously under the light of the late afternoon sun. The room wasn't *technically* called Pepto Bismol Hall (it was the Something Someone Memorial Communal Room or something), but no one called it anything else.

Painting the walls pink wasn't all the church had done with Something Someone's money. They'd also cut away the wall separating the room from the kitchen and put a countertop in its place, because why should the Sunday morning Bible discussion group have to walk through a door to get their coffee and donuts? When it came to community spaces, the United Presbyterian Church of Sheffield was all about efficiency and cheap, garish paint. Pastor Fresh leaned over the countertop. Beneath him was a composition notebook held open by a Bible on one corner and a ceramic sugar packet holder on the other. He had a mechanical pencil tucked behind his ear and a pen between his teeth. Like Pepto Bismol Hall,

Fresh had a proper name: Steve McElfresh. Danica wondered if the nickname sounded cooler when he got it in college. Probably not. Fresh wore flip-flops, one of the dozen Cool Christian T-shirts he owned (today was the one that said OurApostle in the Aeropostale font) and a wood-beaded choker. It was as close to a uniform as he had.

"You need any help, Fresh?" Danica asked.

Fresh jumped like she'd jabbed him. She tried that once, poking him in the ribs to get his attention. He still claimed the sound he made wasn't a scream. "Danny boy! How've you been?"

"All right."

"All right? It's Friday, girl!" Fresh said, his fake enthusiasm at full throttle.

Danica made sure Fresh saw her sarcastic eye roll. "Fine, it's great. Today's super awesome. Do you need help?"

"I think we're all good. Love having an intern again. Love it. How did I live without one?"

"Intern?" Danica asked. They hadn't had an intern all year, since the one with the hand tremors (Timothy, Timmy-boy, T-dogg, etc.) dropped out or changed majors to forensic science or whatever it was the really antisocial interns did when they figured out being a youth pastor meant spending time with teenagers. Danica talked to Fresh once a week — twice, lately, because of camp — and he'd never mentioned a new intern.

"Yeah! I love it when you guys come back and work with us after graduation. It makes me feel like some of you are listening." Fresh was either ignoring Danica's confusion or didn't care. He turned to his comp book, mechanical pencil now in hand, and went back to work. Danica turned to walk away, but froze when saw the new intern descend the staircase at the end of the hall.

"Danica!" the intern shouted, smile on her face, arms outstretched as she closed the distance between them. She wrapped her arms around Danica and squeezed.

The intern was Megan Ashley, once Danica's closest friend. They hadn't spoken in a long time. Almost a year. All of it Danica's fault.

She'd barely changed since graduation: brown hair, chin-length with strawberry highlights, a slight tan, lightly freckled cheeks. The only difference was her body; a little rounder, a little softer, and way bigger breasts. Megan with bigger breasts shouldn't have been possible.

"You're our intern?"

"I know, right?" Megan pulled away, all smiles. Like nothing had ever been or ever could be wrong. "I'm so excited to be back. How have you been?"

There were words she almost said. Words like *Samantha* and *together*. It was too easy to talk to Megan. Too natural. Maybe it was safer not to say anything.

"Okay, I guess," Danica said. "How about you?"

"I don't even know. School's crazy. You can't believe how much work they give you. Five classes doesn't sound too bad until you've got a stack of books to read every week, you know? But I did find this awesome Bible study group. They're amazing. My head is, like, screwed on tighter than it's ever been. It's amazing to be around people who actually *get* your faith." Megan smiled again. "I'm so glad you're still here. I was afraid you'd quit."

"Why would I have quit?" Danica asked. The question was automatic, instinctual, and she regretted it immediately. They both knew exactly why.

Megan frowned and bit her lip. "You know, just... sorry, I didn't mean anything. How's your family? How's Jake?"

Danica relaxed, thankful for the change in subject. "Mom's barely home, but other than that they're good.

Jake got big."

"I bet he did." Megan's hands were still on Danica's shoulders. She seemed so unconcerned, so happy to see her, so comfortable being this close.

She wanted to say more. Things like *why didn't you ever call* and *I missed you.* Emotions and memories intertwined. Samantha, fear of being caught, fear of being left, everything Megan knew about Danica, all the things Danica had once felt for her. Danica wasn't ready for any of it. Megan was the past, a time she'd almost managed to forget.

The metal doors boomed, reverberating like someone had kicked them open. Someone Danica didn't know stalked into Pepto Hall. Mussed hair, dark blue jeans, tight t-shirt. His head moved back and forth, eyes stopping briefly on each and every person.

Danica turned her attention back to Megan. "How long...?"

"Will I be here? Until fall, at least. Do you want to get coffee sometime? We should catch up."

"Coffee would be cool," Danica managed.

"Hey, yo, people. This is where they have youth group, right?" It was the door kicker. The way he looked at her made Danica uncomfortable. As if he'd already sized her up and didn't think much of what he saw.

"This is it. I'm Megan. Is this your first time here?"

"Yeah. I'm Conn. Nice to meet you. And, uh... you are?" Conn asked, turning to Danica.

"Danica. Nice to meet you."

Megan stepped back. "Danica can show you around. I've got to help Fresh. We'll catch up soon, okay?"

She watched Megan go, wishing she could find somewhere to hide, to be alone while she sorted out how she was supposed to feel. Instead she turned to Conn. "Do you go to Sheffield?"

"I'm new. Just got here, you know? My dad was always big on church stuff, so here I am. This is one ugly room."

She didn't like Conn, wanted him gone for reasons she couldn't put her finger on, but she laughed anyway. Like she didn't have a choice.

"Anyway," Conn continued, "I've got, like, one friend and I guess I should meet some other people. You can't get by with just one friend, right?"

Danica led her and Conn toward the chairs. "What's that mean?"

"Like, Alex — that's his name, Alex — he's a cool guy. Easy as hell to hang with. Only this Saturday he's got a date. And it's this group date thing at a bowling alley, right? With all these other girls. Did he invite me along? Nope, because he doesn't want me crashing *his* date. It's no big deal or anything. It's just you can't count on someone all the time."

As Conn spoke, Danica nodded. Never invited along, alone while someone else had plans, afraid they wouldn't be there when you needed. A weird feeling of *togetherness* overcame her, same as the laughter had earlier.

"I know," Danica said. "I hate that."

"Exactly. So I figured I'd stop here and see how it is. I used to like church. It was okay. I had good friends there."

"This is the only place where I don't feel alone." She closed her eyes as she spoke. Between seeing Megan again and everything that was Samantha, Danica's emotions were dangerously raw. Crying in front of the weird new guy was not an option.

"I hear you. And what's up with a bowling party anyway, right?"

"I know!" Danica laughed. "I bet it's the same one my friend is going to. It's a track team thing, right?"

"Yeah, that's it. Track stars and bowling balls." Conn paused, frowned. "Man, I was sure I had a joke for that."

The two sat in chairs at the back of the semicircle. Others filed in as Fresh stepped into the center of the semicircle of chairs. Danica turned to Conn, "Poor Sam got suckered into it. She hates bowling."

"Sam!" Conn slapped Danica on the arm. "Samantha, right? Is that who you mean?"

"Yeah. You met her?"

"Oh, yeah. I was there when Alex asked her out. She's not really my type, but I can see why Alex is into her. Are you two friends? Has she talked about him at all? Sorry, forget it. I shouldn't be asking."

Alex asked her out.

Alex, who'd flirted with Samantha after a meet. Just some guy. No one to be worried about.

Danica's weak hold on her emotions slipped, and she stood, cheeks flushed and eyes stinging, as everyone turned to face her. She fled; out the doors of Pepto Hall, down a hallway stuffed with stacks of plastic chairs, into the girls' bathroom where she finally let herself collapse, sobbing, onto the cold tile floor.

Chapter Seven

AT LEAST FIFTY students were packed into Center Lanes. Alex didn't have a clue who most of them were. Some he recognized from track or class, and a few others were teammates, but mostly it was a sea of strangers. Alex sat on an uncomfortable plastic bench, hands on his lap, while his date did the same beside him. They'd said hello. They'd shared two moments of triumph (Strike!), a few sympathetic glances (Another gutter ball?!), a discussion on favorite brands of root beer, and the briefest chat about movies ever (**Alex:** See anything good lately? **Samantha:** I don't really watch movies.) And those were the high points of the night.

An hour in and they'd finished one game and were five frames into the second. Alex's carefully honed pitching arm did all the wrong things with a bowling ball. He was second to last, hovering just above someone's underdeveloped twelve year-old brother — a gift from parents in need of a "date night" — who rolled the lightest ball using both hands.

"You're up," Samantha said. It was the first thing she'd said in nine minutes. Things were so dire, Alex was timing the silences on his phone's clock.

Alex picked up a swirly green bowling ball with

finger holes that felt too large. He glanced back once, saw Samantha's attention focused somewhere between the far wall and outer space, and threw a powerful and aggressive gutter ball. Not even a sympathetic glance this time. No glance at all. Alex slumped onto the bench beside his non-date. One lane down, Nick pulled a girl he'd met for the first time into his lap. She laughed and ran her fingers through his hair. It seemed like everyone was having a better night than him. Pride kept Alex from calling his dad for an early ride home.

Alex sighed. If pride was going to keep him here, he might as well put it to use. He turned to Samantha and said, "You could have just said no."

"What?" she replied, confused.

"If you didn't want to go out, you could have told me no. I don't need a pity date."

Samantha winced. "That's not what this was."

"But it's not a date."

"It's not a date," she agreed.

He'd already figured that out, but hearing it still hurt. "So what are we doing here?"

"I don't know. I'm sorry. I thought this would make it easier." Samantha gestured at the people around them.

"Did you throw a party to get out of our date?"

"Maybe."

Alex wanted to be angry, but couldn't. She seemed as uncomfortable as him. Why didn't she just tell him the date was off? Was she afraid he wouldn't take no for an answer after how weird he'd been? Ashamed, Alex said, "We don't have to be on a date, okay? We can just hang out. That's cool, too."

"It is?"

Alex had one, small, genuine smile left in him. "It's cooler than you pretending I'm not here."

"Yeah, okay," Samantha laughed. It was sounded

like relief, but still.

"So. We're friends and hanging out. That means we can talk a little, right?"

"We can talk."

"Good. I wasn't going to last long with nothing to do but watch that," Alex pointed his thumb at Nick.

Samantha saw the girl on Nick's lap. "Oh, come on, Lacey. Nick? Really?"

"Freshman?"

"Yeah," Samantha said. "She doesn't know better."

"Wrong person to learn from."

"Like a crash course in advanced douchery."

"I could try to break it up," Alex suggested.

Samantha shook her head. "If you do, it'll take twice as long for her to learn. She needs to get it out of her system."

"There's got to be a better way. I wouldn't wish Nick on anyone."

Samantha's phone screeched out the distorted first notes of a song Alex didn't recognize. She fished it out of her purse while she talked. "I know. I've been there."

"With Nick?"

"With Nick," she said, phone in hand.

"Really? When?"

Samantha frowned. Alex was afraid he'd pushed too hard until he realized she was upset with whatever was on her phone. Her reply was absent, distracted. "Last year. He took me to homecoming. I did stupid things with him in the computer lab."

"Ah," Alex said, trying very hard not to think about *what* stupid things had happened.

"Wait," Samantha said, looking up from the phone. "Not that stupid. He got all gropy and I stopped things. You know what he did when I backed him off?"

Alex shook his head.

"He pulled out his phone and texted someone about it. Seriously."

Alex nodded, then gestured at Samantha's phone. "Everything all right?"

"Oh, yeah. Fine." She shoved her phone back into her purse.

Someone shouted Samantha's name. It was her turn. Alex looked around while he waited, and spotted Krista and her boyfriend leaning against each other on a bench halfway across the alley. A scene repeated by couples at every lane. He was glad Samantha was talking, he really was, but disappointment ate at him. He feared how he'd feel tomorrow, when the reality of Samantha's disinterest sunk in. Without that hope, what was there to stop Alex from falling back into the fog?

"You still here?" Samantha asked as she sat back on the bench. He hadn't noticed her return.

"Yeah. Yeah, sorry, I'm okay."

"Uh huh." Samantha looked concerned.

At least, Alex *thought* she looked concerned. "Maybe a little less than okay. It's nothing. I'm good."

"Hey, hold on," Samantha put a hand on his leg. She didn't seem to give it a second thought. "I'm sorry I was a bitch to you tonight. It wasn't cool. There's just... there's stuff, okay? A lot of stuff. It's not about you."

"Don't take this the wrong way," Alex said, "but I've got 'stuff' too."

Samantha's cheek dimpled in. Was she was biting the inside of her cheek? "So you're saying everything's not about me."

Alex laughed. "Some of it's about you."

"Want to talk about the parts that aren't?" Samantha asked. Her hand: still on his leg.

Did he want to? The only people that asked Alex about the other *stuff* were his dad (a definite *no* to that talk) and people who were paid to. Professionals. Grief counselors. Never a friend. Never anyone he *knew*.

"I really don't know," Alex managed.

Samantha looked down and saw where her hand was. She looked back up, but her hand stayed where it was. "Maybe some other time we could. Outside of a bowling alley."

Alex, ready to say an immediate yes to anything Samantha asked, somehow didn't get an answer out before her phone beeped. She gave him a *hold on* look and pulled her hand away to find her phone. She glanced at it and her eyes widened. "Shit. Oh, shit, shit, shit," she said. Samantha looked up at Alex. There was fear in her eyes. Panic.

"Sorry," she said.

Then stood and ran for the exit like something was chasing her.

~

Samantha kept her phone in hand. Something to squeeze. Something to crush. Danica was here. What was she thinking? How could she show up *here, tonight, with everyone else around?* Samantha didn't check to see who was watching. It wouldn't matter as long as she got rid of Danica quickly and came up with an excuse. A crisis. Danica got dumped. No, *dumped* was too close to what the panic said she should do. Samantha would think of something. First she had to get Danica out.

She'd been getting messages from Danica all night, probably from her friend's computer. That was the only way Danica got online if she wasn't at school or at the library. Samantha didn't want to ignore her, but even messages like **how's it going?** were more than Samantha could handle with Alex there. Her replies got shorter and shorter until she finally stopped. She hoped Danica would get the message and back off. Just for now. Just for a few hours.

Then: **what aren't you telling me?**

Samantha didn't know how to reply and couldn't focus with Alex over her shoulder. Did Danica know? She'd tried to keep her date with Alex quiet, but who knew who he told? What if Danica knew? Was this a test to see if Samantha would come clean?

She tried to ignore it all. Put her phone in her purse. Talked to Alex. Then her phone buzzed again.

ignoring me because you're all over a guy. nice. i'm outside.

Two sets of glass doors separated the bowling alley from the outside. Danica stood in the narrow space between the inner and outer doors, staring out toward the parking lot. She wore loose jeans and a t-shirt at least a size too large. Samantha stopped. For a moment, anger and panic gave way to guilt. What had Danica seen? Samantha's hand on Alex leg while she smiled, laughed, asked to see him again? Only for a moment, though. She remembered they weren't alone, that anyone could see her and Danica together, and fear retook the wheel.

"What are you doing here?" Samantha demanded. Danica turned around. Her eyes were bloodshot, her cheeks glossy. She'd been crying. She'd been crying a lot.

"I need to talk," Danica's voice was rough and quiet, on the verge of tears.

"Now? You want to talk now?"

"I need to."

"I'm not talking to you now," Samantha snapped. "Please go. Please. Before someone notices."

Danica held her ground. "Notices what? You're all over him. Who cares about me?"

"Danica…"

There were fresh tears on Danica's cheeks that she wiped away with the back of a hand holding a chunky purple phone. Danica didn't own one. It had to be someone else's. Her friend's, Samantha thought.

"Leslie's here? Does she know about us?"

"She always knew. She won't tell anyone."

"Great, why don't you just walk in there and tell everyone?"

Danica ignored her. Brushed tears aside. Asked, "Why didn't you tell me you had a date?"

"It's not a date."

"He asked you out at that bonfire and you said yes, right? Why are you lying to me? Are you breaking up with me?" Danica's voice got quieter and quieter as she spoke. Her last question was almost inaudible.

How did Danica know about what happened at the bonfire? Did one of Alex's friends say something? "I was trying to protect us. You know we have to be careful. I was being careful. If I said no to him—"

"Have you kissed him yet?" Danica interrupted.

"I don't want to kiss him." Samantha inched forward until they were close enough that her sandaled toes touched the front of Danica's shoes. "I should have told you. I don't want to be with him. I promise."

Danica leaned into Samantha and pressed her forehead against Samantha's. She whispered, "I thought I lost you."

Samantha placed a hand on Danica's cheek. Met her eyes.

Their kiss was brief. A brush of lips, the sticky touch of drying tears against Samantha's cheek.

"I won't. I couldn't," Samantha said. "We can't talk right now, okay? Will you call tomorrow?"

Danica nodded. She detached herself from Samantha, eyes down, and pushed open the door. Samantha watched her go, waiting for the relief to hit.

"You're seriously doing this again?"

Samantha spun, a spike of electric fear traveling every nerve. Krista. *No, not Krista. Please not Krista.*

"What the hell is wrong with you?" Krista stood, the glass door into the bowling alley held open by her foot. Her face was a shade of red Samantha had only seen once before on a day they'd both tried to forget.

She and Krista, stoned for the first time, lying on the grassy hill behind Krista's house. The giggling, the holding hands. The stupid, silly, meaningless kiss. Krista's anger, her crimson cheeks, her threat to tell everyone unless Samantha swore she'd never do it again.

"What did you see?"

"What do you think I saw?"

"It was nothing. She was upset. Krista, please don't. Please don't tell," Samantha pleaded.

Alex came around the corner before Krista could answer, so fast he nearly ran into her.

"Hey, whoa, sorry. I was just making sure you were okay. I didn't mean to interrupt." Alex raised his hands. *Please don't shoot me, I come in peace.*

Krista looked from Alex to Samantha and back. Samantha could almost hear the words forming in Krista's head. If she had the chance, if Samantha let her talk, there was no turning back. No recovery.

"It was just a fight with someone. It's over. It's totally over." Samantha looked at Krista when she repeated *over.* "It's fine."

"It doesn't look fine," Alex replied.

Krista's mouth opened again.

"Can we go for a walk?" Samantha asked Alex before Krista could make a sound.

"You don't want to keep bowling?"

Samantha grabbed Alex by the hand and pulled him

toward the door. "Can we talk later, Krista?"

Krista nodded in slow motion. "I'll tell them you guys had to book, okay?"

"Thank you." She'd bought herself time. Not much, but enough to run.

Samantha fled into the damp spring night with Alex in tow. She didn't know where she was leading them. Away. Away was all that mattered. As far away as she could get.

Chapter Eight

SAMANTHA DRAGGED THEM past the last street lamp and into the night. The sidewalk ended, leaving only a pitiful guardrail between them and traffic. Eventually the guardrail was gone, too. Headlights cast long, spiraling shadows as cars raced down the darkened road. Samantha kept her hand tight on Alex's, walked as fast as she could pull him. Tires buzzed at the edges of the berm's warning strips. Trees pressed Samantha and Alex closer and closer to the oncoming traffic. It was stupid to be here, dangerous, but going back was worse. She had to keep moving. She had to run.

Run from what, though? If Krista talked, what she said would travel faster, farther. It would find her friends, her home, her father. There was no escape from that. No way to keep ahead of herself. Samantha felt another car rush past and realized she wasn't running. She was tempting fate. Tempting fate and dragging someone along for the ride.

The trees broke at the edge of a parking lot. A single halogen floodlight cast enough light to read the words painted in red and green on the building's white walls: Tessario's Delicatessen. Samantha led Alex off the road into the parking lot. Maybe here, safe from the cars and far from her friends, she could clear her head, decide what to do and where to go. Samantha released Alex's hand. Her palm, sweaty and clammy, tingled as blood rushed back into it. She made her way to an unlit section of white brick wall and slid down onto the cement sidewalk, her back against the wall. Alex faced her and crouched on the blacktop.

"Hey," he said, smiling. His face was flushed from exertion. "You know how you said you were okay back there?"

Samantha nodded.

"You're really not okay."

Samantha shook her head. What was the point in lying?

"You want to talk about it?"

Another head shake.

Alex pivoted on the balls of his feet and took a seat against the wall beside Samantha. He stretched out, set his hands on his thighs, and looked up. Samantha did the same. All she saw was a sky so washed out by light pollution the stars were barely visible.

"You know I'm new here, right? I moved here from Boston."

Samantha replied, her voice weak and strained, "Yeah."

"Anyone tell you why?"

"I asked," Samantha said, "but no one knew. Are your parents divorced?"

"They were."

Samantha took her eyes off the sky and faced him. "Were?"

"Mom died last year. Now I'm with my dad."

Samantha, for the second time that night, put her hand on Alex's leg. "I'm sorry. I didn't know that."

"No one does. I didn't really say anything, and

people don't ask unless you give them a reason to, you know?"

"Yeah. I do."

Alex put his hand over Samantha's own. She liked the warmth of it, the roughness compared to Danica's. She liked having Alex close. She liked *him*. Was that why she'd lied to Danica?

"It was rough when I got here," Alex said, his eyes now on their hands. "Things weren't... I don't know... It was like I was in a fog only I could see."

"Is that still how it is?"

"Don't make me say something really cheesy right now, okay?"

Samantha was surprised to hear herself laugh. "Cheesy would be a nice change."

"I saw you run," Alex said, "and it was the first time I felt something since she died."

Maybe Samantha needed a release, an escape from all the things that were wrong. Maybe it was what he said, or the heat of his hand on hers. Maybe she just wanted to kiss someone and not fear getting caught.

Whatever the reason, Samantha's hand slid up Alex's arm to his neck and turned him to her. He took the hint, and their lips met under the single working floodlight in the parking lot of Tessario's Delicatessen.

~

Danica opened her eyes for the first time since collapsing into the passenger seat of Leslie's car. Her head hurt and her muscles were stiff, but at least she'd stopped crying. She looked out the windows, tried to focus the blur of light and shadow into something she recognized. Home, Danica thought. She was home. Danica pulled free of her seatbelt and opened the door.

"Call me tomorrow, okay?" Leslie asked before Danica could climb out.

"Okay."

She shut the door and crossed her yard. Light filtered through the thin, cream-colored curtains of her double wide's front windows. Mom was still awake. There was no way she'd make it to the bedroom without being seen. Unless Mom was blind *and* sleeping, it would be obvious Danica had spent the night in tears. She considered sneaking in through the back, but didn't have the strength to bother. Danica fished her keys out of her pocket, unlocked the door, and walked inside.

The television was on, its volume set to inaudible. Ian slept with his head against the back of the couch and mouth hanging open. Mom was half-sprawled across his lap.

Danica kept her face down and angled away. "Hey," she said.

"Hey, hon," her mom replied. Then she looked up. Saw. "Danny, what's wrong? Are you okay?"

Ian made a *mmmrrpph* sound.

"Fine. I just want to go to bed."

Moms were not impressed by "fine." Not even tired moms. "What happened? Did someone hurt you?"

Danica stopped at the threshold between the living room and the kitchen. "No one hurt me. Can we talk about it tomorrow?"

"No, Danny, what happened?"

"I'm fine, Mom! Leave me alone!" She was crying again before the words were out of her mouth. Her mom disentangled herself from Ian and tried to speak, but Danica had already fled. She slammed her bedroom door and held it closed until Mom's pleas stopped and she returned, defeated, to the couch. Finally alone, Danica dropped her coat onto the floor next to the pile of unwashed shirts and bras, and fell face first onto her mattress.

Somewhere under the bed, hidden behind books and pants that no longer fit, there was a small plastic art supply box. Her emergency kit, the one she'd hidden from Megan the day they'd thrown out the matches and lighters and needles. She hadn't touched it in over a year. She'd told herself she didn't need it, but she kept it anyway. Just in case. Danica imagined holding the box, laying its contents out on her comforter, choosing the right tool to take the pain out. She might have, too, if not for the terrible wave of exhaustion that swept over her.

She fell asleep in her clothes, but it was shallow, fitful. The world beyond her closed eyes remained, dripping the irregular drumbeat of a broken faucet through her door, flashing the echo of car headlights through her curtains, screaming the cries of night birds as restless as she. Danica dreamed memories twisted into nightmare. Samantha's lies, her hands on someone — everyone — else. Her kiss burning Danica's frozen lips. And always leaving. Always leaving.

Danica woke to find her room aglow with shifting blue light. There was someone on her bed. Her mother? No, someone else. A woman whose face was half-covered by hair that moved as if she were underwater. She was clothed in a thin dress made of woven fog, her skin colorless as a corpse. The woman leaned forward, her face inches from Danica's own.

"I'm so sorry, my love. I am so, so sorry."

Danica's whole body felt numb. She tried to speak, to ask who the woman was, but her mouth wouldn't move.

"It hurts. I know it hurts. I wish I could have come sooner, but I'm here now."

The woman with the swaying hair rose back up and slid a hand under the neck of her dress. She grimaced in pain as her hand reemerged with something held delicately between her fingers. A pin. A fine golden pin, no thicker than sewing needle. It was long, though; nearly as long as the woman's index finger.

"You'll never have to be alone again. I promise you. Never again."

The woman lowered the pin towards Danica's breast. The needle's point went through her t-shirt and into her flesh. It was the coldest thing Danica had ever felt, and her numbness did nothing to dull the pain. The woman kept her eyes on Danica's as the pin pushed deeper and deeper; through Danica's breast, through the muscle beneath, into her heart. A roar built in her head as it entered her. A roar that separated, piece by piece, into individual voices, each speaking over the other, each full pain and rage. The woman pushed the last of the needle into Danica with the tip of her middle finger. When it was done, the voices went silent.

"Never again, my love. Never again."

Danica's eyes closed. She had neither the will nor desire to keep them open. The voices vanished into Danica's dreams, as did the pain of the needle.

When she woke the next morning, Danica recalled only the vanishing image of the woman's hair and the sight of a long, golden pin. There was no mark on her breast. No pin. Only a pain in her heart and head that she couldn't escape. Just Danica, herself, alone, falling into the dark.

Act Two

Love That Never Dies

Chapter Nine

THE CARDBOARD BOX had brown packing tape stretched across every opening, three layers thick. Alex sat on the floor beside it, still dressed as he'd slept: shirtless and in boxers. He held the black metal handles of his father's only pair of scissors, his hand unsteady, unsure where to begin the first cut. He'd unpacked the other boxes a year ago, but shoved this one into the back of the closet and covered it with baseball equipment and dirty clothes. He never forgot it. It stayed there, purposefully unopened, out of sight but always in mind.

His mother hadn't left a note. She'd left the box.

He'd awakened before the sun had risen, and shuffled into the kitchen to find the scissors. His father was already there, reading the newspaper, face covered by the story of a drowning the night before. They hadn't spoken, but his father had taken Alex's presence as the cue to cook breakfast. He could hear the clink of plates and the clang of pans through the bedroom door. If he didn't do this now, before breakfast was ready, Alex feared he'd lose his nerve and the box would spend another year under his laundry.

Now, right now, Alex had strength. He had memories of a kiss, of the unexpected force of her lips, the silence of the moments after, the peace of their walk back to his car, hands clasped. He'd cried in the car as he drove her home. Tried to hide it, too, but she'd seen. She didn't say a word, or ask why, or seem ashamed or uncomfortable. She let his tears come and pass, and kissed him on the cheek when they said their goodbyes.

Alex pierced the tape with the point of the scissors and dragged it, slicing, to one end of the box. He did the same along each side of the box, then dropped the still-open scissors onto the carpet. There was a moment of hesitation when Alex placed his hands on the unsealed flaps. No one knew his mother had left the box for him. They'd have opened it, ensured its contents were safe, appropriate, unlikely to cause more pain. She must have known it, too, because she'd left the box under his bed, not out where his family could find and purge it along with all other traces of what had happened.

He opened one flap, glanced inside. The cover of a book. Poetry. Bukowski. One of his mother's favorites. He opened the other flap, removed the book, and set it aside. More books were below it. Vonnegut, Heller, Frost, Dahl. Had anyone noticed these missing from the shelves when they packed up the house? Had they cared? Beneath the books was a wooden jewelry box inlaid with pearl. His grandmother's, then his mother's. Now Alex's. It was empty, as it had been since the day his mother dumped its contents into the trash, weeping, for reasons she never explained.

Finally, a photo album Alex remembered well. Whenever he saw it on his mother's lap, her fingers on one photograph, her unfocused gaze somewhere beyond its pages, he knew it was one of the bad days. Pictures of him, of them, of his father. Those would have to wait until he was ready. He repacked the box, books first, jewelry box last, and put it back in the closet.

Just in time. His father spoke through Alex's closed door. "Alex, hey, breakfast is ready, okay?"

Alex didn't answer. He closed the closet door, opened the one to the hallway, and found himself face to face with his father.

"Breakfast," his father repeated.

"I heard you."

His father walked down the hallway without another word. Alex followed, stepped into the kitchen, and took his seat at the small, round table. There was a plate of french toast and bacon waiting for him.

"Sleep okay?" his father asked.

"Yeah."

His father took his seat across the table. A cup of coffee and two English muffins were his breakfast, as always. His father took a nibble of the muffin and a sip of coffee, watching Alex as he did, as if today would be different and Alex would speak without being asked.

Two nibbles and a sip later, his father gave up. "Have a good night?"

"Uh-huh."

"You went to, what, a party?"

"Bowling," Alex said. He looked down at his plate, hoping his father would take the hint to back off. He never took the hint.

"With the team?"

Alex sighed and dropped his fork on the plate. This was when Alex would usually stand up, take his food into the bedroom and eat in solitude. It happened most weekends. His father couldn't stop asking questions, and Alex couldn't answer. The longer they spoke, the closer Alex got to the memory of his father saying goodbye; first to Alex's mother, then to Alex himself, before taking his two suitcases to the taxi and leaving them for good. That, and everything after.

He met his father's eyes. He saw the man's pain, the pain Alex *wanted* to cause, and shame washed over him.

"With a girl," Alex answered.

"So," his father said, "it was a *really* good night."

They both smiled, together. He wondered if he should say something. Anything. About the kiss, or the box, or the day of the funeral when his father returned to his mother's house to take Alex away. Anything that mattered. He didn't get the chance. Alex's phone rang, loud even from across the house. Alex gave an apologetic look and took the plate with him into his bedroom to answer the call. It was Conn.

"All right," Conn said, not even bothering with a hello. "Let's hear it, Mr. Can't Send Me a Single Text Before Crashing. How'd it go?"

"It was good," Alex said.

Alex sat on the bed and set the barely-eaten plate of French toast next to him. He looked down the hallway, toward the kitchen, then down to where he'd knelt and opened the box. Again, Alex smiled.

"Things are really good."

~

Danica slumped over the folding table her mother had set up in the kitchen. It only got dragged inside when the family was together for a meal. So, barely ever. Six chairs were crammed around the table. One was empty, as it always was, because Danica's mother never stopped moving long enough to sit and eat. Jake knelt in the chair next to Danica. Even then he barely reached the table. Steve and Pete sat across from her, eyeing each other as they ate. The call to breakfast had interrupted their backyard wrestling. Ian sat alone on the side nearest the window. He hadn't said a thing since they sat down. He never did.

It was almost noon. Danica's mother didn't start breakfast until Danica pulled herself out of bed to use the bathroom. She'd intended to go back to sleep for as long as her body would let her, but Mom was already cooking when Danica stepped back into the hallway.

No one said anything about the previous night. Mom only asked if Danica wanted eggs or pancakes and offered her a glass of milk. Danica ignored Mom's obvious concern. Had to ignore it. If she opened the door to question, Danica knew the first thing Mom would ask.

"Was it a boy?"

Danica focused on her breakfast — scrambled eggs, though now that she had them they looked as unappealing as pancakes had sounded. She poked at a bit of egg, moving it around the plate, her eyes following the slight smear of butter it left in its wake. Last night felt both distant and immediate. The image of Samantha and Alex so clear but so far away, farther than the other side of the bowling alley. Farther than across the gulf of a canyon, or the expanse of the ocean. Danica imagined them touching and heard the rush of coursing water, felt a pinpoint of pain in her heart.

"I'm going to Andy's," Steve declared when he finished eating.

Mom turned on the sink faucet before responding. "I thought we were going to the zoo today."

"The zoo sucks," Steve said. He picked up his dirty plate and handed it to Mom. "Andy's doing flag football today."

Mom closed her eyes and silently counted to five. It was a calming technique she learned after Dad ran off, when she still had them seeing the family counselor. All Danica remembered of the counselor was his toupée and yellow teeth. Mom said, "This is my only weekend off for a month. You're spending today with your family."

"What family?" Steve stomped off to his bedroom and slammed the door.

Mom dropped the plate in the sink so hard Danica was shocked it didn't shatter. She turned from them, face down to the running faucet, hands on the edge of the counter. She wished she could help, but Danica didn't want to go to the zoo any more than Steve did. She didn't want to go anywhere except back to bed. Even sitting here, listening and saying nothing, sapped what little strength she had. Danica wondered if Mom was trying not to cry. She envied that Mom had that option. To fight her tears off.

Ian took his coffee into the living room. Pete left his plate on the table and followed, leaving Jake and Danica in the kitchen with Mom. Jake turned to Danica and quietly asked, "We're not going to the zoo?"

Danica shrugged.

"I wanted to see lions," he said.

Without turning, Mom spoke in a shaky voice. "We'll go see the lions, honey. I promise."

Again, Danica wondered if she should say something. A reassuring lie for Jake, for Mom, for herself. A sudden knock on the back door saved her from having to try.

"I'll get it," Mom said.

"No," Danica replied, needing an escape. "I will."

She brushed past her mom, stepped into the laundry room, and pulled the fraying drape aside. There, sweaty in her windbreaker and track pants, was Samantha. "It's for me," Danica shouted and slipped outside. Samantha took a step backwards. Was it to make room, or to keep distance between them? They faced each other without speaking — Samantha out of breath, Danica out of words — when shouts from the kitchen startled them. Mom and Steve, round two.

Samantha took another step back, toward the line of dying trees beside the house. "Can we talk?"

Danica nodded and followed Samantha. Samantha stopped behind one of the pines. They'd come here many times before, out of sight enough for privacy, though never enough for safety.

"Did you run here?" Danica asked.

Samantha nodded. "From the park. Dad dropped me there. He'll be back soon."

"You could have called." Danica's tone was flat. Automatic. Before, with Mom, she couldn't feel no matter how much she'd wanted to. Now that numbness was a shield.

"I wanted to see you." Samantha took a step closer. "Is that okay?"

There was a slight buzz in Danica's heart at that, like the pins and needles of sensation returning to a sleeping limb. Danica replied, "Yes."

Samantha opened her mouth to say something, but didn't finish. Instead, she closed the distance between them and kissed Danica on the mouth. Shocked, unprepared for affection, Danica placed her hands on Samantha's stomach and pushed her away.

"What are you doing?"

"I'm so sorry," Samantha said. "I'm so sorry for last night. I didn't mean it."

"Didn't mean what?"

Samantha hesitated. "To hurt you. I didn't mean to hurt you."

"It's fine," Danica said, not meaning it and not trying to sound like she did.

Samantha moved back beside the tree. Her voice shook as she said, "Krista saw us."

No more pins and needles. Heat flooded her limbs and face. "Saw what?"

"When I kissed you."

"Oh my God," Danica said. "Oh my God."

"She saw and I don't know if she's going to tell."

"What do you want to do?" The heat built to fire, months of fear now real. Samantha with someone else, Samantha and Danica caught. Samantha gone forever.

"No," Samantha said, understanding exactly what Danica meant. "I don't want that."

"But Krista might say something."

"She might not. Not if I... maybe if I..."

"What?"

Samantha let out a ragged sigh. "Stay with Alex."

"No."

Samantha took a step back toward Danica. Stretched out a hand, but didn't touch her. "Just for show. Just for people to see. If I'm with Alex, she won't talk about us. I can pretend. We can pretend until they forget."

"No," Danica said again.

"Please," Samantha begged. She brushed the back of Danica's hands with two fingers. "I don't know what else to do."

Dozens of responses rushed to mind. She followed them forward and saw they all lead to the same place. To the end. The heat flowed back in her heart, to the pinpoint in her breast. Samantha would stay only if Danica let her hide them where no one could see, and Danica couldn't face tomorrow without her.

"If it's only for them. If it's only for Krista. It can't be real." Danica spoke to Samantha's hand, not to her eyes.

"It's for you," Samantha said. "It's for us. That's what's real."

Danica curled her fingers around Samantha's and nodded. It was her own fault, Danica knew. Her own fault for going to that bowling alley in tears and forcing Samantha to console her. If she hadn't been so stupid this wouldn't have happened. She told herself that again and again, and squeezed Samantha's hand as hard as she could.

"I'm sorry," Danica said.

Samantha didn't reply, except to squeeze Danica's hand in return.

Danica asked, "What now?"

This time, when Samantha kissed her, Danica didn't resist. It was brief, and when it was over they turned away from each other. Samantha looked out to the road. "I need to go or Dad will wonder where I am. If I'm distant at school, just…"

"I know," Danica said.

Samantha nodded and offered a small, tentative smile. "Thank you."

Danica tried to smile back. Probably didn't succeed. Samantha launched into a fast jog and disappeared behind the other double wides. The pain was still there, the deep sting in her heart, clear as when she'd dreamed of the woman and her golden pin. The sound of water returned, and with it an anger that overwhelmed her.

Lying, cheating bitch, she thought, and somehow knew the words were not her own.

Chapter Ten

KRISTA WANTED A cigarette. No, she wanted cigarettes, one lit off the dying butt of the last, until the beer buzz became a full-on beer drunk and she didn't need the things anymore. "I hate it when you taste like an ashtray," Evan always said when he'd ask her to quit smoking. The arrogant prick. Like he cared what her mouth tasted like when he was just going to push her down on him after thirty seconds of making out. Krista wasn't giving him shit for playing quarters until he was too drunk to get it up. Again.

There were seven of them riding out the night in Nick's field. Evan stood across a folding card table from Nick and Logan, each with a quarter in front of them and a six-pack on the ground at their feet. The orange light of the fading bonfire was barely enough to make out what was happening. Logan stood with his hands on the edge of the table, impatient as a five-year old with a wrapped present. Not for his turn, but for someone to land a shot and tell him to drink. The hulking slob could lose every game and stay sober. The rest of them stayed near the fire. Krista on the log with two other girls, and Ferris on the ground facing them. The taller of the girls was perched like a gargoyle on the balls of her feet. Hallie. Her hair was dyed black and pulled into unbraided pigtails. Her friend Linda kept running her hand through her recently cut blonde hair. What had once come down to her waist now ended above her ears. Some kind of hipster pixie cut nonsense that Krista hated.

It was a typical Saturday night in Sheffield with nothing better to do. Krista on the same overturned log, surrounded by the same people, drinking the same cheap beer, and watching the same bonfire sputter and spark and smoke until the night was over and the memory of it all was lost in a bored, drunken fog. It was better than being home, trapped between a brother even the Army didn't want and a stepmother that chewed Xanax like they were Pez. At least when her dad was home (which was never) fake mom bothered to make dinner. Better to escape, even if it meant being surrounded by morons.

Krista fidgeted with her phone. Every few minutes she'd thumb it out of sleep, stare at green and white **CALL** button below Samantha's number, then relock it.

"You know who I miss?" Linda asked. "Your sister. How the hell is she?"

Krista looked up from the phone. Ferris finished her beer while Hallie sipped out of the transparent purple water bottle she always had with her.

Ferris replied, "She's good. Back in town, sorta. She interns at the church so she stays with us, like, two nights a week."

Linda nodded. "I should call her. Her number's still the same, right?"

"Dude, you don't even call *me*," Hallie said. "The only way we stay friends next year is if you come to IUP with me."

Hallie and Linda were seniors, which was obvious because they brought up going to college *every chance they got*. Krista couldn't wait until Hallie took Linda and that idiot pixie cut to a dorm somewhere very far away. She returned her attention to the phone. She needed to call Samantha, but what was she supposed to say? The last thing she needed was to catch Samantha mid-make out with that weird little lesbo. She'd spent a lot of time drinking and smoking away the memory the day Samantha kissed her. Had told herself it was just the weed and almost believed it. Anyone else and Krista would've walked back through those glass doors and shouted to everyone in the bowling alley to come and see — come and see who's all over another chick! —   but not Samantha.

"Yeah! Shit, yeah! Drink, you sloppy bitch!" Nick shouted, pointing at Evan with both hands. When it came to drinking games, no one could match Nick. People didn't play him to win, but for an excuse to get drunk fast.

"Remember when he used to think I was his sloppy bitch?" Hallie asked. "You think he'll try to feel me up without asking again? I haven't kicked anyone in the shin for weeks."

"Just do it. He deserves it for something," Linda said.

Hallie shuddered and frowned. "Hell no. I'm not getting close to him on purpose."

"Throw a rock," Krista said, kicking at a chunk of stone on the ground. "Aim high."

Linda and Hallie laughed. Ferris shook her head, all disapproving. She could be such a bore.

Something over Krista's shoulder caught the girls' attention. Krista turned and saw a silhouette walking across the field. People dropping in on one of Nick's bonfires was nothing new, but there was something about the approaching figure that made Krista anxious.

"Oh, it's just some guy. I thought it might be

Samantha. Where is she, anyway?" Hallie asked.

Krista could tell Ferris had the same question. She'd been texting Samantha without reply since last night. She knew Krista wasn't telling her something and it pissed her off. That part Krista didn't mind so much.

"Well hello there, ladies. I hope I'm not crashing," the figure said as he stepped into the circle of bonfire light. Krista squinted. It wasn't someone she knew, unless… was that Alex's friend? Krista tried to remember his name.

Hallie grinned. "You're totally crashing. I'm Hallie."

"Conn," he responded, stopping beside the log. Beside Krista.

"This is Linda," Hallie said, pointing, "and that's Ferris. And—"

"Krista. I know. Nice to meet all of you." Conn's eyes stayed on Krista.

Great, he's here for me. Krista leaned back onto one hand and gave Conn a long once-over. "Do I know you?"

"We met, but you were puking on your friend's shoes."

"Right." Krista winced. Not her best night.

"So, what brings you to our fire, crasher?" Ferris asked, the flirt so obvious Krista wanted to smack her.

"Slow night, nothing to do, thought I'd come by and say hey. I needed a break. A little fun, you know?"

"A break from what?" Ferris asked.

"I keep busy." He noticed the phone in Krista's hands. "You waiting for a call?"

"About to make one. So, y'know, thanks for stopping by. Say hi to my boyfriend on your way out, 'k?"

Conn laughed, glanced at Evan, then turned back to Krista. "That's it? I don't even get a shot?"

"I think you had it," Linda said.

"Better luck next time," Hallie added.

Conn leaned close to Krista and whispered, "Should I have tried to impress you?"

Krista gave him another long up-and-down look and whispered back, "Sorry, not impressed."

"What if I kicked the shit out of your boyfriend? Would that be a start?"

"Okay," Krista laughed. "At least you're funny."

Conn didn't laugh, just stared at her, smirking, until she got the message. He wasn't kidding.

Krista shrugged. "Fine, whatever. Go for it. Let's see what you've got. *Conn*."

Conn kissed her on the lips, hard. For a second, Krista forgot that she should have been disgusted. She actually kind of liked it, and it was over before she could decide she didn't.

"What was that?"

"Me picking a fight with your boyfriend."

Something hit the card table. Evan's fist. "What the hell are you doing?"

Conn turned to face Evan. Everyone's eyes followed. Evan slammed his can of beer down and took three steps toward Conn. Krista could only see the side of Conn's face, but she was pretty sure he was smiling. He wasn't scared. He thought this was funny.

"Getting your attention." Conn closed the distance between them. "I've got a bet with Krista. I don't think you'll last a minute against me. She's giving you five. True love, am I right?"

There wasn't anything attractive about Conn. He was too small, too grungy, too full of himself. A creep with a crush she didn't need. Yet Krista felt herself go still as the two boys circled each other. Did she *want* Conn to win?

"Do you know this guy?" Hallie asked, laughing

nervously.

"Met him once," Krista replied.

Nick and Logan flanked Conn, but Evan waved them off. "You think I need your help? With him?"

"Yeah, guys, wait your turn." Conn said, still grinning. "When I'm done, maybe I'll kick your asses in quarters as an encore."

Nick burst into laughter. "You're on, asshole."

"You sure attract the fun ones," Linda said, and Ferris nodded in annoyed agreement.

Conn made a show of cracking his neck, rotating his shoulders, and hopping up and down on the balls of his feet. Evan didn't bother with any of it. He stepped in and put everything into a right hook to Conn's head. Conn didn't raise his arm to block it, didn't try to dodge. The punch hit Conn in the temple. The force of it knocked him sideways and onto his knees. Nick and Logan cheered. Ferris gasped. Krista fought down a rising tide of disappointment.

"That... okay, that was a hell of a swing, man. Better than I thought you had." Conn pushed his hair out of his eyes and slowly stood. "Round 2?"

Krista couldn't be sure, but she thought Evan looked afraid. The blow should have knocked Conn unconscious, but he wasn't even dazed. They closed on each other again. Evan clipped Conn on the forehead with a jab, then followed with another wild right. Conn stepped into it and caught Evan's right forearm on his own left. Then, with his free hand, he hit Evan under the jaw with an open-palmed strike. Conn didn't let him recover. He swung with his left, then his right, then his left, connecting with Evan's head every time. After the third punch, Conn stepped back and let Evan wobble, stumble, and fall to his hands and knees.

"Holy shit," Nick said.

"Huh," Linda added.

Krista stared at Conn in disbelief. Who the hell was this guy? No one moved as Conn brushed himself off and returned to Krista's side. He knelt, looked her in the eye, and smiled. Maybe he'd never stopped smiling.

"Are you okay?" Krista asked.

"I'm tougher than I look. But, hey, you have a call to make, and I'm interrupting. I'll leave you to it. I've got to make nice and get these guys drunk. Tell Samantha I said hi."

Conn didn't try to kiss her again before he walked away. He didn't even touch her. Krista sat in silence, aware of but unconcerned by her recovering boyfriend, as Conn spun the fight to Nick and Logan as some kind of joke. She looked down at the phone in her hands, absently locking and unlocking her phone as she listened. Whatever Conn was saying to everyone was working. They were all laughing. Evan, who was struggling back to his feet, was laughing, too. It didn't make sense. Conn didn't make sense. Had she even mentioned to him that it was Samantha she needed to call?

Hallie turned to Krista. "Okay, I'm a *little* impressed."

Krista smiled absently, and said, "I'll be right back. I have to make a call." She walked across the field and unlocked the phone a final time. It was time to talk some sense into Samantha. Force it on her, if she had to. Krista hit **CALL**.

~

Samantha struggled with homework to the scratch of her father's fountain pen on a yellow legal pad. Mom was in the kitchen, cleaning up dinner's mess. The occasional clink of glasses and thud of cabinet doors were the only reminders she was home. Samantha glanced up at her father, at the photocopied blueprints, land surveys, and permit requests spread out across the coffee table. There was a deadline approaching — some kind of out of town meeting — but Samantha knew better than to ask about work (or anything at all) when he was stressed. The closer his trip got, the quieter the house became. Samantha returned her attention to her own work. She'd been stuck on the same chapter of *The Grapes of Wrath* since she got home from her talk with Danica.

Dad's pen stopped scratching. He looked up and the absurd and irrational fear that he knew Danica was on her mind froze every muscle in her body.

"Think she could make any more noise in there?" His eyes locked onto the kitchen doorway. Samantha wasn't sure if he expected an answer or not. Agreement could be an interruption. Silence could be an insult. She waited. If he turned to her, she'd nod and agree. She was ready.

Dad returned to his work. Silence was the right call. She wanted to sigh, to release the tension somehow, but knew it would be a mistake. Instead, she pretended to read as her mind drifted back to the blank despair in Danica's eyes. She'd seen Danica hurt, seen tears and anger and fear, but nothing like that. Samantha had intended to tell Danica about Alex: That she'd kissed him. Kissed him and liked it. Didn't want to be with him, though. Didn't want to lose Danica, didn't know what she was doing or why. She was prepared to be dumped (maybe *needed* to be dumped) but the sight of Danica, emptied out by what she already knew, stopped her.

Samantha's phone rang. She dug it out of her pocket and hastily silenced it, but her father had already looked up.

"It's a little late for a call," he said.

She eyed the caller ID. *Shit.* "It's Krista. You know how she is. I'll be fast."

Her father nodded but didn't look away.

Samantha brought the phone to her ear. There was no way to move to the bedroom without raising Dad's suspicions. No choice but to try and make it work. Samantha had to know what Krista was planning.

"Hey," Samantha said.

It was noisy wherever Krista was. Windy, too. "You have a second?"

"Sure."

"Last night."

"Yeah," Samantha said, keeping her voice as steady as possible.

"What was that?"

"It was nothing, like I said."

Krista sighed, loudly, like she needed to be sure Samantha heard her over the noise. "Give me a break. You're hot for her. It's so fucking obvious."

"That's not true." Samantha hoped her smile looked less phony than it felt.

"For a closet dyke, you suck at lying."

Samantha channeled all of her anger into her hold on the phone. "Stop it."

"Then admit it."

"What?"

"That you're into girls. And I swear to Christ if you lie to me I'm going back to the fire and telling *everyone* about last night."

"You're at Nick's?" Samantha felt her calm slip. Could they hear Krista talking?

"Last chance," Krista said.

She heard drunken laughter and shouting through the phone. She couldn't risk calling Krista's bluff. "Yes, okay? I am."

"And what about Alex?"

"I don't know," Samantha admitted. Her father dropped his pen on the coffee table. He was getting impatient.

Krista sighed again, but this time it sounded unforced. "I don't care what you do with her. Hang out in her trailer, feel each other up, whatever. But if you're stupid like that again…"

"I know. I won't be."

"I'll burn you so damn fast."

"I know you will."

"But you know I don't *want* to, right?" Krista asked.

"You won't have to. I already texted Alex. We're going out Wednesday."

"You're gonna use that poor boy, aren't you?" Krista sounded proud.

"I like him. I do."

Krista's laugh was harsh and unkind. "You don't know what the hell you like."

Samantha didn't answer. She needed to end the call before her father *told* her to end it.

"Use him, screw him, I don't give a shit. Just be smarter. Peace, bitch."

The call went dead. Samantha put the phone on the arm of the chair and chanced a cautious glance at her father. His face was blank. Samantha smiled apologetically. "Sorry that took so long."

Her father nodded, picked up his pen, and went back to work. He tapped the nib on his legal pad three times. Looked back up. "Who's Alex?"

This was it. Her first real test. "A guy who asked me out."

"Boyfriend?"

Samantha nodded. It was too early for a spoken lie, at least with him.

Her father nodded. "Bring him by some time. I should meet him."

Mom dropped another pan into the sink. One interruption too many. Her father set his pen on the coffee table. Samantha waited until he was in the kitchen to move. With practiced haste, she gathered her things, rushed to her bedroom, and jammed her earbuds in. Music drowned out the worst of what followed.

~

She floated on a limitless sea, its surface still and clear as diamond. There was no division between her and the water, no point where her skin ended and it began. She was the sea, for the sea flowed through her. The sun shone down, reflected off the unbroken expanse of her skin, warmed her to her very depths. She was endless and serene and forever at peace.

And then, she wasn't. No longer the water but herself. Danica. A girl in the embrace of the sea. Only it wasn't a sea, but a river that stretched to the horizon. She was Danica, and the water was the river, and she was not alone.

There were dozens of others beneath and around her. They swam without need of air, without fatigue, without fear. They encircled Danica and laid their hands upon her, spun her onto her stomach so that her face dipped below the surface. The women — and they were all women — stared up at her, touched her face and arms and legs, beckoned to her to follow them down. Down into a river which had again become as wide and deep as the sea. Danica knew who they were, knew their names and thoughts and deepest pains. She loved them, for they were her sisters and she had finally come home.

Embedded in the heart of each was a shard of radiant

gold. When they swam, the points of light swirled like a storm of stars, leaving trails that crossed and connected; an unbroken knot that bound them together. A shape made its way through the tangle of light, weaving between threads with a grace Danica had never before seen. Another woman, like the others in all ways but one. Her heart was empty and dark.

Danica knew her, had seen her before, though she couldn't remember when. The woman approached and reached out a hand that came to rest over Danica's heart. Danica looked down, saw the same glow in her own heart that she'd seen in the others', and knew that it belonged to the woman before her. It was wrong somehow, that light. A seed of blackness rested in its center, drained its vitality, corrupted the bond she shared with her sisters. A disease. A curse.

The woman lifted Danica's head out of the water and turned her until they faced a towering cliff shrouded in dark, rippling clouds. Rain fell with enough force to erode the cliff as she watched, sending slabs of grey stone plunging into the deep. A man watched them from the top of the cliff. Danica knew him, knew him though she'd never before seen him, and felt a hatred so potent it echoed out through her sisters. The women scaled the cliff, clawed their way up the decaying wall of rock to drag the man down, down, down into the river, into the sea.

None laid a hand on him. Any that reached the top of the cliff were driven away and cast back into the water. A hand gripped Danica's own, the woman's hand, and Danica knew she'd felt it before. Warm and strong, it gave her strength and banished her fears.

Lightning struck the top of the cliff. In the brief flash of light, Danica saw the face of the man she hated, saw it wasn't a man at all, but someone she knew. Someone she loved.

Samantha.

The woman who gripped her hand said, "We're waiting," and Danica awoke from the dream before the sound of her voice died.

It was 3 a.m.

Danica stayed awake until sunrise forced her out of bed and back into the world.

Chapter Eleven

ALEX WOVE THROUGH a slow-moving herd of students and dashed into the stairwell. He was in a bit of a rush. Sunday morning, he'd woken up to a text from Samantha. **hang out wednesday? <3**, it said. Today was Wednesday, and he'd counted every hour between then and now.

Someone kicked the stairwell door open so hard it cracked against the wall. "Alex, dumbass, slow the hell down!"

Alex swore quietly (though not as quietly as he intended) and turned. It was Conn, taking his sweet time now that he'd gotten Alex to wait. They'd barely spoken since the bowling party. Slowing Alex down was probably Conn's revenge.

"Hey, man. Where've you been? I haven't seen you around."

"Been busy with Krista," Conn said. He slapped Alex on the arm and headed up the steps beside him. "Yeah, you heard me. Krista's on the hook, no thanks to you."

"Doesn't she have a boyfriend?"

"No, she *had* a boyfriend."

Alex held the door at the top of the stairwell open for his friend. "Oh yeah, I heard something about a fight over the weekend?"

Conn grinned. "Already a thing of legend. What did you hear?"

"That you crashed Nick's bonfire, leveled Krista's boyfriend, and were last seen helping her into your death trap of a car. Oh, and you're the Tiger Woods of quarters."

"Lies. Krista got into my car all on her own."

Alex put a hand on Conn's shoulder and turned his friend around to get a closer look at his face. He leaned to one side, then the other, examining him closely. "I heard the guy got in a shot on you."

"So?" Conn brushed Alex off and kept walking. "He had a fast right."

"Yeah, but where's the bruise? I wanted to see some damage."

"You athletes are all sadists and perverts, you know that? All that matters is I beat the hell out of the dickbag and Krista was even happier about it than I was."

"All right, all right. Hail the conquering hero. Is she everything you hoped?" Alex couldn't figure out how Conn took a punch to the face without so much as a bruise. He'd been the target of his fair share of line drives as pitcher. They all left a mark.

"Everything and more," Conn said. "What's up with you? You've got plans with Sammy, right?"

"Yeah. I've got a date. We're going to a movie." Alex smiled like an idiot. He couldn't help himself.

"That's more like it, man. Wait, this isn't another track team group date thing, is it?"

Alex held up his hand to cut Conn off. They'd reached the Graphic Arts room and he didn't want Samantha to hear them talking. Alex entered the room ahead of Conn. It was empty save for one person. Alex didn't know her, but he'd seen her with Samantha. Danica. That was her name.

"Oh, hey," Alex said.

Danica glared. "What?"

Alex was taken aback by her hostility. "Is Samantha around? I'm meeting her here."

"She's in the bathroom."

Alex realized she was looking past him. He turned. The only person there was Conn, who didn't look well. He was pale and sweating, practically hyperventilating, with his arm against the doorjamb for support. It looked like another panic attack, but over what? The only thing in the room other than desks and chairs was Danica.

"You okay?" Alex asked.

"I'm late for something." Conn said, and was gone before Alex had a chance to respond.

Alex turned back to Danica. "What was that about?"

"He's not what you think," Danica said. She had her hand over her left breast. It looked like she was in pain.

"What does that mean?" Alex had a sudden urge to follow Conn out the door. There was a sound like water rushing past in his ears.

"Nothing. I don't know," she replied, suddenly as unsure and uncomfortable as Alex felt. "Sam should be back soon."

Alex took a few tentative steps into the room and sat two desks over. "You're Danica, right?"

She nodded. "You're Alex."

"Yeah. We haven't really met, have we?"

"No," Danica replied. "Sam mentioned you. That's all."

"Right. Cool. Well, it's good to meet you."

Danica nodded and returned to her work. She was looking over black and white photo prints. Alex considered leaving her be, but he didn't like the flatness of her voice. He pressed on. "So, you two are friends? You and Samantha, I mean."

She met his eyes and Alex saw in them something that scared him. Behind the fatigue was something else: an empty hopelessness Alex recognized too well. It was the same despair he'd seen on his mother's face, and Alex felt just as helpless in the face of it.

After a moment of silence, Danica said only, "Yeah."

"Alex, hey." Samantha stood in the doorway, her eyes moving back and forth between Alex and Danica. "Have you been waiting long?"

"No. I just got here. You ready to go?" Alex walked to Samantha, arms out to give her a hug, but she stepped around him.

"Yeah. Oh, this is Danica."

Alex said, "We met."

"Oh. Good."

"Let's go, I guess. Danica, do you need a ride home? My dad wouldn't mind," Alex offered.

Danica shook her head. "I'm getting coffee with a friend."

"Cool," replied Alex. "It was awesome meeting you. Have a good one."

"Yeah," Danica said.

Danica and Samantha stared at each other, neither speaking, as if wrestling with what to say. When Samantha finally broke the silence, she said nothing but, "Bye."

Samantha grabbed Alex's hand and pulled him out of the room. Alex waved on his way out, but Danica had already looked away. When they were far enough down the hall not to be heard, Alex pulled back on Samantha's arm, forcing her to slow.

"What?" Samantha asked, her smile forced.

"Is she okay?"

"Danica?"

Alex nodded.

Samantha shrugged, then shook her head and sighed. "There's a lot going on with her right now. It's fine. She'll be fine."

"All right," Alex said. "Just… be there for her, you know?"

She looked back in the direction of the Graphic Arts room. "I will."

"Thanks."

"So," Samantha said, the smile returning, "are we going to do this or what?"

"Yeah, sorry. I'm killing our date before it starts, aren't I?"

Samantha rolled her eyes. She grabbed his hand again, this time staying beside him instead of dragging him down the hall. Alex tried to make sense of what had happened; Conn's unexplainable panic, Danica's hollow despair, Samantha's awkwardness. Even later, after they'd been dropped off at the theater, after they'd found their seats and Samantha kissed him when the lights went down, after the best day Alex could remember having in a year, he couldn't shake the memory of Danica's eyes and the powerlessness he hoped he'd never feel again.

~

Danica shifted in the stiff-cushioned chair, searching for a position where she wouldn't slide off of the vinyl upholstery and onto the floor. She kept expecting to see people staring, snickering. Danica had chosen one of the comfortable chairs at the back of the shop before realizing they were on a foot-tall riser. It was like being on stage. Danica felt herself slide forward, caught herself on the arms of the chair, and tucked her legs underneath her. For the moment, she was stable.

That was how everything felt: stable, but about to

slip. Though the numbness remained, it had begun to erode. Monday had been terrible but simple. She and Samantha acted like strangers stuck at the same desk. By today, Samantha had gotten bolder. After half of the period of silence, she'd placed her hand on the desk, close enough to Danica's that they just touched. "It won't be forever," Samantha said. Hope weakened the walls between Danica and her emotions, just in time to watch Alex take Samantha out on their date.

The coffee shop was nearly empty. Two Catholic school girls had more books than Danica had read in an entire year spread out on their table. Beside them was a middle-aged man in cut-off sweatpants and ratty t-shirt, his attention on a battered laptop. Megan waited at the counter for a barista with bleached hair to make their drinks. Danica looked back and forth between Megan and the television, where a towering chef chopped tomatoes and onions and gestured emphatically at the viewers with his cleaver. Eventually, Megan caught Danica staring at her and smiled, so Danica turned to the television and didn't look back.

Why was Megan doing this? Why take her out for coffee, all smiles, like everything was fine? Danica wondered if this was some kind of closure thing, the proper goodbye they didn't get before Megan went to college. They'd see each other every week at youth group, though. A goodbye now wouldn't do any good. Danica couldn't make sense of it. Everything seemed wrong, false, hostile. She told herself it was Samantha — not Megan or Leslie or Mom — who was to blame. It didn't help.

Megan sat beside Danica and set a small hot chocolate down on the table, keeping her own drink in hand. "So," Megan said.

"So," Danica repeated.

"What's been up with you?"

Megan was concerned. There was nothing Danica wanted less from her than *concern*. "Not much. How about you?"

"Okay, fine, I'll go first," Megan said, laughing. "College is great, but I miss home. Like, a lot. I could have interned somewhere closer to school, I guess, but this seemed like such a good excuse to come back. It's weird working with Fresh, though. I was one of his kids last year, right? And now I'm helping him run things? It's crazy. But it's good, mostly. I think he's really happy to have me back."

"He was pretty desperate for a new intern."

"I know. I wasn't supposed to start until the summer. He gave me this pitch about how it would be better to start before attendance crashed over vacation. Totally rehearsed. Like a speech class thing, you know?"

"Sounds like Fresh," Danica said.

"Right? Otherwise, I don't know. It's just so different in college. I told you about the bible study group I found, right?"

Danica nodded.

"It's amazing. Everyone is awesome. You'd love it. I thought about you as soon as I found it."

"Why?" Danica asked, more suspicious than she intended.

"They're just, I don't know, *accepting*. They took me for who I was, you know? It's not like it is here. You'd love them."

Danica knew exactly what Megan meant when she said *accepting*. It meant they didn't care that Megan was gay. Danica didn't know how to respond. "Cool," she managed.

Megan set her drink on the table and leaned closer to Danica. "I know it hasn't been easy for you here."

"How do you know how it's been for me? You

haven't called once. We're only getting coffee because you came back for Fresh. You didn't even expect to see me. You said you thought I quit." Danica was surprised by how angry she still was, how easily that anger boiled to the surface. It felt good, that anger.

"I know." Megan sighed. "Things got weird."

Things didn't get weird. Danica got weird. Megan was the first person to know about Danica. Not only that she was gay, but about the matches and the lighters and the scars on her thighs. Megan never judged her, not even when Danica fell hard for her. She let the crush pass without ever pushing Danica away or leaving her alone. Megan was a hard girl to chase off. It took Danica a whole year to find a way.

"How is it? Is it better?" Danica asked.

Megan hesitated. Danica didn't have to say what *it* was. They both knew. Megan grabbed the left cuff of her shirt and closed her eyes as she raised the sleeve. There was a straight white scar on her wrist that began at the bottom of her thumb and ran most of the length of her forearm.

"I'm sorry."

"It's fine. It's totally fine. I never blamed you." Megan pulled her sleeve back down. "It was just my family, you know?"

"Yeah," Danica said, needing to change the subject to something, anything, else. "Are you seeing anyone?"

Megan shook her head. "I did for a little while, but it didn't really work. I don't have time for it right now, you know? She was cute, though. How about you?"

If there was anyone she could tell about Samantha, it was Megan. Despite everything, Megan could be trusted. She might even be able to help. Danica tried to make herself say *yes*, to say Samantha's name, but something twisted in her heart and stopped her. Danica put a hand over her breast, but it didn't hurt to the touch. The pain was deeper, small and sharp and hot.

An electronic bell sounded as two people entered the coffee shop. Danica knew them both. One was Krista. The other was worse: Ferris, Megan's sister. Megan turned her away and swore.

"I should go," Danica said.

Megan shook her head. It was too late for that to matter. There was no way to keep from being seen. They sat in silence while Krista and Ferris made their way to the counter and cased the coffee shop. Danica prayed for protection. She prayed they wouldn't be seen, for escape of any kind.

It was Krista who noticed them. She tapped Ferris on the arm and pointed. Then, without a word between them, they turned back to the counter and ordered drinks. When the bleached barista returned with them, Ferris snatched the paper cup and marched toward Danica and Megan.

"Hey," Megan said, no longer her normal, cheerful self. "What're you two up to?"

"Can I talk to you?" Ferris reached across Megan's body, careful to grab her by her unscarred arm, and pulled her to the front of the coffee shop. Krista stayed with Danica. She sat down in Megan's chair, smiling. It was a predator's smile.

"What was that about?" Krista asked.

"You already know," Danica said, then added, "don't you?"

"Nope. Is she afraid you're going to lez out with her sister or something?"

"Shut up." An instinctual anger filled her, one much like the unexplainable fury she'd felt when she met Alex's friend. Less, though. As if she were catching the scent of something far in the distance.

"Oh, no way. Was I right?" Krista glanced at Ferris and Megan. Ferris looked angry. Megan looked ashamed. Afraid. Krista said, "Yeah, Ferris, I know the feeling."

"What do you want?"

Krista shrugged. "You out of Sam's life."

"I don't know what you're talking about."

"Bullshit, bitch. I saw both of you and you know it." Krista lowered her voice and continued. "I don't give a shit what you are. No one does. I could post a pic of you going down on those two girls and the only thing anyone would say is, 'Huh, I didn't know she was a pedo.' You don't matter enough for people to care."

"Then get out of my face," Danica interrupted.

"Shut up. You think I didn't know about Sam? I knew way before she got desperate enough to slum it with you. All you had to do was keep your shit with her to yourself. You two could've screwed every night and I wouldn't have cared. But you barged into *my* party and stuck your tongue down *my* friend's throat where anyone could have seen."

Danica had been afraid Samantha was *slumming it* for too long to hide how much Krista's words stung. "Why do you care who knows? It's not your problem. It's ours."

"Yeah? How do you think Ferris would feel if she knew? Want me to call her over and find out? I bet she'd love it if her sister *and* her best friend were all over you. You think I want to deal with that shit? You think *Sam* wants to deal with it? You should be *happy* it was me who saw you. I'm not the one hurting Samantha. I'm protecting her."

"She doesn't need protected. I love her."

Krista laughed so hard she doubled over. Ferris and Megan looked up from their argument. Everyone in the coffee shop turned. Danica shrunk into her chair, waiting for them to join in, to laugh at stupid, naive Danica, who thought she was in *love*.

"You're adorable," Krista said. "I bet that's why Sam likes playing with you."

Shame overwhelmed Danica. "Please leave me alone."

"Then leave my friend alone."

The electronic bell went off again as Ferris stormed out of the coffee shop. The look on Megan's face said everything. This would be their last time out for coffee.

Krista stood. "I don't think it's me you need to be afraid of."

Danica waited until Krista was gone to join Megan at the front of the shop. They walked to the car in silence and stayed that way until they reached Danica's double-wide.

"See you at youth group?" Megan asked.

Danica nodded once before fleeing the car for the safety of her bedroom. There was no point in prayer, nothing to ask for that she could hope to receive. There was only one thing left for her. Her plastic art supply box. The emergency kit. It was there, under her bed, waiting for the day she'd need it. Waiting for today.

The scorched end of an unfolded paperclip was the first real thing Danica had felt in days, and the tears were enough to keep her sane while she passed into the unquiet mercy of sleep.

Chapter Twelve

SAMANTHA SAT IN the shade of the bleachers to recover between races. The shade wasn't helping. Cool, breezy spring had been overthrown by a thick and cloying humidity that made every run misery. Her clothes were damp with sweat after a single relay and it was only going to get worse. The 200m and 400m dashes were still ahead.

At least she was out of sight of her father. He was back after a month of being too busy to come. She could feel the physical pressure of his gaze wherever she went. He was analyzing her, searching her for weakness. It was only a matter of time before he saw something was very wrong. Her only choice was to hide and hope she'd be safe for one more day.

How long until she ran out of days, until the tower of lies she'd built collapsed on her head? She lied to Danica about her dates with Alex. She lied to Alex about what Danica meant to her. She lied to Krista, to her teammates, to friends and to family. Samantha wasn't sure if she had anything real left.

"Samantha! You're up!" the coach shouted. It was time for the 200m dash.

Samantha brushed the grass off of her legs and shorts

and headed for the starting line. It was time to focus on the race. Her father was watching, and the only way to hide was to win. She settled into her blocks and cleared her mind of distractions. Tried to, anyway. Danica was front and center no matter how hard she tried to push her aside. She was even there when Alex kissed her — kisses she wished she didn't enjoy, wished felt like an obligation so the guilt didn't have so much fuel. She liked Alex, but it was Danica she *wanted*. No one cared what Samantha wanted, though. Least of all her father.

The starting pistol fired before Samantha was ready. She pushed off her blocks last, which gave her opponents a head start she couldn't afford. With survival on the line, Samantha's world narrowed down to her lane. There was nothing but the push on her heels, gaining with every step.

Samantha ran.

She crossed the finish line first. Even with a lead, the others were too slow to outrun the push. She hunched over, hands on her knees, and looked into the stands. Her father didn't applaud. Never did. He either nodded, or he didn't.

He nodded. It would have been a relief if not for the other thing she saw: her father was no longer alone. A boy in a blue and gold baseball uniform sat beside him, applauding. It was Alex. Samantha knew what came next, and it made her sick with dread. Alex would be invited to dinner. Her father would judge Alex and, in the end, he'd approve. The relationship would be encouraged. And if it ended, well...

Samantha returned to the shade of the bleachers. She was tired of pretending. The harder she tried to hide behind Alex's attraction to her, the less hidden she felt. The lies were eating away at her, but they were the only way to endure. There was nothing stronger than her need to survive. Not hope, not compassion, and not love. That was a lesson her mother — too scared to fight, too weak to run — would never learn. Samantha knew that some fights couldn't be won, could only be escaped. If she'd listened to her instincts, if she'd been able to leave Danica behind, they'd both be safe. Now her only hope was to be faster than the consequences.

When it was time for the final race, her father and Alex were still there, watching. Samantha took her place at her blocks. The push was coming. It would follow until she had nothing left, until it chased her down and dropped her, alone and exhausted, at her father's feet. There was nothing faster than the push, not even her, not in the end.

The starting pistol fired.

Samantha ran.

~

The chains holding the rubber seat creaked with every move Danica made. She kicked back off the ground hard enough to glide back a foot, then let herself swing until she came to a stop. Over and over again, enough to keep her friends from noticing she wasn't there. Her sweatpants chafed against the raw skin of her thighs. Danica could have bandaged herself, but she was pretty sure Mom still watched the first aid supplies for signs of a relapse. Danica could take the pain. Welcomed it, in a way, as proof she could still feel.

Texas was to her left, pumping his legs so hard that the top of each swing was nearly parallel to the ground. Will was less ambitious. He kept the swing moving with the minimum possible effort. They were all high. Especially Leslie, who was currently hanging off the edge of the multicolored playground carousel. Every time the carousel spun her toward Danica, she smiled. Danica had stopped returning the smile minutes ago.

Will skidded to a stop. He asked, "Hey. How've you been?"

"Fine," Danica said.

"Haven't seen you in a while. I was getting worried."

She hadn't spoken with Will, or any of her friends, in over a week. She'd finally let them drag her out of the house, but only because it was easier to pretend for an afternoon than to deal with them asking why she was avoiding them. The questions came anyway.

"Sorry," she replied.

Will frowned. "How're the kids for Christ?"

Danica dragged herself to youth group the previous night to see Megan. It was the only way to learn how much trouble she'd caused. Pastor Fresh crushed her hopes with his opening announcement: Megan was catching up with schoolwork and would return next week. Danica wondered if she really would be back. She'd probably chased Megan off for good. Danica was poison to anyone she loved.

You aren't poison, my love. They are.

"What?" The word was out of her mouth before she realized the voice hadn't been Will's.

Will's frown deepened. Leslie stopped spinning. Texas either hadn't heard or didn't care. He continued to swing. Danica's chest tightened. Her heart raced. She recognized the voice, knew it wasn't real. It was the woman in her dreams, the one with hair like water, a dress like fog, and a voice like the waves. Danica reflexively placed her hand over her heart.

"Are you sure everything's okay?" Will asked.

"Yeah. We're worried about you," Leslie added.

The burn on Danica's leg itched. "What, you've all been talking about me?"

"It's not like that. We're just concerned is all." Will spoke with more wounded sincerity than Danica could take.

"Fine. I feel like shit, and I don't want to talk about it. Thanks for asking."

"Hey," Leslie said, her voice as sticky with pity as Will's. "Don't get pissed. He's just trying to help."

"Maybe I don't want Will's help."

"You don't have to talk to me, okay?" he said. Danica hated way he whined when he was hurt. "I'm here for you. That's all."

"Yeah, I know why you're here for me. Everyone does," she snapped. Danica immediately regretted it. A jab at Will's crush was too far. She shouldn't have come. She should have known better.

Texas dug his heels into the gravel and jolted to an immediate stop. He waited for everyone to look before speaking in his typical laconic monotone. "You need to break up with that girl already, D. She's not worth it."

"I need to what?" How did Texas know about Samantha? Danica turned on Leslie, whose head hung in shame.

Will asked, "Break up with who?"

"You told him?" Danica demanded.

Leslie stared at the ground. "Danica…"

"Is Danica seeing someone?" Will begged.

"I told you not to tell anyone. You *promised* you wouldn't!"

"I didn't know what to do. I was scared for you, okay? You can trust Texas."

Will's voice rose to a shout. "Trust Texas with *what*? What the hell is going on?"

"Danica's dating Samantha Rowland. But, like, in secret," Texas replied.

Danica fixed her white-hot glare on Leslie, who

closed her eyes and sighed. "Texas, dude, I just said you'd keep your mouth shut."

"Why am I the only one who didn't know?"

Danica ignored Will's pleas. She wasn't done with Leslie. "If it gets out it's *over*. You *know* that. I'm going to lose her because of *you*."

"I won't tell anyone," Will said. "I promise. Neither will Texas. I'll make sure."

Leslie talked over him. "Maybe that's what you need, you know? Her hiding you is bullshit. You deserve better than that."

Danica screamed; a brief, ragged wail that turned to tears before the sound died. She was powerless, adrift. Her friends had turned against her. The ground opened beneath her, and this time there was no escape. She was alone. She'd always be alone.

You're not alone. You have us. We're waiting for you.

Hair swirled before Danica's eyes. Cool, soothing water touched her skin, and her friends' voices dropped to dull reverberations. She saw the cliff rise above her, and rose with it this time. She saw the man waiting, waiting. Saw the women thrash in the sea below. The pin burned hotter than anything she'd pressed against herself in desperation. The man's face changed, as it had in the dream, and it was Samantha looking down from the tower of stone.

She screamed again. Terrified, she grabbed at the sound of Leslie's voice, and at once was back on the playground. She'd fallen off the swing, landed on the ground on all fours. Leslie's hands were on her shoulders. Will and Texas were further away, their voices too quiet to be understood. Danica allowed Leslie to help her up and lead her to the car. Leslie didn't ask Danica what had happened, only waited for Danica to calm and for the tears to stop before she spoke.

"I'm sorry, Danny. I really am."

Danica nodded. It didn't matter if Leslie took it as forgiveness or dismissal. Danica was still in the dream, halfway between the top of the cliff and the water below, falling endlessly forward. Only after she'd returned to the safety of her room and the heat of her lighter did Danica realize it wasn't the fall she feared, but how much she wanted it.

~

Alex flicked a smooth, grey pebble back and forth across the cement step of his front porch in time with the *click click click* of Conn's cheap plastic lighter. They'd been out here for a half-hour, killing time until Krista picked Conn up for their date. The beater Conn called a car was, he'd explained, in a deep coma from which it might never wake. Alex felt a little safer knowing the thing was off the road, hopefully for good. Conn's cigarette — his third in the last hour — twitched back and forth in his mouth, as if it was as impatient to be lit as Conn was to smoke it. Finally, the dying lighter sparked and produced an anemic flame.

Conn took two long drags before answering the question Alex had asked minutes earlier. "She's probably just worried you'll hate her family and get weird with her. Dinner with a girl's parents is no-win."

Alex nodded. By chance, he'd ended up sitting directly beside Samantha's father. He'd turned to Alex, no idea who he was, and started in on what a dominant track star his daughter was. "Samantha's your daughter?" Alex had asked. That led to a moment of scrutiny so intense he almost apologized for asking.

"You're Alex," her father replied, and Alex had

nodded. The man smiled, shook Alex's hand, and spent the rest of the race alternating between track and field analysis and probing questions about Alex's background. When Samantha joined them after the meet, her father said, "Alex is coming for dinner this week. Any day is fine."

He'd never asked Alex if he *wanted* to come to dinner, and Alex wasn't about to say anything other than *yes*. Samantha looked uncomfortable, though, and didn't say much the rest of the afternoon. She looked almost relieved when he left for his plans with Conn.

"Maybe. I don't know," Alex said. There was something about Samantha's father that put Alex on guard. It was almost like he *wanted* to worry Alex, like the friendliness was just a threat of what would take its place if Alex gave him cause.

Conn blew smoke out of his nose and shrugged. A car turned onto Alex's road. Krista's car. Conn said, "What the hell do I know? Ask Krista what she thinks. I'll even give you two some privacy. I've got to piss." He was up and into Alex's house before Krista came to a stop.

"Yo!" Krista shouted from the street. "Where the hell is he?"

Alex gestured at the door. "Boys' room. He'll be out in a minute."

"Whatever." Krista took a seat on the steps next to Alex and picked up the pack of cigarettes Conn had left there. She looked at the pack and frowned, but pulled a cigarette out anyway. "Menthol. What a girl."

"So, what's up with you two? You dating or what?" Alex asked.

Krista stared at Alex through squinted eyes. She lit the cigarette before answering, just like Conn had. "We'll see. How's it going with Samantha?"

"Good," Alex said, uncomfortable with the way

Krista was studying him. It was like being with Samantha's father all over again. "I'm having dinner with her family this week."

"Ow, good luck with that. Conn had better not try that crap with me. I don't do family time."

Alex smiled politely. It was time to change the subject. "Do you know Danica? She's one of Samantha's friends, right?"

Krista coughed hard and threw her half-smoked butt into the grass. "Goddamn fiberglass. Danica? I guess. Why?"

"I don't know," said Alex. "I met her the other day and she didn't seem to like me much."

"Aw, poor thing. Can't take someone not liking you?"

"Lots of people don't like me. It's nice to know why, is all."

"Who cares what she thinks? She's nuts, and Sam treating her like some kind of charity case is just making things worse."

"Making what worse?" Alex asked.

Krista flicked stray pieces of grass and pebbles off of the cement steps. "Forget it. I don't know anything for sure. It's just, like, a guess."

"What's just a guess?"

"Danica's gay. That's not the guess. She's a straight-up lez. Anyway, I'm pretty sure she's got a thing for Sam. She's probably pissed you've got what she wants." Krista grabbed the cigarette pack and fidgeted with it, opening and closing the flap. "Just ignore her like everyone else."

Alex felt sick. Sure, Krista struck Alex as the kind of person who'd say things just to cause trouble. Yeah, it was probably nothing but a rumor. Except... it sort of fit. Maybe Krista was right. "I didn't even think about that."

Krista shrugged dismissively.

"I should probably talk to her," Alex said.

"You don't want to do that."

"Huh? Why not?"

Conn reemerged from the house and jumped off the top step. He landed on the grass beside Krista and put an arm around her waist. "What's going on?"

Krista ignored Conn. "You don't want to mess with her. I meant it when I said she's nuts."

"Whatever," Alex sighed.

"I'm not screwing with you. Ferris is terrified of the little freak. Won't even tell me why."

"Terrified of Danica? Seriously?" Alex asked. Danica looked depressed, not dangerous.

"Jesus Christ, drop it already. Ask Ferris about it if you care so much." Krista spun and headed towards her car. Halfway there, she looked over her shoulder at Conn. "You coming or not?"

Conn nodded, but turned to Alex first. "You okay, man?"

"Yeah. Trying to figure out what to do."

"About that girl?" Conn asked.

"I didn't know she was into Samantha. I think I might have really hurt—"

"Who cares?" Conn interrupted, his voice a little too loud. "You think you need to apologize to everyone else who wants a date with your girlfriend? That's their problem."

Alex, taken aback by Conn's outburst, stammered, "I'm just worried about her."

Conn's smile returned, the anger gone in an instant. "Nothing to fear, dude. I'll protect you from her. Anyway, got to run. The lady awaits."

Conn dashed to Krista's car. Alex, still shaken by his friend's sudden anger, stayed on the porch until the vehicle pulled away. The more he got to know Conn, the less he made sense. It wasn't just Conn's sudden shifts in moods that had Alex on edge, but his inexplicable concern for Alex's relationship with Samantha. Why had he gotten that angry over Danica? And what was with his joke about protecting Alex? He'd laughed it off, but it hadn't sounded like a joke. Alex didn't actually know much about his friend. He'd never been to his house, or met his family. Hell, he'd never even seen him in class.

A gust of wind swept up from the reservoir. It whistled through the trees like a voice whispering words he didn't understand. Shivering, Alex remembered different words, the ones Danica said about Conn the day they'd all met.

He's not what you think.

Chapter Thirteen

By the time Samantha made her way to Alex's locker, most of the other students were gone. She'd been ambushed at her own locker by one of her relay partners, Brandy Haller, who'd heard a rumor that their coach was changing up the relay team and, panicked, demanded to know what Samantha knew. *If you ran as fast as you talked, we wouldn't be having this conversation.* Samantha stayed silent, desperate to escape, until realizing she had an excuse: her boyfriend was waiting downstairs. She'd forgotten how much easier it was not having to lie when she had a date. The thought made her sick with guilt.

Samantha expected Alex to be waiting, maybe even impatient. She wasn't ready to see him talking to an angry-looking Ferris Ashley. Whatever they were discussing, it couldn't be good. Could Krista have told Ferris about Danica? No, that wasn't possible. Ferris wouldn't be yelling at Alex. She'd be at Samantha's throat. Nothing other than Stinky Vince made Ferris that angry, though.

Ferris noticed Samantha watching, forced a smile, and waved. No way to hang back, now. Samantha headed for Alex's locker, but Ferris didn't wait for Samantha to reach them. She was down the hall and out the door by the time Samantha got there.

"What was that about?" Samantha asked.

Alex hugged her instead of answering. "Ready to go? My dad's probably waiting."

"Yeah, sorry about that. I got caught upstairs." Samantha let Alex take her hand and lead her to the door. She continued, "Is everything okay?"

Alex held the door open for her with his free hand. "Yeah. I mean, I guess I'm a little nervous about tomorrow."

"Dinner with my family, you mean?"

"Uh-huh. I know I shouldn't be freaking out, but…"

"It'll be fine." *For you.*

They walked down the long, twisting sidewalk that led to the parking lot. Below, out of sight, Samantha could hear the lawnmowers on the football field, and the laughter and shouting of students loitering in the stands. She wished she could join them. Smoke a joint under the bleachers, get lost in the hum of the lawnmowers, put aside the worry, let down the walls. That life seemed so far away.

"You'll be there," Alex said. "That's enough."

Alex's father's car was waiting in the nearly empty parking lot. Samantha could see her own further back, alone under the shade of two towering pine trees. Samantha pulled Alex to a stop. "Hey, seriously, what was that with Ferris? Is something going on?"

He hesitated. "I shouldn't keep my dad waiting. I was worried about Danica, is all. We can talk about it later if you want."

Samantha's panic came to a rolling boil. She let go of Alex's hand. "You asked Ferris about it?"

"Long story." Alex looked like he was weighing whether to make a run for it. Samantha had never seen him this uncomfortable. What had Ferris told him?

"Why are you worried about Danica?" Samantha pressed.

"Aren't *you*?" Alex sighed. "Look, I really need to go. We can talk tomorrow. It's cool, I promise. Just, maybe you should check in on her."

Alex paused to give Samantha a chance to say goodbye. When she said nothing, he offered a wan smile and ran to the waiting car. Samantha couldn't understand why Alex was so concerned about someone he barely knew. If something was wrong with Danica, wouldn't Samantha have noticed? Or had she become so good at pretending Danica didn't matter that she'd actually stopped paying attention?

Samantha got into the Accord and buckled her seatbelt. She needed to get home. She didn't have an excuse ready for being late, and Samantha couldn't count on anyone to cover for her. Danica's was out of the way, so far in the boonies that it would be almost an hour driving there and back. It was the only safe place to talk, though. Samantha started the car. She remembered the last time she'd been to Danica's. The last real visit, not the morning after the bowling disaster. Samantha wanted to feel safe like that again. She wanted Danica to feel safe. Samantha pulled out of the parking lot and headed for the boonies. An excuse would come to her eventually. It would have to.

Samantha was used to coming to the back door, but she hadn't thought to call Danica to let her know she was on the way over. Front door it was, then. Danica's mother answered after the second knock. She'd only met Danica's mom a few times, and when she opened the door — Samantha was expecting Ian, the deadbeat boyfriend — she struggled to remember her name.

"Samantha," she said through the screen door. "It's been a while."

"Hi, Vicky." Samantha said the name without actually remembering it. Instinct or something. She wasn't going to question it. "I know. Track is driving me nuts. Is Danica home?"

Vicky held the door open and showed Samantha in. Ian was either asleep or trying to look like it. Vicky talked like she didn't care if it kept him awake. "In her room. Like always. You should just walk in. She won't answer if you knock."

Nodding, Samantha headed for the hallway. She stopped when she reached the corner. "Has she seemed, I don't know…"

"I think she could use a friend right now." Vicky returned to the couch. Samantha got the message.

Danica was playing music so loud that Samantha could hear it clearly from the end of the hall. Samantha hopped on the tips of her toes, like she did before a race. Then, before doubt could set in, she strode down the hallway and opened the door to Danica's room.

The first thing Samantha saw was Danica's bare legs. Something small and metal fell on the floor, but Samantha wasn't sure what it was. Then Danica swore and shouted, "I told you to knock!"

It wasn't the first time she'd seen Danica's bare legs, but never because she'd stormed in on her in her own bedroom. Samantha put a hand over her eyes. "Sorry, your mom told me I could just walk in!"

"Samantha?" Danica said. Samantha heard rustling sounds, sheets being pulled up, before Danica spoke again. "You can open your eyes."

Samantha lowered her hand. Danica was half under the covers, legs no longer visible. Her cheeks were flushed, and there was the glint of what looked like tears in her eyes and on her cheeks. Samantha shut the door.

"Are you all right?" asked Samantha.

"Yeah. Fine. I'm fine." Danica pulled the covers over her waist. "You surprised me."

"Sorry. I didn't even think." Seeing Danica on the bed hit Samantha harder than she expected. It had been a long time since they were alone. "It's really good to see you, Danny."

Danica looked down and blushed. A smile broke through for just a moment. It slipped away just as fast. "Now's not a good time."

Samantha sat down on the bed and put a hand over Danica's. When she didn't respond, Samantha leaned close and whispered, "I missed you."

"You did?" Danica looked up.

"Of course I did."

"You don't talk to me. You barely look at me. I don't think you've smiled at me since before..." Danica closed her eyes. "You smile when you see him, though."

"Danny, he's *nice*. That's all. And we need to be careful."

"I'm sick of being careful."

This wasn't how it was supposed to be. Samantha wanted Danica, and needed Danica to want her back. "We don't have to be careful here," she said, and ran her hand up Danica's arm. Their eyes met. Samantha didn't hesitate. She pushed Danica back onto the bed and fell on top of her. Samantha kissed her, on the lips, on her neck, on the lobe of her ear. Her right hand took Danica's left and held it against the pillow.

"Sam," Danica whispered.

"Shh," Samantha replied. She slid to the right, rested one of her legs between Danica's own, and returned to kissing Danica on the mouth. Now wasn't the time to talk. It could be a long time before they got another chance. They might never have it again.

Danica turned her head a bit, breaking the kiss. More firmly, she said, "Sam."

Why was she being like this? Samantha let go of Danica's hand and slid it down her side, onto her thigh. At the touch of Samantha's hand on her leg, Danica gasped so sharply that Samantha pulled away.

"What?"

"Get off of me," Danica said.

"Danny," Samantha said, confused. She leaned back in for one more kiss. That's all it would take. One more kiss.

"STOP!" Danica put both hands on Samantha's chest and shoved. Samantha rolled off the bed and landed on the small of her back.

Pain shot up her spine and down her legs. "Jesus, Danica!"

Danica yanked the covers over the rest of her body and leaned over the edge of her bed. "I told you to get off of me! You can't just come over and *have* me. I'm not a toy!"

The words hurt more than the fall. Samantha was so ashamed it made her queasy. She couldn't even look at Danica. Her own voice sounded weak and pathetic as she said, "I'm sorry. I'm sorry."

"I can't do this anymore," Danica said, voice wavering. "I love you. I love you, but you have to love me, too."

She'd never told Danica she loved her, and Danica had never said it to her. Samantha never considered whether it was love or not, and answered without thinking. "I do. I do."

Danica calmed and lowered a hand over the edge of the bed. Samantha grasped it and pulled herself up.

"I'm so sorry," said Samantha.

"Break up with him," Danica said, like she hadn't heard Samantha's apology. "If you love me, break up with him."

"I can't. Not yet. But it's not forever. It's only until Krista backs off," Samantha pleaded.

"Krista," Danica said, her voice low. "Do you know what Krista did today? What she did to *me*?"

Samantha shook her head.

"She was writing on my locker in lipstick after lunch. I told her to stop, so she grabbed me by the hair and yanked so hard I fell on the floor. Everyone thought it was funny."

Samantha couldn't bring herself to ask what Krista was writing. Instead she said, "I didn't know."

"Break up with him. Or me. One or the other."

"Danny, he met my *father*. If we break up now, he'll want to know *why*."

"Then just tell me you don't want me anymore." Danica wasn't crying, but she was close.

Samantha backed toward the door. She stepped on something hard as she did. A metal butane lighter. She kicked it aside, looked back up, and said, "If you don't believe I care, then *you* end it. I'm not giving you up."

Danica said nothing.

"I'll talk to Krista. She'll leave you alone. I promise."

Again, no response.

"I need a little more time, okay?"

"What if I don't have more time?" Danica asked.

That scared Samantha more than she could take. All she could say in response was, "I'll make it work."

Samantha closed the door behind her. She took a moment to regain her composure, then headed for the front door. Vicky looked at Samantha expectantly, but Samantha said nothing but a quick goodbye as she dashed outside. Samantha was halfway home before she realized she hadn't thought of an excuse. Her clothes and skin smelled like Danica, and her hair was a mess. She was running out of lies. Maybe Danica was right. Maybe they didn't have any more time. Samantha would have cried if she remembered how.

~

Conn was still half under the covers when Krista slipped back into her bedroom and set her phone on the nightstand. He was bare chested, propped up against the headboard with a pillow. His eyes were closed but he wasn't asleep. There were long, thin scars all across his chest. They were faded, old-looking, like he'd had them for a lifetime. When she had asked how he got them, he snapped at her and told her to mind her own business.

Krista returned to bed without removing the thigh-length nightshirt she'd slipped on when her phone rang. The top was all she had on. Not counting the covers, Conn wore even less.

"How's Samantha?" asked Conn.

"Why do you care?"

"Just curious." His eyes were still closed.

The call had interrupted them before things got serious. Krista expected Conn to be all over her as soon as she got back into bed, but no, he was asking about Samantha. The boy made no sense. The night he'd beaten the hell out of Evan, Conn drove her home. She vaguely remembered trying to drag him into the back of his car. He let her kiss him once, then sent her into her house. When they ended up alone again, this time in her room after school, she expected the kind of fumbling, semi-virginal bullshit she always got from the chivalrous guys. Conn was not that. Conn knew what he was doing. In fact, Krista wasn't sure she'd known what *knew what he was doing* meant before this. Krista had been with college guys more clueless than this grungy...well, how old was Conn? Krista assumed he was a junior like her, but she'd never asked his age.

"She asked me to leave Danica alone," Krista said, answering despite her irritation.

Conn's eyes opened. He turned to her, eyebrow raised. "Well, they *are* going out. What did you expect?"

The lie came out automatically. "What do you mean they're going out?"

"Don't you know how chatty you are when you're drunk? You told me the whole story, like, three times. Playing footsie in class, sneaking off to make out, blah, blah, blah. All of it."

There was no way she'd told him. Did a few drinks really make her *that* stupid? "Who else have you told?"

"You think I'd tell someone and spoil this lovely thing we have together?"

"It's just drinking and sex. What do you think's going on?"

Conn grinned. "Drinking and sex. Look, I didn't tell anyone. I don't know why you care, but I didn't tell anyone."

Everything was a joke to him. Krista stood and searched for her pants. They were definitely not picking up where they left off. "Good. I don't need the headache if people find out Sam's been experimenting with that psycho. Anyway, don't you care that she's cheating on your friend?"

"She's cheating with him, not on him, right?" Conn watched Krista dress as he spoke. "Either way, it's his problem."

"I don't get you," Krista said.

"Most people don't. Oh, and she isn't experimenting. You're the one with no heart. Not her."

"So, what, Samantha's in *love* with her? Fuck off." She pulled her arms in through the her sleeves and put her bra back on under her nightshirt. If he was going to be an ass, he wasn't getting a free peek.

"They're in love with each other," Conn said, suddenly serious. "It's the real deal. Hate it, but call it what it is."

"What do you know about love?'

"More than you." Conn leaned over the other side of the bed and came back up with her purple t-shirt. He tossed it to her. "More than most people ever will."

"You're so full of shit. If you're Doctor Love, why haven't you told your idiot friend to leave Samantha to her soulmate? Why are you here when I'm the one screwing with their *perfect love*?"

Conn grabbed Krista by the wrist too quickly for her to react and pulled her onto her back. Krista let the t-shirt fall out of her hands. Maybe things *were* going to pick up where they left off. Anything was better than talking about Samantha. Conn leaned close to her ear. "Take it from me. A love that never dies will poison your heart."

He pulled away and met Krista's eyes. She was dizzy, her heart racing. The grungy clown was gone. This was the Conn that fought Evan, the Conn that she couldn't stop thinking about.

Krista wondered if he was going to kiss her. He didn't. He said, "Sometimes, you've got to put love in the ground before it gets people hurt."

"I never told you about them, did I?" Krista asked.

"No," Conn replied. "You didn't."

"Then, how did you know?"

"I know things. It's who I am." Conn smiled.

"And who are you?" Krista asked.

Conn didn't lose his smile. "Stick around. Maybe you'll find out."

Krista realized the fingers of her free hand were making little circles on the back of Conn's. She should have been afraid. He knew things she hadn't told him. He was playing with her, with her friend. There was an obvious and searing anger beneath his smile, a rage that Krista shared. She grabbed the back of Conn's neck, pulled herself to him, and kissed him viciously.

The phone rang. This time, Krista ignored it.

Chapter Fourteen

IT WAS TOO dark to see the clouds, but Alex could feel them. The sticky humidity was smothering. Light from inside stretched long and rectangular across the boards of Samantha's overwhelmingly large, second-story deck. Alex sat on one of the two reclining deck chairs, facing a backyard he could barely see. Samantha was still inside. She'd asked Alex to wait outside while she washed dishes and promised to join him as soon as she could. When he'd offered to help, Samantha practically pushed him onto the deck.

Alex had spent most of the night confused. Samantha's parents were aggressively friendly from the moment he walked in. Samantha's mother, Jenny, took his jacket before he even had it off, while Heath, Samantha's father, handed him a bottle of locally made cream soda that he swore would be the best Alex ever had. Alex barely had time to say hello before Heath led him into the living room to show him the dizzying array of blueprints, spreadsheets, and contracts that would lead, he promised, to the biggest strip mall development Heath had ever planned. He was there twenty minutes before he saw Samantha, and only long enough for a hello before she disappeared back into the kitchen.

"I wanted them to roll out the red carpet for you," Heath explained. That's when the questioning started, an interrogation that lasted until Samantha brought out a tray of lasagna that could have fed twelve people. Heath smiled the whole time.

Dinner was perfectly choreographed, from the serving of the food to the clearing of plates to the reveal of Samantha's apparently famous devil's food cake (which lived up to the fame). Heath told jokes, Jenny and Samantha laughed and kept plates full, and the spotlight fell on Alex at regular intervals so he could repeat stories he'd already told Heath in the living room. Alex was relieved to finally have a quiet moment out on the deck. Something about it all put Alex on edge, though he couldn't put his finger on why.

"Sorry that took so long," Samantha said. Alex hadn't heard her join him. "You doing okay out here?"

Alex smiled. "I'm good. Better, now. Obviously."

"Yeah, yeah. Thanks for putting up with that. It was intense, I know." Samantha sat in the open recliner.

"It was cool. I mean, yeah, it was pretty intense, but it was nice, too."

Samantha leaned back in the reclining chair, stretched her arms above her head, and yawned. "Well, thank God that's over."

"Do you cook every night?"

"No way. I'd die. Dinner parties only. The rest of the time Mom cooks and I eat."

"Mom hated cooking," Alex said. "If I didn't make something, we'd end up having popcorn. And I suck at cooking, so we pretty much just had popcorn."

Samantha smiled, but she was obviously impatient to change the subject. After a brief pause, she asked a question he knew was coming. "What were you talking to Ferris about?"

"Do we have to talk about this?"

"You told me we could talk about it today," she said.

Only because she wouldn't leave him alone until he promised. "I know."

"You said it was about Danica. What about her?"

Alex couldn't hold eye contact with Samantha. He spoke to the wooden beams of the deck. "I was worried about something and Krista said I should ask Ferris about it. That's all."

"Wait, so you were talking to *Krista* about Danica."

"I don't know why this is such a big deal."

"Alex, I really need you to be straight with me," Samantha said, something close to fear in her voice. "What did Krista tell you?"

"Nothing! Just that I should stay away from her because she was crazy and might, you know, hate me."

Samantha slowly pushed herself upright. "Hate you because…"

"Because of us being together."

"Why would she hate you for that?" Samantha asked, her voice as tense as her body.

"Well, Krista said… you know…."

"Said *what*?"

Alex shifted in his seat, embarrassed. "That she was interested in you."

Samantha stared hard at him. "Is that all?"

"What else would she have said?" Alex asked.

"Nothing. I don't know. What about Ferris?"

Alex was sick of being interrogated, but it was impossible to say no to Samantha. "She didn't say anything. She got pissed off at first. Then she got *really* pissed when I told her Krista said I should talk to her. I don't know what's going on, honestly. All I did was ask about your friend to your *other* friends, except they all hate her and won't tell me why. I was trying to help. I'm sorry."

There was a long pause while Samantha stared at Alex, like she was deciding if she believed him. Finally, Samantha said, "You were just worried about Danica."

"Yes."

"Who you don't even know," said Samantha.

"Yeah."

"So you talked to someone who hates her."

Alex nodded. "Because I was worried."

"I don't understand."

"You don't understand why I'm worried?"

"I don't understand why you care," she said.

Alex waited for reflex to take over and find the perfect lie that would deflect Samantha onto safer topics. No lies came. If Alex wanted to talk, his instincts weren't going to stop him.

"I told you that my mom died," Alex said tentatively, "but I didn't tell you how."

Samantha shook her head, confused.

Alex inhaled through his nose. Exhaled through his mouth. He closed his eyes, repeated the cycle of breaths three more times, then reopened his eyes. "She killed herself. She did it in the basement while I was at my aunt's. No one told me how. I didn't want to know."

"Oh my God. Alex, I didn't know."

"No one does. Not at school, anyway."

"I'm so sorry," Samantha said. "Did she talk about it? I mean, did you have any warning?"

"I don't know." Maybe he wasn't ready for this. "After it happens it seems really obvious. You see all these signs. Then you can't really stop seeing them."

"And you think, you know, that Danica...?" Samantha's voice wobbled and trailed off.

"No. I'm not sure. It's not like you can know. It's more like, when things happened with Mom, I knew she was falling, but I didn't know how hard she'd land."

Samantha turned toward the empty black of the back yard. "Maybe this is just a tough time for her. Maybe she'll be fine."

"Probably. Most people are. But..."

"But what?" Samantha asked, still staring into space.

"If someone's about to fall, you've got to try to catch them."

"What if you're afraid you'll fall with them?" Samantha asked as she turned back to Alex.

When Alex was still seeing the counselor, they'd said something similar: if someone wanted to fall, Alex couldn't hold them up forever. The counselor wanted Alex to repeat it to him, to accept that he wasn't responsible for things he couldn't control. Alex still wasn't sure if he agreed. Maybe falling together would have been easier than surviving alone.

"I don't know," he said.

Samantha gripped Alex's hand and pulled him to her so hard that he almost fell off the recliner. She wrapped her arms around him, buried her face into his neck. Samantha didn't make a noise, only shook while Alex held her. He wondered if there was something he was supposed to say, something that would help, but the words stayed out of reach.

After Samantha's shaking subsided, she pulled away and said, "I'm so sorry about your mother."

Before Alex could reply, Samantha's father opened the door and told him it was time to go. Samantha led him through the house and to the front door. Alex stopped in the open doorway and leaned in to kiss her. She stopped him, put a hand on his chest, and forced a smile that was so believable Alex wondered how many of the ones he'd seen had been real. Then she said goodbye.

~

The metallic thud of the car door slamming shut. The click of the seatbelt locking into place. The murmur of nearly inaudible voices through the closed windows. The tap of her own finger on the hard plastic of the dashboard. Danica lived from sound to sound. In the silence she ceased to exist, only to return with each click, thud, tap and murmur. She preferred the silence.

The snap of the door latch opening. The creak of the seat's springs. The scrape of the key sliding into place. The rumble of the engine coming alive. The whine of her mother's voice.

"If they think I'm not going to fight this, they're wrong. I'm going to fight this, Danny, I promise. You'll be back next week."

Danica sunk into her chair as her mother spoke, waiting for the next silence into which she could disappear.

"They can't do this to you," Mom said. "I know they can't. I know it. I'm going to fight this so hard."

Danica realized what was coming when they'd gotten the call. Pastor Fresh wanted a quick chat with her and her mom. The kind of thing Fresh avoided at all costs. Her mom had seen through it, too. She'd only been asked to a meet with Fresh once before, last year, after the spring lock-in. The day Danica called an ambulance for Megan. Danica was proud of her mother for not asking what she'd done this time, even if the answer would have been laughably boring.

Megan and I went out for coffee and got caught.

That was all they needed, though.

Fresh — Pastor McElfresh for this meeting — wasn't alone. With him was Bill Ashley, the only church Elder whose daughter had been sent to the emergency room by

Danica Perlich.

Certain words were said. Words Danica expected to come up. Words like *bad influence* and *needs help*. A few times, Elder Ashley's mask slipped and he said *lesbian* and *crazy* instead. Vicky never argued. She heard *lesbian* and *Danica* in the same sentence and showed no surprise. She let Elder Ashley pronounce his sentence and dismiss them. Only now, in the car, was she saying all the things she hadn't said when it mattered.

"You didn't do anything. It's not your fault she came back. I'm going to call the head pastor as soon as I get home, Danny. As soon as I get home."

The click-clack-click of the turn signal. The tick-tick-tick of the keys striking the steering column. The hum of the idling engine.

Elder Ashley had looked at Danica only once, before saying, "When my daughter came back, I'd assumed Danica already moved on. I would have sent Megan to another church if I'd known. Since she *is* here, though, I think it's best that we handle this as we should have last year."

Fresh was as silent as Danica's mother. He wore a polo shirt and khakis. Dressy for Fresh. The way an Elder would want him to dress. When Elder Ashley said one of the words, like *lesbian* or *crazy* or *doesn't belong,* Fresh met Danica's eyes. He looked ashamed, but only enough for sympathy. Not enough to help.

The only time Danica's mother spoke was to meekly ask, "Are you kicking my daughter out of youth group?"

Elder Ashley replied, "We think it would be best if she found a church more suited to her situation."

The only time Danica herself spoke was to say, "Your daughter is gay, too."

"My daughter's burdens are our concern," he responded. "She never assaulted anyone with a pocket knife."

The car came to a stop at a traffic light and Mom turned to Danica. "Danny, what he said. About you being gay."

"I don't want to talk about it."

"You know you can talk to me, right?"

"I said I don't want to."

"I thought you might be. I wasn't sure. I didn't know how to ask. Maybe I should have," her mother said.

The honk of a car horn when the light turned green. The screech of the tires when her mom stepped on the gas.

"Should I have asked, Danny?"

"I don't want to talk about it," Danica repeated.

It didn't matter. There wasn't enough left to matter. One last thing to lose. Just one. Just Samantha. Danica knew it wouldn't be long before she was gone, too. A day. A week. Soon enough.

After gym, she'd found her shirt and bra in pieces on the floor. No one admitted to doing it. Everyone laughed. Especially Samantha's friends.

The whisper of voices that only Danica could hear. The buzz of a golden pin that only Danica could feel.

Samantha could stand by while they tore Danica to pieces. She was protected. She was safe. If Samantha couldn't hide anymore, maybe she'd have to choose. If she was exposed as Danica. If she was forced to tell the truth.

The crash of waves on the shore. The whistle of wind past her ears as she dove into the deep.

~

Alex flipped his pen from finger to finger, stuck on the last word he'd written. A yellow legal pad rested on his knees. Its topmost page was half-covered in dense, sloppy handwriting. A warm breeze blew over the reservoir and through the trees. Alex looked up, through the rustling leaves to the cloudy sky above. If it rained now, he wouldn't have to finish the letter. He could stop where he'd left off and never return to it. A day ago, Alex would've been happy for the rain. He wasn't sure what he wanted anymore.

He'd been out here for hours, long enough for his legs to fall asleep and for the dawn sun to climb into the sky. He hadn't been able to sleep, not after his dinner with Samantha and the talk that followed. So Alex had snuck out of the house as soon as his father went to bed, legal pad in one hand and a flashlight in the other. There were things he needed to say, things he couldn't imagine giving voice to until he'd admitted them to Samantha. That's why he was writing the letter. Because it was time.

Alex looked at the last line he'd written.

I was at Aunt Sharon's that night. Maybe they told you that already. That's why I wasn't home. I had a game in the morning and Mom

No one would read the letter or know it existed. When he finished, he'd tear it carefully off of the legal pad and send it where he had all the rest: down the cliff, into the reservoir. Dozens of letters had gone into the water. They weren't all to his father like this was, but most were. The point wasn't to send them, but to finish. He'd failed to finish this letter too many times.

Alex placed the tip of the pen on the paper.

Mom was doing really bad so I decided to sleep at Aunt Sharon's. She drove me to games a lot when Mom was doing bad. Mom was usually fine with it. But that night before I got out the door she

Alex stopped again. He dropped the pen on his stomach and returned his attention to the rippling surface of the reservoir. The letter writing was the only useful thing he'd learned from his former grief counselor. It took four months of pointless, weekly sessions for the counselor to realize Alex wasn't going to talk and suggest they part ways. At the end of Alex's last session, the counselor gave Alex the legal pad and a pen.

"I know you don't want to talk to me," he'd said, "but I think you do have things you need to say. Sometimes, when I want to talk someone but don't know how, I write a letter to them. I don't usually send it, but if I write it down, I know what to say once I'm ready. Give it a try. If it helps, and you decide you want to, you can always come back. Okay?"

Alex never went back, but he'd used half of the pad on letters in the months since. The counselor had hoped Alex's letters would eventually get him to talk (to someone, to anyone), but they hadn't until the last letter he wrote. The one to Samantha. The one about his mom. He wondered if that was why this letter scared him. If he was finally able to finish it, was it time to speak? Alex didn't know if he was ready for that. He didn't want to be ready. But he might not have the courage to start this letter a second time.

If Alex couldn't forgive himself, at least he could admit why. His eyes already stung with tears when picked the pen back up.

she asked me if I was sure I wanted to leave. She said we could watch a movie and have dinner together. But I was already packed and Aunt Sharon's car was outside and so I told her she'd just oversleep like she always did and I'd end up being late. I don't think she said anything back, but I didn't really give her the chance.

Alex threw the pad and pen aside, leaned his weight against the dying oak tree behind him, and stopped fighting the tears. He didn't need to write anything else. The rest was obvious. The last thing he said to his mother wasn't even goodbye. He told her she couldn't be trusted and left her there alone. That wasn't what ate at Alex, though. Alex blamed himself for the nights just like it that he'd said the same thing to her, in words and in actions. Alex gave up on his mother long before that, and whether or not he realized it, she must have given up, too.

The crying passed quickly, like a brief but violent storm. When it stopped, he dried his cheeks on the sleeves of his shirt and turned to retrieve the pad. It wasn't there. In its place were two bare feet. In all his time on the cliff, he'd seen anyone he hadn't brought with him. He should have been afraid, but that wasn't what Alex felt. The last of the wetness on his cheeks dried, and the memory of having cried faded. He couldn't recall what he'd been writing, or why he'd come out to the reservoir at all. Then he knew. He'd come to see *her*, the woman who stood before him. Alex forced his eyes upward. They lingered on each spot where they fell: on her ankles, on her bare knees, on the hem of her shimmering silver dress, on the curve of her breasts, on her pale neck. Alex was smitten before his gaze found her perfect, beautiful face.

She held the legal pad with long, delicate fingers. Her eyes met Alex's and her red lips turned up in a smile. Her teeth were perfectly white. "I'm sorry, it was rude to read this before you were finished. I couldn't help myself."

"It's fine. I don't mind," Alex replied, shaking his head, needing her to believe him.

"I usually wait until you've thrown them away." The woman knelt and placed a hand on Alex's thigh. "I got impatient."

Her touch distracted him, made it hard to form thoughts into words. "You read my letters?"

She leaned in, close enough for Alex to feel her breath on his cheeks. "All of them."

"Why?"

"Because they surprise me," she responded. She began to slide her hand up Alex's leg, but stopped to add, "You aren't what I expected, Alex. You aren't what I hoped."

Words poured out of Alex's mouth. "But how did you get them? I threw them away. Into the water. I didn't mean to disappoint you. I didn't—"

"Shhh," she said, placing a finger against his lips. "When you threw them into the water, you were throwing them to me."

"I don't understand."

"The water is my home." Her hand moved downward, over his chin and onto his chest. Her hair seemed to move and flow at the edges of Alex's vision. "Would you like me to show you?"

"I can't swim."

"I'll teach you. Would you like that?"

Alex nodded. He'd only met her, didn't know her name, didn't have a reason to trust her. Yet he wanted her. Wanted her and needed her to want him back. Anything she wanted was hers. She was the only woman he'd ever known, and the only one he ever wished to know.

"Then come with me. Live with me in the water. There's nothing here for you, is there? Nothing for you to leave behind."

A word tore through the haze of infatuation. "Samantha," he said. As her name passed his lips, the woman before him changed. Her skin was pallid. Her silver dress became a ragged, grey thing that seethed like fog. Her touch was cold and damp. Alex's heart thudded painfully as fear swept over him. He pulled away and slid backward across the ground.

"Oh," she said with a curious smile. "I thought I had you."

"Who are you? What do you want?"

"To hate you. It's so much easier when I can hate you."

Alex scrambled to make sense of what was happening. The woman had been beautiful, yes, but he'd never been so smitten by beauty alone. There was something more to it, something he couldn't explain. But whatever he'd seen, it was gone. An illusion smashed when he'd found his way back to thoughts of Samantha. Alex now felt a less strange, but equally disconcerting sensation. An unexpected familiarity. Like he should know her. Did she remind Alex of someone? Was that it?

His mind fixed on was the last thing she'd said. *It's so much easier when I can hate you.* Alex replied, "I've never met you before."

"No, but I've met too many just like you. Stumbling blindly into someone else's story and making it your own, turning love into pain and never knowing what you've done. And never to blame, because, in the end, you're simply someone's excuse to misbehave."

"I don't understand. What did I do to you?" The things she'd said — that he'd stumbled into *someone else story*, turned *love into pain* — came together. Alex realized who she reminded him of. "Is this about Danica?"

"She is not your concern." The woman grabbed Alex's face, her palm under his chin and fingers on his cheeks. She squeezed as she spoke. "You keep dangerous company. Constantine's filth is all over you. That would've been reason enough to drag you into the water."

Alex trembled when the woman said *Constantine*. Conn said his name was short for something, but not what. He thought of Conn's fear of this place, of Danica's reaction to Conn and the warning she'd given Alex. "You know Conn? Did he do something to you? Please, just tell me what you want."

"I want you to leave and never return. Very soon we'll make this place ours, and my sisters won't care if you refuse to come with them. Be smart and keep your distance from your friend. From your girlfriend, too. You deserve better than what's to come." The woman let go of Alex's face and stood. She looked at the legal pad in her hand, carefully tore off the top page, and dropped the pad itself onto the ground. Then she folded the sheet twice and slipped it into the side of her dress, as if into a pocket Alex couldn't see. "I'm sorry about your mother, Alex. I wish I could promise things would get better."

Disoriented and afraid, Alex could think of only one thing to say. "Would you at least tell me your name?"

She smiled the same curious, surprised smile as when he saw her for what she really was. "Lenka," she said, and vanished into the trees while the word still hung in the air. Alex heard the distant sound of a splash echo up the cliff.

It took Alex a long time to find the strength to stand. He stumbled up the hill, away from the water. There was something terrible and strange happening that he didn't understand. Didn't *want* to understand. He knew he should take the woman's advice to leave the woods and never return, forget the things she'd told him. Forget he'd even seen her. This wasn't his problem. Even if it was, there was nothing Alex could do. He had a life again. He had Samantha.

None of which made a shred of difference to him. All that mattered was the memory of standing at the door, the decision to leave his mother alone, the morning that followed. He wouldn't walk out again, even if there was nothing he could do to help. He'd stay. He'd try.

First, he needed to find out what was happening, and the woman had given him the key. Her name. Lenka.

Alex returned home and locked himself in his room. He began another letter that he wouldn't send. This one, driven by anger and not guilt, would be easier than the rest. He wrote the first two words.

Dear Constantine.

Chapter Fifteen

"I'M GOING TO be late!" Samantha yelled through her mother's closed bedroom door. "We need to leave!"

There was no response but the sound of feet stomping and the occasional slam of a dresser drawer. This fight had been going on for twenty minutes, though truthfully they'd been arguing about *something* since Dad went out of town. He'd flown to Charlotte the morning after the Alex dinner, and the meetings he thought would be done by Sunday had apparently run long. Bitterness and frustration, compressed by months of enforced silence, finally escaping as fast as it could be put into words.

"Mom, I have a test first period. I can't be late!"

The weekend should have been great. Dad gone, no meets, no obligations. A few weeks ago, a weekend like that would have been blissful. Two whole days of freedom. If only there'd been someone to spend it with. Danica hadn't been to school since she demanded Samantha break things off with Alex. At first it had been a relief. Samantha hoped that a few days away would clear Danica's head. Now she was staring at Danica's number on her phone, wanting to call but worried it would make things worse. As for Alex, Samantha had done everything she could to dodge him. There was no way she could break up — not yet, not so soon after what he'd told her — but she couldn't pretend things were fine.

Samantha knocked on the bedroom door. What was taking her so long? "Mom!"

"One minute!" Mom shouted back.

Samantha didn't have one minute. If her father was home, there'd be no choice but to wait quietly. Her father was not home. She threw open the bedroom door. Her mom was in the center of the room, blouse on but unbuttoned, startled. On her mother's stomach, half-hidden by the red fabric of her shirt, were three large, yellow-purple bruises. Samantha's mother turned her back to her daughter and buttoned the blouse.

The bruises weren't supposed to seen. He was careful where he left them. Always on the back or stomach, never visible when dressed. That was why Samantha avoided her parents' room, even when he was gone. It was Mom's fault Samantha was there now. If she'd been on time, if she'd gotten dressed faster, Samantha wouldn't have had to see anything.

Nor would she have opened her mouth to demand, "Why do you keep letting this happen?"

"Close the door," her mother replied, quietly.

"You know how he is. Why do you always make it worse for us?"

Samantha's mother turned, shirt half buttoned, cheeks flushed. She snatched the keys off of the bed and threw them into Samantha's chest. The keys fell to the floor with a thud.

"Drive yourself to school," she snapped.

Samantha picked up the keys without taking her eyes off of her mom. "Everything is your fault."

Her mother's response was a weak, wounded glare. Samantha hated that look. Cowardly. Stupid. Defenseless.

Samantha would never be like her. Never.

The last thing Samantha heard before she escaped the house was her mom's impotent scream as she slammed the bedroom door.

Monday got worse from there. Samantha made it to her test on time only for her mind to go blank. If she got every problem she finished correct, there was a solid D in her future. Then came chemistry lab, where she knocked over a beaker of citric acid and ruined her experiment. She'd have to stay after school to redo it. Better yet, acid splashed onto the front of her shirt and left faded circles where it hit. Ruined.

Between periods, Samantha rushed to her locker and grabbed her sweatshirt. She wasn't cold, but at least it would cover the acid stains.

"S'up, slut? Where's Alex?" It was Krista, one arm propped against the adjacent locker, the other around Conn's waist. Samantha had no idea how long they'd been standing beside her. Ferris was with them, too. She looked impatient to get to her next class.

"How am I supposed to know? Ask your boyfriend."

Conn shrugged. "He hasn't called me in days. Not even a text. Figured he was busy with you."

"Yeah, well, he wasn't. I have to get to class."

Samantha pushed past her friends and stopped. Danica stood in the center of the hallway, her hair pulled into a sloppy ponytail, circles under her eyes dark against her skin.

"Can we talk?" Danica asked.

Samantha wanted to talk, so much that she almost said yes with Ferris and Krista right there. "Later, okay?"

"No. Now."

"Danica," Samantha implored.

"Go away, psycho. Sam's busy," Ferris said.

Danica ignored Ferris. "Please."

Krista and Conn — both of their mouths turned up in a half smile, like they were sharing one between them — flanked Danica while Ferris stepped in front of Samantha and said, "She doesn't want to talk to you. No one does."

"When are you going to tell them?" Danica demanded, staring hard at Samantha.

"Tell me what?" Ferris demanded.

Why couldn't she have waited until 8th period? "This isn't the time, Danny."

"Tell her or I will," said Danica. Her arms were shaking, but her voice was firm. "You can't keep hiding me."

"Tell me what, bitch?" Ferris shouted.

"Ferris, can you give us a minute? You, too," Samantha said, turning to Krista.

"Oh my God, you have a thing for Sam, don't you?" Ferris laughed. "I can't believe this. You're out of your mind."

Samantha grabbed her friend's shoulder and squeezed. "Ferris!"

"I love her." Danica's eyes never left Samantha. "She loves me, too."

Silence. People passing in the hall stopped to look. Krista's smile vanished. Conn's did not. The push lurked behind Samantha, ready.

"Just like Megan did, right?" Ferris's voice was a growl.

Danica finally turned to Ferris. "Shut up."

"Shut up or what? You'll cut me like you cut my sister?"

Samantha kept trying to pull Ferris back. "What the hell are you talking about?"

"What, she didn't tell you how she was hot for

Megan?"

"I didn't do anything!"

Ferris kept talking. "Why do you think Megan had to get all those stitches? Psycho lezzie cut her arm open when she got shot down."

"No shit!" Krista said, suddenly amused again.

Samantha looked past Ferris to Danica. "Is that true?"

Danica was shaking her head, but not in denial. She looked like a cat that had been cornered. Samantha stepped around Ferris and stared down at Danica.

"Is that true?" she asked again.

The rest happened very fast. Danica put her hands on Samantha's cheeks and kissed her on the lips. Anyone in the hall who hadn't already stopped came to an immediate halt. Samantha put a hand on Danica's breastbone and tried to push her away. Danica forced herself forward and wrapped her arms around Samantha's back. As Danica pulled them together, Samantha raised her right arm, palm open, and swung. Her hand caught Danica on the face. The *smack* echoed through the hall. Danica released Samantha and stumbled backwards.

Someone gasped. Samantha wasn't sure who. Someone else laughed. Krista.

Danica looked up, confused, betrayed, her cheek already red. Samantha's hand tingled. What had she done? That couldn't have been her instinct. She would never have slapped Danica. That wasn't who she was.

Ferris got past Samantha and shoved Danica as hard as she could. Off balance and stunned, Danica fell backwards onto the floor.

"Don't you ever touch her!" Ferris screamed.

Someone said *holy shit*. Someone else yelled *catfight*! Krista kept laughing.

Ferris continued forward. She pulled a foot back, a

soccer player's wind-up. The kick hit Danica in the knee, and Danica finally reacted. She screamed. The sound turned Samantha's stomach. She nearly vomited there, in the hallway, while Ferris moved in for a second kick.

And then Alex was there. He jumped between Ferris and Danica and roared, "What the hell are you doing?"

Samantha withered at the sight of him. How long had he been here? Did he see what she'd done?

Danica stumbled to her feet. With one final, pained glance at Samantha, she fled down the hallway. Ferris shrunk away, aware suddenly of how many people were watching. Krista's laughter finally died.

Samantha scrambled for words, searched for something to say, some explanation.

"I can't believe you all," Alex said. He turned to Conn and added, "Hang around after school. We need to talk."

Alex sprinted down the hall in the direction Danica had escaped. He'd never so much as looked at Samantha. The crowd broke apart and dispersed. Ferris slunk off in the opposite direction of Alex. A teacher stepped into the hallway, so uselessly late that on any other day it would have made Samantha laugh. Krista took Conn by the hand and pulled him toward the stairwell.

Conn touched Samantha on the arm on the way past. "I'm sorry that had to happen."

Samantha collapsed against her locker as the hallway emptied around her. She was still there, alone, when the bell rang for 3rd period.

~

Alex waited at his locker after the final bell, unable to shake the memory of what had happened between Samantha and Danica. If first seeing Samantha run had dragged Alex out of the fog, today was like waking to realize he'd been living a dream. Samantha lied to him about Danica. Maybe about her feelings for him as well. Alex wasn't sure Samantha ever said she cared about him. Maybe she'd only let him kiss her to keep from having to.

He put it out of mind. There would be time to make sense of it later. First, he had to talk to Conn. Somehow, all of this — Samantha, Danica, the woman at the reservoir — led back to him. Alex needed to understand how, and why.

Though Alex was waiting for Conn, he searched the passing crowds for Danica's face. He'd tried to find her after she escaped, but there were too many exits and places to hide. If she was still in the building, she was keeping out of sight. Alex couldn't blame her. Still, he looked at every face, hoping. The crowd thinned, became a trickle of stragglers that eventually ceased.

When the last student cleared the hallway, Conn stepped out of a stairwell. Alex suspected the timing was intentional.

"Well, if it isn't the mighty avenger himself." Conn approached, hands in his pockets, a smirk on his face. "That was brave, getting between two pissed off ladies like that. Have you seen Ferris' legs? It'd be something to get kicked by those."

"Braver than the dick who stood there and laughed at it," Alex said.

Conn sighed. "Sure. Fine. Bullying is wrong and I should be ashamed of myself. Is that all? I've got plans."

"Hold on. That's not what I wanted to talk about."

"Whatever. Go for it," Conn replied, obviously bored.

This was it. Time to see if he was crazy.

"Tell me about Lenka," Alex said.

Conn's jaw set. His eyes narrowed. "What was

that?"

"Who's Lenka, Constantine?" asked Alex.

Conn shook his head and laughed. Then, without even looking at him, he grabbed Alex by the collar and shoved him into the lockers. Alex tried to break free, but Conn was stronger than he looked. Way stronger.

"Dude, that is not cool," Conn said.

"Sore subject?" Alex tried to sound confident, but getting jacked up against a locker hadn't been in the plan.

Conn's smile was cruel, mocking. "I don't know, how's your mom doing? I hear hanging yourself is a shitty way to go if you don't die right off. Which, by the way, she didn't."

Alex had never talked about his mom with Conn. Not once. Furious, he struggled futilely to get free of Conn's grip. "You don't know anything about her!"

"I know more than you think. I did my research, you know? I wanted to know who you were before I wasted my time with you."

Alex went slack. Had *everyone* been playing him? "Waste your time? I thought we were friends."

He stared at Alex for a moment, confused, then carefully released his hold on Alex's collar. "Shit, man, don't be like that. We were. We are."

"Then act like one. Tell me who Lenka is."

"Where did you even hear that name?" Conn asked.

"You wouldn't believe me if I told you."

"Ah," Conn said, nodding. "One of them actually talked to you? That's new."

"One of them? How many are there? And what are they?"

"Too many. Back home we called them Rusalka. Drowned women who were too pissed off to die. Out for vengeance and whatnot, you know how it goes. The point is, they're dangerous. You should stay out of their way."

"Seriously? Drowned women out for vengeance?" Alex asked, wishing he was more skeptical than he felt. *Drowned* was exactly how Lenka looked.

"Yeah, I know. Back in my day we believed all kinds of crazy shit. Just happens we were right about this."

"In your day? When was that?"

Conn laughed.

"Conn, please. I need to know what's going on."

"You really don't, man. You don't even *want* to. You asked me to be straight with you, so I will: you're not crazy. You're just caught up in something insane. But it's nothing you have to worry about. It's passing you by. Go back home, bond with your dad, and feel like a winner. You got the girl."

Alex was sick of being toyed with. He gave in to his anger and punched Conn as hard as he could, a clean shot to Conn's jaw. If it hurt him, it didn't show. Conn grabbed Alex by the neck and slammed him back into the locker so hard it knocked the air out of Alex's lungs.

"A long time ago, there was a girl. Her name was Lenka. I loved her more than you've loved anything in your life. Only I screwed up. Things went bad. Seriously bad. Samantha's about to get a taste of what I'm talking about."

Alex grabbed Conn's wrist with both hands and pulled himself up to relieve the pressure on his throat.

Conn continued, "Here's the truth, and it might hurt to hear. You don't matter. I mean, not even a little bit. You know how a chess board has pawns? That's a really charitable view of your situation. I needed to get your girl's attention. That's it. Now you're done. I appreciate your help. But — and, seriously, this is the truth — your girlfriend is in a shitload of trouble. I'm the only thing that can protect her. Without me, she's going to die."

Alex felt Conn's grip loosen and withdraw. It took all

of Alex's strength not to double over and hack out his own lungs. Conn straightened his shirt and stepped away from Alex.

"What about Danica?"

"Who do you think I'm protecting Samantha from?" Conn asked with a laugh. "Oh, hey, look who's here."

Alex followed Conn's line of sight. Samantha was in the doorway, holding one of the double doors open. She looked panicked. Conn smiled at Samantha, then at Alex. Finally, he turned and walked in the opposite direction of Samantha.

Samantha ran to his side. "Are you okay?" she asked. She put a hand on his cheek. Alex pushed it away.

"Don't touch me," he said. "What was that this morning?"

"Alex..."

"Was what Danica said the truth? Is that why you hit her?"

Samantha looked away.

"Were you lying to me the whole time?"

Samantha wrestled with her answer. She settled on a single nod.

"Were you lying to both of us, or just to me?" Alex asked.

She ignored his question. "No one's seen Danica since this morning. I called her house. She's not there, either. I'm really worried. It's fine if you're angry at me. I don't care. But I need help. I'm afraid she might... I don't know who else to ask."

Alex hurt. His throat was sore, his lungs burned, and nothing he'd cared about was real. He wanted go home, lock the door to his bedroom, and wait for the fog to sweep back in to dull the pain. Wanted to, but couldn't. Not until they found Danica and made sure she was okay. But where was she? How was he supposed to find her?

Something clicked. Not the details. Not why or how, but where. It fit, even if it still didn't make sense. Alex grabbed Samantha's hand.

"We need to get a ride to my place."

"What? You think she went to your house? Why?" she asked.

"Please, just trust me. We need to go. I'll call my dad. He can pick us up."

"Wait." Samantha reached into her pocket and pulled out a set of keys. She sounded relieved. "Mom gave me the car."

He didn't, couldn't, share Samantha's relief. If his guess was right, if Danica was headed where he thought, they might already be too late.

Chapter Sixteen

DANICA WALKED FOR hours. The knee Ferris kicked throbbed with every step. The pain had become a sharp and constant thing, present even when she stopped to rest. Danica was happy for it. She lived in the pain, let it drive her forward. It was the only thing she had.

She'd left the school not knowing where to go. After hours spent crouched in a field house bathroom stall, legs cramping and tears running dry, Danica knew only that she had to leave. She'd stood, walked into the cloud-dulled sunlight, and felt a now-familiar heat in her breast. It soothed her, the return of the pin's burning touch. Its voice called to her, gave her strength.

Come to us, my love.

And she did.

She'd made her way out of Sheffield, down smaller and smaller roads, until she found herself on a gravel path that wound its way towards a dairy far off the road. She followed the path behind the dairy, where the gravel turned to dirt and plunged into the wall of a dense forest. Fog seethed beyond the tree line. Danica continued, limped into the trees, into the mist. The path ended, but Danica didn't need it. The voices were clear, now, and she knew where they would lead. The cliff, the deep black waters below, the distant, swimming forms of those who were waiting for her.

Danica saw a shape ahead, a shadow in the fog that slowly coalesced into the form of a woman. *The* woman. The one Danica had seen in her dreams for so long. Her hair flowed above her head, her clothes weightless over her skin. Danica hobbled forward until she stood before the woman. The pin buzzed and hummed and burned the closer she came.

"You're here," the woman said. She was smiling.

Danica nodded.

"Tell me why you came," she said.

"It hurts so much."

"I know, my love, and this is the end of it. But that's not the only reason, is it?"

Danica shook her head.

"Tell me."

"Samantha," Danica said. She thought of Sam's hand descending toward her.

"What about Samantha?" the woman asked.

Danica's knee throbbed. Her cheek stung. There were weights on her shoulders, hanging from her hands, pressing on her head. The ache of it all saturated her skin, her heart, her brain, and her bones. She hurt, and she hated, and she knew there was only one way to be rid of the pain forever.

"I want her to hurt like I hurt," Danica said.

"She will, my love. I promise she will." The woman put her arms around Danica and embraced her. "My name is Lenka. You're safe, now. You won't be alone anymore. Come and meet your new sisters. They're waiting for us."

Lenka released Danica from the embrace and took her hand. They walked together into the fog, toward the welcoming embrace of the water. Toward escape, she thought. *Toward revenge*, the pin replied.

~

Samantha pulled Alex to a stop when they came into view of the forest. A thick mass of fog blanketed the woods, like a storm cloud had descended over it. Alex had seen mist roll in from the reservoir, but nothing like this. Never fog that ended so cleanly at the edge of the trees, a wall protecting something within. The sight of the shrouded forest nearly panicked him. He remembered Lenka's warning to stay away, that she and her sisters intended to make the forest *theirs*.

"You think Danica went in there," Samantha said.

It had only been a guess, but now? "Yeah."

"But why?"

"Trust me," Alex said, and started forward again.

Samantha yanked on his arm. "There's only so far that 'trust me' goes."

Alex had no idea how to explain any of this to her. There was a connection between this place and Lenka, between Lenka and Conn, between Conn and Danica. That was all he had, and even that sounded delusional. He couldn't make Samantha understand. He didn't have time.

"You don't have to follow me," Alex said. "I don't know how to explain, and you wouldn't believe me if I tried. I have to find her. I have to try."

"But why?"

"I told you. I won't let her fall alone."

Samantha swallowed, and looked back to the forest. "That fog doesn't look, I don't know... right."

"I don't think it is," Alex replied.

She squeezed his hand. Hard. "Then we need to stick together."

They pressed forward together. A wet chill penetrated Alex's clothes and skin as they approached the tree line. Samantha must have felt it too; she shivered and pulled Alex closer. He reminded himself that it didn't mean anything and never had. Her feelings for him had been a lie. One that led him out of the fog, but blinded him from seeing it had taken someone else in his place. Still, Alex was glad she was with him. He didn't want to be alone. Not here. Not yet.

The mist closed around them. The normal sounds of the forest had been replaced by something. Something unnatural. Footsteps rustling through fallen leaves, maybe, or whispered voices. Alex kept a tight hold on Samantha's hand and stepped carefully around the roots and brush. He went by memory and instinct, unable to see far enough through the fog to be sure that he wasn't wandering down one of the trail's many branching dead-ends. The fog was a living thing, always moving, flowing like water as they passed through. Alex's foot came down on a divot and his ankle twisted. He nearly fell, but Samantha's firm grip on his hand was enough to keep him balanced.

"Careful," Samantha said.

Alex took a moment to steady himself and get his bearings. Just ahead, the path turned sharply downhill. They were halfway to the reservoir, maybe a bit more. If he was right, that's where Danica was headed. Or where she already was. Or... Alex stopped himself. He had to believe they weren't too late.

"It's going to get steep," Alex warned.

"Don't worry about me. I'll catch you if you fall."

Alex chose his footing as carefully as he could. He took slow, deliberate steps so Samantha could follow his path. There was a calm that found Alex when he stood on the pitcher's mound. A focus, a sharpening of the senses.

It was as if he could hear things that *might* happen, sense actions the batter *wanted* to take. Alex felt that same heightening of self and gave himself over to it.

The ground shifted suddenly beneath his outstretched foot, crumbled and scattered down the hill under his weight, but he was ready. His mind sensed the shift in balance and direction before his body had the chance to fall forward. Alex let go of Samantha's hand and swung both arms to regain his balance. Samantha shouted his name, afraid he was falling. He ignored it, found solid ground with his outstretched foot and planted it like he was bracing for a pitch.

"What was that about catching me?" Alex laughed, overcome by the relief of having caught himself.

"Are you okay? Where are you?" Samantha asked. She sounded far away, though they couldn't have been more than a few feet apart.

Alex looked over his shoulder but saw nothing but trees and mist. He reached out a hand and called out her name. Nothing. He shouted again. "Samantha?"

A hand touched his. Alex grasped it before noticing something wasn't right. Samantha's hand had been warm, her grip firm. This hand was cold, damp, and limp. Alex released it and lurched away. His right foot came down on another loose clump of earth, but this time he wasn't ready. He tumbled sideways and his shin came down on an exposed root. He rolled, tumbling down the hill. His head glanced off a rock as he twisted in a futile attempt to slow his descent. A yard from the bottom of the slope, he crashed into the trunk of a maple and came to an abrupt and painful stop.

Alex pushed himself carefully into a crouch. Though his whole body hurt, nothing seemed to be broken. He called for Samantha again, searched the fog frantically, but the only reply was the rustle of leaves and the whisper of things deep within the fog. Alex got back to his feet and brushed the dirt off of his legs. He was about to climb back up the hill when he heard something behind him.

It was a voice, Alex was sure. He couldn't make out the words, but he recognized it nonetheless. Danica. Somewhere up the hill, Samantha was alone with whatever had touched his hand. Somewhere ahead, Danica was about to fall beyond his reach. He knew he'd hate himself no matter what he did, but there was only one choice he could live with.

Alex turned and continued down the hill.

~

Alex was gone. He'd let go of her hand, left her alone at the top of the hill, the sound of his voice receding into the mist. She didn't know where she was or where Alex was leading them. He was down there somewhere, but she could no longer hear him. Samantha tested the ground in front of her with her feet. If she followed, she was as likely to get lost as she was to find him. Still, it was her only option. She'd have to try.

A twig snapping was her only warning. Something wrapped an arm around Samantha's waist and yanked her backwards. She clawed at it, dug nails into its cold flesh. Samantha was no stranger to fear. She lived with it every day. In her home, there was danger in carelessness, in misspoken words, in every accident. It was a minefield where, though every mine was flagged, it was only a matter of time before she stepped somewhere she knew she shouldn't. That was the fear Samantha could handle.

Not this. Not lost and alone, abandoned in an unfamiliar forest, in the grasp of something or someone she couldn't see.

The arm around her pulled her off the trail and into

the brush. Samantha didn't scream. Screams were deadly, dangerous things that made everything worse. She held her fear inside and fought, dug heels into the ground, tried to slow the thing that had her. She reached for a rock or a branch, anything she could use to fight. Her hand brushed something, but before she could grab it her attacker threw Samantha on the ground. It didn't give her time to recover. Before Samantha could get to her feet, something leapt onto her and pushed her back down.

She heard the murmuring of a river and felt cool water running along her legs and up the sides of her chest. A delicate hand brushed Samantha's bare arm. Its touch stole her breath. The will to fight left her, and her fear went with it.

The thing straddling her was a girl — Samantha's age, or close to it — with wet hair and moist, porcelain skin. She pressed down on Samantha's shoulders with her hands. There was something about her smile that Samantha couldn't resist. Or it might have been her eyes, or the curve of her neck, or the pressure of her hands on Samantha's body. It was something. It was everything.

"Don't leave," the girl said, leaning closer. "Stay with me."

Thoughts of Danica and Alex were swept away by the water flowing across her body. There was nowhere she wanted to be but here. The girl's lips were so close. So very close. Samantha imagined the girl bending forward, bringing those lips into reach of her own.

One of the girl's hands slid down Samantha's arm and clasped Samantha's hand. "You remind me of someone I loved. She was beautiful and tall and strong, just like you. I miss her so much."

Samantha wanted to speak, but words were an effort she couldn't afford. Not with this beautiful creature so close. Samantha wanted to be taken; to do, to *be*, anything the girl asked of her.

"I loved her, and she loved me. At least, she loved me until people found out. Then it was like she didn't know me. I never stopped loving her, though. Not even when her servants came for me and held me under the water so I couldn't tell anyone the things we'd done when her family was asleep." The girl leaned closer, but not enough. "Now you're mine, like I made her mine. I could do anything I want to you. You'd thank me for it, beg me for more, offer me everything. You'd thank me for the water if I promised to stay with you while it filled your lungs, wouldn't you?"

Samantha nodded.

"I wish they'd let me, but you belong to the new girl. My sisters would be cross if I stole you." She sighed, continuing, "But they won't mind if I play while we wait."

The girl let go of Samantha's hand. Samantha closed her eyes as the girl touched gently her on the cheek. She tried to sigh, but her face was covered, surrounded by water. It took Samantha a moment to realize she couldn't breathe. There was liquid in her throat, in her lungs. She gagged, tried to cough. She thrashed and kicked, but only out of reflex. She didn't need air. The only thing that mattered was the girl's hand against her face. It was all she wanted.

Then it was gone, and cruel and unwanted air took its place.

"That was fun, wasn't it?" the girl asked as Samantha gasped. She smiled and licked her lips. "Do you want to play some more?"

Samantha didn't answer. It didn't matter what she wanted. Even the notion of *wanting* was gone.

The girl's smile vanished at once. She screamed, a high-pitched, warbling sound that hurt Samantha's ears.

Still screaming, she leapt backwards and landed her feet yards away. Samantha's head cleared. Thoughts that had seemed so distant a moment before flooded back. Danica, Alex, the fog. The girl's skin, so smooth and beautiful before, was now grey and mottled. Her hair hung over her face in matted ropes. She took three tentative steps backwards, her eyes on something behind Samantha, then turned and disappeared into the fog.

An open hand reached down and offered itself to Samantha. It wasn't pallid and dead, nor was it delicate and pale. It was normal. Human. She took it and was pulled to her feet. She looked up at the person's face, expecting to see Alex, hoping to see Danica.

It was Conn.

She wanted to ask what he was doing here. How he'd found her. What he wanted. Who (or what) the girl was, and why she was terrified at the sight of him. There wasn't time for questions, though. Danica was out there somewhere, alone, in danger. Samantha stared into mist so thick she could barely see the tree in front her, then turned back to Conn. He was smiling.

"Shall we?" he asked, and started down the hill.

~

Alex stepped out of the fog and into the small clearing where he'd come so often before. It was as if a bubble had formed in the mist. It encircled the overlook, swirling around and above him. A boiling, hemispherical wall. There had been sounds as he'd made his way here, footsteps and whispers and others he couldn't place, but the only sound here was the lapping of the reservoir against the cliff wall, far below.

He leaned against the nearest tree and caught his breath. The walk shouldn't have exhausted him like this.

It was as if the woods had grown larger under the influence of the mist. Alex tried not to worry about Samantha, still back there somewhere, trapped and lost with the things he'd heard circling. Samantha could handle herself. She could outrun anything if it came to it. It was Danica who needed him now.

Alex heard the soft crunch of feet on dead leaves from the other side of the clearing. Someone else was here. Alex peeked around the trunk of the tree. It was Danica, emerging from the fog and limping noticeably. A dozen shadows stood behind her, unmoving, their forms obscured by the thick haze. Alex kept his focus on Danica. Whatever they were, if they came for him there was nothing Alex could do to stop them.

"Danica," Alex said, sidling from the cover of his tree in the direction of the drop. She was closer to it than he, but the limp slowed her. So long as she didn't run, he might be able to cut her off.

"Who's there?" she shouted. She stumbled back and searched the clearing. When Danica's eyes found him, she took another step toward the mist. "Alex?"

Alex nodded and put his hands up, palms out. The gesture felt silly, but it was all he could think to do to stall. He continued sideways, angling himself between Danica and the only clear drop into the reservoir.

"Why are you here?" she asked. Danica limped forward, but cautiously.

"I know it feels like this is all you have left, but it's not. You don't have to do this, okay?" There'd been a speech in his head on the drive over, but it was gone, shattered by the reality of the moment.

"It's what I want." Danica continued forward. "It's what she wants, too. No one will even know I'm gone."

"That's not true." Alex reached the center of the clearing and stopped. No matter which way Danica went, he could stay between her and the water. "I know for a fact that's not true. I know you probably hate me, but I'd miss you, too."

Danica paused. "I don't hate you. What you did for me today was... I mean, no one's ever stopped them from..." She shook her head. "It doesn't matter. I'll be with them after this. I'll be free."

"Did they tell you to do this?"

"No." Danica moved her hand over her left breast. "I have to do this on my own. It's my choice."

"Then they'll let you leave, right? If you come with me, they won't stop you."

"Alex, please. Stop. I don't want to be alone anymore." She pressed forward, faster now despite her injured leg.

"You're not alone now. I won't let you be alone. Samantha won't, either. She came with me. She's out there, looking for you."

Danica stopped less than a yard away from him. Her voice went cold. "I don't care. She's yours. You should enjoy the time you have with her."

"What does that mean?" He was losing her.

"Let me past." Danica took a step forward, but Alex put a hand out to block her. She slapped it down. "They're waiting for me. I'll be one of them, and she'll wish she never hurt me."

Out of options, Alex tensed. He'd fight her off the cliff if he had to. "Danica, she never wanted me. She used me so she could hide what she had with you. I know how much she hurt you, but I can't let you do this. I just can't."

For a moment (just a moment), it looked like he'd gotten through. The anger bled from her face, and a tear fell down her cheek. She opened her mouth to speak, but never got the chance. That was when the things in the fog began to scream, a wail that chilled Alex's spine.

Over the screams, he heard Samantha shouting. "Alex? Danica? Can you hear me?"

"Sam?" Danica replied. She turned to see Samantha and Conn crash out of the brush and fog. Conn stepped in front of Samantha, blocking her from getting any closer to the cliff. Danica's face hardened again. "She came with *him*."

"Danica, wait…"

She lurched to the side so suddenly that she almost passed Alex before he could throw himself in front of her. Danica saw him move and tried to change direction. Too late. Her shoulder struck Alex's chest and pushed him backwards toward the drop. Off balance, he flailed his arms and drove his heels into the ground to brace himself. Samantha screamed his name. He glanced back, saw the water below. There were things swimming, circling, breaking the surface then diving back down. Desperate, Alex shoved Danica with his own shoulder. When she stumbled, a path to escape opened to her left. He could flee now, before she took them both into the water. He imagined those hands pulling him into the enveloping deep, the water in his mouth and nose, the blackness closing over him. He could leave her, let her jump. It was what she wanted. No one would question him. He had every right to escape. Every reason.

Alex stayed where he was, and readied himself for another charge.

"Danica, stop!" Samantha screamed. Conn had his arms around Samantha. She struggled, fought to run to them, but he was far too strong.

The swimmers thrashed and called out. The fog rippled at the edge of the clearing. Danica turned to Samantha, stared at her for a long moment, then looked back at Alex. She nodded to him and took a step away from the cliff. Tears returned to her eyes, and Alex felt his own welling up in response.

Alex didn't hear the shale of the cliff crack, only felt the sudden movement of it beneath his feet.

He'd sat here, at the edge of the drop, so many times. He'd watched the water from the place he now stood and it had held his weight every time. Maybe something in the ground had shifted, the cliff responding to the demands of the things below. Very little of the rock crumbled, but it was enough to tip Alex's weight in the wrong direction. He reached out reflexively, searching for anything that could stop his fall. Danica did the same, and her hands caught his in a desperate grasp.

All sound but that of the water faded. The women's wails, Samantha's screams; all of it was gone. There was Danica, there was the fall, and there was Alex caught between. His feet slid and brought him closer to the edge. Danica struggled to pull him back, but there was nothing she could do. Time expanded, slowed, offered two choices. Only two. He could keep his hold on Danica's hand and drag her over the cliff with him. Or he could release her and fall alone.

Danica cried out his name as he let go. His feet left the ground. The cliff rose above him, the wind whistled in his ears, and the queasy weightlessness of falling twisted his guts. He thought of the girl on the edge, feared none of this would matter, hoped he was wrong. He thought of Samantha, of his father, of his last day in his mother's empty house. Then his back broke the surface of the water, and cold hands pulled him down into the darkness of the lake, and there were no more thoughts at all.

Act Three

Splinter In Your Heart

Chapter Seventeen

Samantha ran until she couldn't take another step, and all but the memory of the things in the fog were far behind her. She fell to her knees and sunk into the muddy ground. It was raining. Had been raining since she fled the clearing. Samantha's clothes and hair were soaked through and her feet squished in sodden shoes. She looked up at the fat drops of water falling off the leaves above. The last traces of the fog were gone, driven away by the downpour.

There hadn't been fog in the clearing, either.

She'd stood helplessly at the mist's edge while it happened. She watched Alex stand his ground between Danica and the water. Watched him force Danica back when she fought her way toward the edge. She'd wanted to run to them, run to Danica, but Conn was too strong. Then Alex fell so suddenly it was like he'd simply vanished. Samantha screamed, her voice joining the cries of the things in the fog. She saw Danica's mouth open, but couldn't hear her over the cacophony. Conn grabbed Samantha by the shoulders and shoved her toward the edge of the clearing. He told her to run. Samantha could still picture the girl in the mist, the one who wanted her to beg. She could still feel the water in her lungs, hear the thing's mocking laughter. Samantha turned from the clearing and fled.

Now, with the fear and adrenaline draining from her system, shame rushed in to fill the void. How could she have run? Alex had fallen. He could have been injured. He could have needed her help. If he died because no one had gone into the water after him...

Except it wasn't the water itself she had to fear. It was the drowned women, the things that had watched Danica and Alex fight at the cliff's edge and chased Samantha through the fog after Alex fell. They were in the forest and the water, waiting. Waiting for Danica.

Samantha never considered herself a coward, but what else was she? She'd always run at the first sign of danger. Always. If anyone tried to stop her — if they refused to let her go, as Danica had — she did anything she could to escape, even if it hurt them. She thought of Danica's cheek, reddening where Samantha had struck it. She thought of Alex, lost in an instant. What if Danica had followed him into the lake after Samantha ran? Alex's death would have meant nothing. Both of them gone in the same day, over the same cliff, into the hands of whatever monsters Danica had come to join. And all Samantha's fault.

Shaking, Samantha fumbled her phone from her pocket and unlocked it. It was wet, but still working. She needed to get help before it was too late. Samantha tried to key in in **911**, but her trembling fingers couldn't find the keys. She deleted and retyped the numbers three times before finally getting it right, then held her thumb over the send button. What would what she would say when they answered? Not the truth. Not the whole truth, anyway. Better to say nothing. Beg for an ambulance, tell them someone fell into the water, and figure out the details while she waited.

Something slapped the phone out of Samantha's hand. She gasped and clawed herself across the muddy earth until she felt the trunk of a tree against her back. Instinct took over, and she raised her hands over her head and pulled her knees in front of her chest. She looked up, prepared for the attack to come.

It was Conn. Only Conn.

"What the hell are you doing?" he shouted.

"I thought you were one of them!"

"I mean what were you doing with the phone? Who were calling?"

"My phone? An ambulance. I was calling an ambulance." Samantha searched the ground for where she'd dropped it.

"And what was your story going to be?"

Samantha ignored his question. "What happened to Danica? Did you see what happened to her? Is she okay?"

"For now." Conn crouched and ran his hand along the ground until he came away with Samantha's mud-covered phone. He frowned and added, "She didn't jump, if that's what you're asking."

"What about Alex?"

Conn wiped the mud off of the back of Samantha's phone with his fingers. "I told him to stay out of this. He should have listened to me. I liked him."

"Liked," Samantha mumbled, noting the past tense.

"He's gone. Get over it and focus."

"Focus on what?" Samantha yelled. She thrust out a hand. "Give me my phone. I need to call for help."

Holding the phone out of reach, Conn asked, "Do you want to survive tonight or not?"

Samantha's arm fell to her side. "What?"

"There, now you're focused." Conn said. "You think this is over? Those things you saw want you dead. What that girl did to you before I saved you was playtime. They won't just kill you, Sam. They'll keep you like a trophy. Forever."

"Why?"

"For your girlfriend. You were going to be all hers."

Samantha remembered what the girl in the fog said to her, that Samantha belonged to the *new girl*. "But, she didn't... Alex stopped her."

"Yeah, that I wasn't expecting. Never saw anyone do that before. Danica missed her chance," Conn said with a smile that made Samantha uncomfortable. He put a hand on her leg. "But that doesn't mean you're safe."

"I don't understand. None of this makes sense."

Conn shook his head. "Does this look like the time to explain? We need to call the cops and get out of here."

"That's what I was trying to do," Samantha said. She reached out again for her phone.

"Tell me what happened today?"

"I don't know," Samantha replied. "Alex fell. He tried to help Danica and he fell."

"He didn't fall. He was pushed," Conn said.

"No, he wasn't."

"Danica pushed him. He got in her way, so she pushed him into the water. That's what happened."

"That's not what happened! She wasn't fighting. She wasn't going to jump. He fell, but she didn't push him." Samantha was desperate, confused. Why did Conn want her to lie?

"I don't care what you saw. I'm telling you what you're going to tell the police." Conn put the phone into Samantha's hand. "You're going to tell this story exactly like I say it happened, or tonight will be the prologue to a very short and ugly tragedy."

"You can't threaten me," Samantha said.

"I can, and I will if I have to," he replied. "But I'm not. I'm the only reason you're still alive. If you want to stay that way, you're going to do what I tell you."

"Why do you want them to think Danica killed him?"

"It's a little late for you to care what happens to her, isn't it?"

Samantha clutched her mud-covered phone. "I can't do this to her."

"Fine. Then let's get you home. I'll drive."

Suspicious, Samantha said, "I thought I had to do what you tell me."

Conn leaned back and shrugged. "You don't have to do anything. If you don't want my help, I'll take you home, get you inside, and make *sure* your father understands that it *wasn't* his daughter's girlfriend who pushed the guy he *thought* was her boyfriend off a cliff. You know, get the truth out, since we're all sick of lying."

Samantha, shocked, could only shake her head. How did he know about her father?

"If you're not going to do what I tell you, I can't keep you alive. If you want to get yourself hurt that bad I might as well speed things along."

Too exhausted to fight, too afraid to refuse, Samantha gave in. "Why do you even care?"

"Because technically this is my fault. You got caught up in a fight that I started. You aren't the first one, either, but if you do what I say, you might be the last," Conn said. "We're a lot alike, Sam, and I'm all you have right now."

Samantha raised her phone and unlocked it. A thought came and went, that there was no way her phone should still be working after its fall into the mud and water. "I can't do that to her. I can't say she pushed him."

"Fine. Get them here and I'll do the talking. All you have to do is keep your mouth shut. It's that or tell your father the truth. I know how much he scares you. I used to be scared, too. When this is over, and those *things* are gone, I can teach you things that'll give him a reason to be afraid of you. But for now, the best you can do is survive." Conn reached over and hit **SEND**.

She wanted to help Danica. Save her from the pain Samantha had brought down on her. But who would save Samantha if Conn told her father the truth?

A voice came over the speaker of Samantha's phone. The only way she could help Danica was if she got through today. She had to survive. Samantha raised the phone to her ear.

~

The rain was still falling when Danica woke and found herself huddled against the wall of an unfamiliar house. She didn't remember leaving the forest, or how she'd gotten here. Wherever *here* was. The eaves of the house had protected her from the worst of the rain, but the grass beneath her was so sodden it hardly mattered. Danica's hands were cold and pruney, her clothes soaked and stuck to her skin, her hair plastered against her face and neck. The sun had set and all the lights in the house were out. Danica pushed herself to a crouch and squinted at the brightly colored hands of her watch. 4:30? In the morning?

Her eyes drifted from the watch to her hand. There was something clutched in it, something crumpled and yellow. Her hand — numb, asleep after hours crushed under her body — squeezed whatever was in it reflexively. She pried open the fingers of her left hand with her right and let it fall onto her lap. Paper. A crumpled piece of yellow notebook paper, written on with blue ink. Where had it come from? Danica shoved it into her pocket. Whatever it was, it would have to wait.

Pain radiated from her injured knee when she stood. The joint was swollen and locked up. Danica took a tentative step and the motion hurt so much tears welled in her eyes. She couldn't stay here, though. She had to move. Find out where she was. Find a way home. Danica took two more steps. Each hurt less than the last. Limping, she made her way around the house to the street.

There had been no escape from the image of Alex falling backwards toward the water, not even in sleep. She saw him vanish every time she blinked, heard the splash of Alex's body breaking the surface in every raindrop. She'd stayed in the clearing long after the fog had lifted and the rain began and the women in the water had vanished. After Samantha fled into the trees and left Danica alone. Danica had no idea how long she'd waited before stumbling away from the precipice. There was nothing between that moment and waking against the house, a void filled only by the memory of Alex releasing her hand and falling into the arms of Lenka's sisters. A death that was meant to be hers.

She still heard the low murmur of the pin, but it had changed. It was as if it had grown roots and become a piece of her. The longer it was inside, the more her heart grew around and into it. She could no longer hear Lenka's voice. She could *feel* her. Her thoughts and emotions lived alongside Danica's. That was how she knew she'd been abandoned when she didn't jump. Her own heart had turned against her in that moment.

And for what? The water took Alex in her place. Another casualty, punished for believing Danica worth saving.

The house was at the end of a short road that terminated in a cul-de-sac. Danica reached the end of the street before recognizing where she was. Her house was less than a mile away. She must have walked through most of the night. Danica turned towards home. There was no sidewalk along the main road, so Danica was forced to hobble through a water-filled drainage ditch. She wondered what she'd say to her mom when she got home. What had she already heard? Someone — Sam, maybe — would have called 911 by now. Word must have spread, but what word?

Danica's answer came when she crested the hill above the flat patch of her yard. Parked across the street from her doublewide was a single police car. Danica could make out two figures sitting in the front seats. There was only one reason they'd be waiting for her, and that was to arrest her. They thought she was responsible for Alex's death. Maybe they were right. She hadn't killed him, but he'd be alive if not for her.

Danica was happy to surrender if jail was the worst she had to look forward to. Juvie (or even prison) were better than where she'd end up. They'd bring her back to where she'd gone after they put Megan, bleeding, into an ambulance. The place where they forced pills and food on her, where they took away everything but her clothes because they couldn't be sure she wouldn't hurt herself. It took a week that time for them to decide she wasn't a danger anymore. This would be worse.

It wasn't hard to keep out of sight of the cops and slip through the trees that bordered her yard. The true danger was being seen by her family. It wouldn't matter if Mom believed she was innocent. She'd still let the officers take her to that cold, fluorescent-lit hell. She'd demand it and promise Danica it was for her own good.

The back door unlocked with a soft, metallic click. Danica turned the knob, opened the door an inch, and waited. The house was quiet, the only sounds were the leaking kitchen faucet and the refrigerator's hum. The nightlight in the hallway cast a narrow blue oblong of light across the threshold of the kitchen. Danica crept through the doorway. She didn't hear any snoring from the living room, which meant Ian had found his way into the bedroom. That made things easier. Danica left her shoes on. Harder to stay quiet, but easier to run if she got caught.

She snuck into her bedroom, found her backpack, and laid it on the bed. She changed into dry clothes and a jacket, then packed by the dim glow of her nightlight. She fit in two changes of clothes and an unopened bag of pretzels she'd left on her dresser. She paused, returned to her wet clothes, and retrieved the soggy notebook paper. She placed it, still crumpled, into one of the backpack's pockets. Her emergency kit — the lighter, the razors, the compass needle — poked out from under the bed. Danica should have thrown it out when she and Megan cleared her room of her tools. Taking it now would be an insult to what Alex had done. She kicked it back under the bed and grabbed her things.

She returned to the hallway and paused. Danica didn't know where she was going, had no idea when or if she'd be back. There was nowhere to hide and no one to help her. The police would find her eventually and take her away. She couldn't leave just yet, no matter how dangerous it was to delay. Danica set the backpack on the floor and inched her way to the next bedroom.

Pete and Steve snored in time with each other on the bunk beds opposite the door. The two of them could sleep through anything. She picked her way through the scattered toys and clothes that littered her floor and stopped at Jake's small bed along the left wall. She knelt and touched his cheek with her fingertips. His eyes fluttered open. Danica put a finger to her lips and said, "Shhh."

"Danny?" he whispered.

"Hey, Jake."

"What's wrong?"

"I love you, Jake. I just wanted to tell you that." Danica stroked her brother's hair. There wouldn't be anyone to take care of him when Mom was at work, not with Danica gone.

Jake smiled. "I love you too, Danny."

"Now go back to sleep," she said, and kissed him on the forehead. Danica backed out of the room. By the time she closed the door, her youngest brother's eyes were closed. She returned to her backpack and slung it back over her shoulders. Something moved just at the edge of her vision. Inside her room. Danica spun, expecting to see her mother, expecting to have to run.

A pale figure sat on her bed, water dripping off of its bloodless skin. Danica froze. It was Alex. Though he was looking directly at her, he didn't seem to notice she was there. His mouth was open slightly, his eyes empty. Heat flared in her breast. She wanted to escape, or to fall to her knees and apologize, or to scream. Anything but stand there under his unfocused gaze.

She blinked. That was all. Just a blink, and when her eyes opened, Alex was gone. The heat in her breast faded. The only sounds she heard were the dripping faucet and the buzzing refrigerator. Danica was alone again.

The floor of her mother's bedroom creaked. Someone was awake. Still unsettled by what she'd seen, Danica limped back through the kitchen and out the door. By the time the bathroom light clicked on, she was back amongst the trees, fleeing through the rain as the sun rose above the horizon.

Chapter Eighteen

SAMANTHA WATCHED DAWN break from the floor of her deck, sheltered from the downpour by their enormous patio umbrella. It was easier not to think surrounded by the relentless noise of the pounding rain. She couldn't sleep, couldn't even rest or sit longer than a few minutes. Samantha passed long, dark hours moving from place to place, chair to chair, room to room. Thought moved with her, unwanted, a step behind so long as she didn't stop. The storm hid her for now, but it was only a matter of time before memory found her again.

The police had questioned her in the parking lot of the dairy. They'd put her in the back seat of a police car but left the door open, a thermal blanket from one of the EMTs draped over her shoulders. Samantha stared out the front window of the cop car as a detective asked question after question. Across the street, two men stood outside the Ribeiro house. One was Alex's father, frozen like a statue as a police officer explained that his son was gone forever. Samantha didn't know if he was crying. The rain made it impossible to tell. That was one of the things she saw if she tried to sleep: Alex's father on his porch, sometimes crying, sometimes not. Better to stay awake. She could stay awake as long as she had to.

The glass door behind her slid open. From within the house, Samantha's mother said, "I'm making breakfast. Want to come inside?"

Breakfast was a thin excuse to get her talking. Still, Samantha didn't want to be alone, and she hadn't eaten since lunch the day before. She followed her mom inside and sat on a stool at the granite island. Maybe it was better to talk now, before her dad got home with his own questions.

"Are pancakes okay?" her mother asked.

Samantha nodded.

Mom pulled a bowl down from a high shelf and dug out the pancake mix from the back of the pantry. Samantha found her mother's efficient mastery of the kitchen hypnotic, the way she knew where every item was without looking or even thinking about it. She was in control here. Confident and as close to secure as Samantha ever saw her. It was an illusion, that safety. The illusion that let her mother feel brave when she knew she wasn't. Her mother would tear this kitchen down with her bare hands if *he* told her to. Tear it down and hide the tears until no one was looking.

Mom paused and turned to Samantha. "How are you doing?"

Samantha shook her head.

"Do you want to talk about it?"

"I don't know."

Mom dumped the powdered mix into the bowl, then sat beside Samantha. "I know only met him once, but Alex seemed like a really good person."

Samantha nodded.

"Were things serious between you?"

"I think it was for him," Samantha admitted. "It was still really new for me."

"I liked seeing you with someone who was good to

you," her mother said.

She didn't want to meet her mother's eyes. "I didn't deserve it."

"Samantha. Don't say that. That's not true."

Samantha slid a finger back and forth along the cold granite of the countertop and said nothing.

"The police said your friend was responsible. Danica?"

Samantha didn't reply, didn't move.

"You were close with her, weren't you?"

Samantha looked slowly up at her mom and asked, "Why would say that?"

"You seemed happy when I saw you with her," said Mom. "More than with your other friends."

Samantha felt an unexpected desire to say something *true*. "I could be myself with her, you know?"

"I do. I'm glad you're a little better this morning. The police said you were in shock last night."

"I guess." Shock had been the police's suggestion, and Samantha let them believe it. She couldn't bring herself to confirm Conn's version of the story, nor did she have the strength to contradict it. The police had tired of repeating questions to a silent girl while the rain soaked their clothes, so they'd driven her home with a promise to return for a statement when she was ready.

"Do you want to tell me what happened?"

Could her mom tell she hiding something? Did she have the same doubts as the police, that a girl of Danica's size could have forced Alex over the cliff? Samantha couldn't risk confirming those doubts. If she told the truth now, her mom would tell the police. Word would get back to Conn. To her father.

Samantha shook her head.

Her mother stood back up and began mixing ingredients. "I should get breakfast going. I'll call the school and tell them you won't be in. You're staying home today."

Samantha didn't argue. At school, people would want to know things. What happened. What she'd seen. Better to face the quiet than questions she couldn't answer.

There was one question, though, that needed to be answered. One Samantha had to force out.

"Does Dad know what happened?"

Her mom set the bag of mix back on the countertop, but kept her back to her daughter. "I called him last night. He said things aren't going well and he won't be home for another day or two. He said he'd talk to you when he gets home."

Her hands trembled. When her father got home, Samantha would do what she'd done her whole life. She'd put someone else between herself and him. She'd say whatever would keep her safe. She'd speak the words Conn put into her mouth because they were the only escape she had left, and the one person who'd ever made Samantha feel safe would suffer in her place.

People thought Samantha was strong. They told her that, said they looked up to her, wanted to be as tough as her. She knew how to make people believe it. She knew how to make herself believe it.

Alex saw past the lie to what Samantha really was, and when he fell into the water, the lie died with him. Samantha sat in silence, wishing her mom would be strong for her now, wanting to hate her because she couldn't. Wanting, and failing, and finally seeing who it was she truly hated.

~

The cigarette hissed when it hit the puddle at Krista's

feet. She kicked the butt into the mulch beneath an overgrown shrub and blew a last cloud of smoke out of her nose. The small overhang protected Krista from most of the rain, but only if she stood with her back against the school's metal doors. Her jeans were already soaked halfway up her shins, and her hair was soggy from the humidity. She was miserable, she was wet, and she wasn't letting any of that stop her from having a fourth cigarette. Anything to avoid returning to the cafeteria.

There'd been an announcement during homeroom by the principal, one so vague it wasn't even clear Alex was dead. By that point, everyone already knew. People stopped Krista in the halls, came up to her before and after class, texted her relentlessly. Did she know what happened? Was it true that Samantha was there? Why wasn't Samantha at school? Was she okay? Did that Danica girl really push Alex? Exhausted, Krista slipped away from lunch before anyone could stop her.

Krista glanced at her phone and threw out the half-smoked butt of cigarette number four. The bell was about to ring.

They'd renovated the school when Krista was a freshman, which left a few corners of the old building intact but mostly unused. Krista pushed through the doors into a fragment of hallway that had been a popular exit before they dropped a computer lab in the way. Now the only way to the exit was a narrow passage behind the cafeteria. Perfect for anyone desperate for a moment alone. Krista stopped at the end of the hallway, made sure no one was looking, and swung around the corner into the lunchroom.

Eyes followed her as she walked to the table. Krista knew they had more questions. They wanted the inside scoop, the dirty details. Information. Gossip. None of which bothered Krista. The problem was what came next.

There was blame to be cast. For now, it rested on the girl who'd pushed Alex. On Danica. But only for now. Eventually, someone would wonder why Danica and Alex were there in the first place. Eventually, someone would ask who pushed Danica. When people decided a poor, depressed cutter couldn't possibly be the villain, Krista didn't want the role.

Conn was speaking as she approached, his feet up on the table, his chair rocked onto the two back legs. "Just tell them to call me if they see her, okay?"

Nick nodded. His moron of a friend Logan did the same. Ferris, thumbs tapping madly on the screen of her phone, spared a brief glance up at Krista. She took the empty seat beside Conn, next to the empty one that would have been Samantha's.

"What are you talking about?" Krista asked.

The bell rang. Nick and Logan sprinted for the door. Ferris dropped her phone into her purse and said, "Danica."

"What about her?"

"Just wondering where she is," Conn said. He took her hand and walked with her out of the cafeteria.

Ferris followed. "The cops still don't have her."

"So?" Krista demanded.

"Maybe we want to find her first." Ferris gave Krista a cold stare before walking off.

Krista turned to Conn. "What does that mean, 'find her first'?"

Conn smiled and said nothing.

"What, is she going to kill again if you don't stop her? When did you turn into Batman? Let the police deal with her."

The door to one of the janitors' closets was open, and as they passed it, Conn pulled Krista into it and shut the door behind them. With the door closed, the closet was pitch black. She heard Conn breathing, and felt a hand slide across her shoulder. His touch sent a shiver down her back, an involuntary reaction that pissed her off even more. If he tried to kiss her, she was going to knee him in the balls.

Conn's hand found the light switch and flipped it on. He didn't kiss her, but his face was very close to hers. "There. Now we can talk."

"So, talk."

"I asked your friends to help me find Danica because I don't *want* the police to find her."

Krista shook her head. She wanted to forget she knew Danica, not follow her trail. "Congratulations, you're nuts. Please leave me and my friends out of it."

"Don't you even want to know why?" Conn leaned back, giving Krista more space.

"You're angry about your friend. I get it. I hate the bitch, too, but so what? She'll get arrested and get what she deserves."

"Wrong," Conn said.

"Bullshit, I'm wrong. They'll catch her by tomorrow. She's not some criminal mastermind."

"Not that. Even if the cops don't find her, she'll probably turn herself in. I meant you were wrong about Alex. This isn't about him. It's about her."

Krista grabbed the doorknob. "Forget it, I don't have time for this."

"Wait." Conn put his hand over Krista's. She tensed, ready to elbow him if he tried anything. "I'll be straight with you if you stay."

"Like you care if I stay or not."

He laughed. "Yeah, I didn't expect to, either. But I do."

"Falling in love with me already?"

"Don't get sappy," he said. "It's been a long time

since I met someone who understood me. A really long time. That's all."

"How long?" Krista asked, her body tensing.

"I might be a little too old for you, that's all."

Krista got in his face. "Stop screwing around and answer the question."

"Centuries."

"Fuck you."

"It's the truth." He touched the back of her hand. "I can't die, Krista. A long time ago, I hurt someone. Her name was Lenka. She wanted revenge, and she almost got it. I had to rip out a part of myself to stop her. My spirit, my soul. Whatever you want to call it. Now? Nothing can kill me. Not guns. Not knives. Not time. But you don't really feel things after that. Happiness, anger, pain… none of it. So here I am, half-alive forever, with things out of your nightmares chasing me wherever I go."

The more he talked, the more nuts he sounded. Yet she wasn't laughing. She wasn't reaching for the door, either. The doubts she wanted to have were nowhere to be found. All she had was the sound of his voice and the touch of his fingers on her hand. By force of will alone she managed to say, "I don't believe you."

"Yes you do," Conn said.

And she did. She didn't understand, but she believed. She asked, "Why do you want Danica?"

"Samantha and Danica are like me and Lenka. That's why I'm here. It's why we're both here. Lenka was waiting for Danica at that cliff. If she'd jumped, she would have become just like Lenka."

"And then she'd have come for Sam," said Krista. She'd never heard that name, Lenka, and yet she knew exactly who Conn was talking about. It didn't even occur to her that was impossible.

Conn nodded. "I've watched this happen too many

times."

"You didn't *watch* it. You helped. Jesus Christ, you practically pushed Alex and Sam together. You *wanted* this to happen."

"Because this will never end, not until Lenka admits that I didn't have a choice, and that anyone would do the same thing in my place. *Anyone.* One day she'll understand, and then…"

"Then?"

"She'll forgive me." Conn's voice sounded smaller than Krista had ever heard.

"You said it's always the same," Krista said after a moment. "But Danica didn't jump."

His smile was confident and unsettling. "No, she didn't. That's why I need to find her."

"What are you going to do to her?"

"Lenka feels what Danica feels. She cares about her. Loves her. She'll do anything to protect her."

"Fine, you get Danica and you make Lenka forgive you. What then?" Krista asked.

"I get a part of myself back." Conn pulled on Krista's hand, drawing her closer. "And we can see if there's something real between us."

Conn reached past Krista and opened the door, then walked into the hall. What little resistance that remained in her died. Her only choice was to follow him. If there had ever been a chance to turn back, it passed when Danica pushed Alex into the reservoir.

Chapter Nineteen

SAMANTHA GRABBED HER mom's car keys without asking and drove. She wasn't ready to leave the house, but the two phone calls she'd received hadn't left her much choice.

The first call was from her father. He'd be home tonight after all.

The second, from the school's principal. There was a memorial for Alex tomorrow. He wanted Samantha to speak.

Fifteen minutes later, Samantha pulled into the wide driveway of the Ashleys' enormous house. It was identical to the other prefabricated rectangles on the street, save for the brick around the windows and doors. She remembered when Ferris and her family moved into the development. It was only half built, and they'd run through the empty lots and climbed over piles of plastic piping and mounds of dirt left by the bulldozers. It had been months since she'd come to see Ferris, though. Since Danica.

Samantha rang the doorbell and waited. It was Bill Ashley, Ferris' dad, who answered. Something about him unnerved Samantha and always had. He offered one of his plastic grins and said, "Ferris isn't here right now."

"I'm not here to see Ferris, Mr. Ashley," she replied. "I was hoping Megan was here."

The smile stayed on his face, but his eyes narrowed. Still, he let her in and sent her up the stairs without another question. Lucky, since Samantha couldn't have explained if she wanted to. She hadn't planned to come here. She'd gotten into the car to drive, to keep ahead of herself for a little while longer. It wasn't until she pulled onto Ferris' street that she realized what she was doing and why.

Megan's room was at the far end of the hallway, past the door to Ferris' room. Samantha didn't know Megan well. She and Ferris weren't much alike, and the two ignored each other unless they were fighting. Samantha couldn't even remember what the inside of Megan's room looked like, though she had to have been in it at least once. Samantha paused outside of Megan's closed door, thankful Ferris was out and that luck had gotten her this far. From here, she was on her own. Samantha knocked.

The door opened before Samantha's hand fell back to her side. Megan wore a fitted red t-shirt and jeans. She had a bottle of liquid eyeliner clutched in her hand. Unsurprisingly, she seemed confused to see Samantha. "Hey," she said.

"Can we talk?" Samantha asked.

"Sure. Yeah." Megan stepped back from the doorway to let Samantha enter. Samantha closed the door behind her as Megan walked to the dresser. She set the eyeliner tube down and turned back to Samantha. "I heard about what happened. I'm really sorry."

Samantha looked away. "Yeah. Thanks."

"Were you really there?"

"Yeah."

"I just don't believe that Danica would..." Megan trailed off and picked nervously at one thumbnail with her other thumb.

"Did you know her well?"

"We were close. Last year."

"How close?" Samantha asked.

Megan frowned. "I'm sorry, what did you want to talk about?"

"This, I guess. Danica."

"What about her?"

"I don't know. I sort of drove here without realizing it," Samantha admitted. "I thought maybe you wouldn't be surprised about what happened."

"What does that mean?" Megan asked, suspicious.

"It's just… you know, after what she did to you…"

Megan took a seat beside Samantha. "What is it you think she did to me?"

"Ferris told me what happened." Samantha gestured at Megan's arm.

"Ferris doesn't know what she's talking about."

"Danica didn't cut you?" asked Samantha.

Megan rolled up her sleeve, exposing a long, pale scar on her wrist. "Did you ask Danica what happened?"

"No." She shook her head, ashamed. Samantha wanted to say she didn't have time, but she was past excuses.

"Maybe you should have."

"I know." Samantha paused, then asked, "Will you tell me what happened?"

Megan sighed and ran a finger along the length of the scar. "Danica went through a bad time last year. She was hurting herself."

"Hurting herself?"

"She burned herself. On her thighs, mostly. Where no one could see. I only found out because she told me."

"I didn't know." Samantha's stomach sank. She'd seen the raised white lines, had run her fingers over them, and never thought to ask what they were.

"She stopped after we got close but, well, Ferris told you Danica had, you know, feelings for me... right?" Megan waited for Samantha to nod before continuing. "I was interested in someone else. Danny found out, and things got bad again. We had a lock-in at youth group and Danica disappeared, so I went to find her. She was in a bathroom stall with the pastor's Swiss Army knife. I don't know how she got it. Anyway, I was stupid and tried to grab it off of her. I should have backed off and talked her down, you know? But I was upset, so I reached for the knife and she tried to get away. That's all."

"It was an accident?"

"Yeah, it was an accident," Megan said, like believing anything else was insane. "It was totally my fault, but no one listened. My family thinks she's, I don't know, a psychopath or something. Now they're looking at me like, 'See? We told you so.'"

Samantha looked down at her hands and stayed silent.

"It's a little late for you to act like you care, isn't it? Ferris told me what happened at school. She was bragging about it."

"Oh," Samantha replied.

"Weren't you friends with her or something?"

Samantha nodded.

"Did you really hit her?"

"I didn't mean to."

"How do you not mean to hit someone?"

Shaking her head, Samantha said, "I don't know. No. She tried to kiss me, and I just...forget it. You wouldn't understand."

Megan studied Samantha. "Was there something going on with you and Danica?"

"Yes," she whispered.

"I thought you were seeing Alex."

"I was."

"So people wouldn't think you're gay?" Megan didn't sound angry, or even like she was judging her. She sounded concerned.

"I don't know what I am," Samantha stared hard at her own knees. "There are guys I like, too. I liked Alex, you know?"

"That must be convenient."

Samantha felt like she'd been slapped. Her laugh was so bitter it hurt. "Not really."

There was a long, awkward moment of silence, then Megan said, "I'm sorry. That was mean. You don't deserve that."

"Yeah, I do." Samantha replied. "I hit her. I... that's not who I want to be."

"Then be someone else," Megan said, matter-of-fact, again without a note of judgment in her voice.

If what Megan said before had been a slap, this was a punch that knocked the wind out of her. She closed her shaking hands into fists and rose. Samantha walked to the door and spoke without turning, "Thank you for telling me what happened."

"Danica didn't push him, did she?"

Samantha was too afraid to answer. She left the room, closed the door behind her, and hoped Megan saw through her silence to the truth.

~

Danica waited under the cover of an overgrown maple tree until the church parking lot emptied. The sun was setting, and she hadn't slept since she'd woken against the wall of that unfamiliar house. It took most of the day to walk from her home to the church, sticking to side roads and cutting through yards to keep out of sight. She didn't know where she was running, or what she planned to do once she got there. It was something she'd worry about after she had food and found a dry place to sleep. Maybe things would make sense after that. She sloshed across a parking lot full of puddles to the church's broken side door, the one that never locked right.

Constantine came to the village to study with the smooth-faced man. He spent the winter in the man's wattle and daub hut, it was rumored, learning unnatural and forbidden arts. What brought the noble son of their lord to learn such things, no one could say. Lenka's parents swore that the smooth-faced man had lived in the village for generations without aging a day. He was a heretic, hated by the faithful, but allowed to stay for the services he provided. Thriving crops and healthy animals meant more than piety. Lenka first saw Constantine on a snowy day as she collected wood for a fire. He stood ankle deep in a drift of snow, his boots beside him, his shirt off. He saw her as well, and when their eyes met, she no longer felt the cold.

The memories came when she thought of Samantha, or the cliff, or the women in the mist. They were entwined, now. Samantha and Constantine, Lenka and herself. Danica struggled against an anger she wasn't certain was her own. Lenka's heart was her heart, and hers was Lenka's. When Danica cried, she cried for both of them. When rage overpowered sadness, it was a fury that had built for centuries. Danica was losing herself to *their* sadness, *their* rage.

She walked down a small flight of stairs and through Pepto Hall, leaving a trail of water behind her. At the far end of the hall was the kitchen, and in the kitchen, the pantry where they stored supplies for their food bank. She could stock up on something more filling than pretzels, then find a little-used room where she could sleep. There were probably dry clothes somewhere, too. Danica hadn't counted on how quickly and thoroughly her backpack would soak through. Nothing she had was dry. She thought she remembered a collection for charity after last week's service; maybe she could find where they were storing the donations. An umbrella wouldn't hurt, either.

Constantine kissed her behind the smooth-faced man's house. It was safe there. No one dared trespass or spy on a man whose powers they so feared. The snow had begun to melt, and their feet and ankles were cold and wet by the time they parted. They met there day after day, until winter had turned to spring and their need grew beyond too-brief kisses in the sorcerer's yard. She knew of a secret place, a home long abandoned to the woods, and it was there they first made love.

The pantry was a walk-in closet nearly the size of her bedroom, and was lined with shelves full of food. Most of the worthwhile food was canned, so Danica headed back to the kitchen for a can opener and an empty plastic grocery bag. She wouldn't be able to fit everything she needed in her backpack. Danica returned to the pantry and filled the bag with canned vegetables, soup and beans. She pulled a bag of cereal out of its box and added it to her haul. Danica moved back into the middle of the room and gave the shelves a second look. Was there anything else she needed? How long was she planning on running? She didn't have anyone to hide her, nor anywhere to sleep. If the rain stopped, things would be easier, but Danica knew the rain had just begun. Knew because Lenka knew.

Just as thinking of Samantha brought on Lenka's memories, thinking of the drowned woman led back to Samantha. There was no escape from it. Alex was dead because of Danica, but it was Samantha who'd led both of them to that point. She'd lied to Danica. Lied to Alex, too. Samantha used them both. Every time Danica closed her eyes, she felt Samantha's hand strike her cheek.

Constantine told Lenka he loved her every time they met. He said they'd marry once his time with the smooth-faced man was done. Until then, they had to be careful. If his father found out he'd force them apart. He'd never allow his firstborn to marry a woman from the village, but after Constantine had learned the smooth-faced man's ways, there would be nothing his father could do. Lenka could be patient. She could wait forever if she had to.

The wait ended the day Constantine's father rode into the village, a curtained carriage riding behind him. He demanded to know where his son was hiding. There was someone he wanted him to meet.

Danica packed two bottles of water in the bag, the last things she could fit, and looked up. Leaning against the shelves, droplets falling from his clothes and hair, was Alex. He was as he'd been in her bedroom; eyes unfocused and fixed on a distant point behind Danica. She was close enough this time to see that he wasn't breathing.

"Alex?" she asked.

The kitchen floor creaked. Light poured in through the door, a light she hadn't turned on. Someone was here.

"Hey, is that you Megs? Didn't think you'd be here already," Pastor Fresh shouted.

Danica froze. There was no way he'd fail to check the pantry before leaving the kitchen. She glanced back at the shelves, but Alex was gone. Danica was alone, and she was caught.

Fresh yelled again, now uncertain. "Megs?"

"No," Danica called back, her voice hoarse.

Fresh poked his head cautiously into the pantry. "Danny boy? What are you doing here?"

It was the daughter of his family's rival that put an end to things. A strategic marriage. That was how Constantine described it. Lenka asked him when he'd tell his father he was already engaged. He wouldn't, he said. He couldn't. There was nothing he could do. He'd be disowned, cast aside. One of his brothers would inherit their lands. Lenka cried and begged and never forgave herself for the humiliation of it. He ignored her, dismissed her like she was his servant. She never forgave that, either.

Backed against the shelves, Danica stuttered out, "I'm sorry I was stealing. I'm so hungry. I'm sorry. I'm sorry."

"The police were here this morning. They wanted to know if I'd seen you."

"Did they tell you why?"

Fresh nodded. "Is what they said true?"

She shook her head.

"They said someone died."

"Alex."

Fresh's voice dropped. "They said you pushed him."

"I didn't. I swear I didn't."

"The police asked me to call if I saw you," Fresh said, his voice tight, his expression conflicted.

Danica hung her head. What did it matter? They were going to find her eventually. She mumbled through tears. "Okay."

"I didn't believe them for a second when they said what you did. That's not you."

"What?" she asked, looking up.

"Why don't you go to my office and get changed into something dry. I'll make some tea, and then you can tell me what happened."

"You aren't going to turn me in?"

"Do I look like the kind of guy who'd Judas his own flock?" Fresh flashed one of his dumb-looking smiles.

Danica had never been happier to see it. "I prayed about it after they left and… I don't know, Danny, I just don't like how things felt after what happened with Elder Ashley. We'll have to go to the police eventually, okay? But not until I'm sure it's safe."

Danica couldn't stop crying, but now it was a release. Fresh reached out his hand, and Danica took it gratefully.

Chapter Twenty

SAMANTHA AWOKE TO the unnatural quiet that fell only when her father was home, a silence the house itself seemed afraid to break. She knew he was due back. Had gone to bed before he arrived to avoid him. Her dreams had stolen what little relief sleep offered, stranding Samantha in an endless sea of mist and screams. Samantha crept out of bed and opened her closet. The smart thing to do was to get dressed and wait, not leave her room until just in time for school.

Samantha would have done anything for one more day free of him. Today would be difficult enough as it was. Alex's memorial awaited. It was too much and far too soon. Samantha focused on what she'd wear to the memorial. She'd figure out the rest as it came. The only black dresses she had weren't memorial appropriate, so Samantha settled on dark blue jeans and a long sleeved, purple blouse. She combed out her hair, put on makeup, and found a small pair of silver ear studs she hadn't worn since her grandmother died. When she was ready, she looked at the clock and her heart sank. There was still twenty minutes before she needed to leave for school. Too much time to be discovered, and if she were caught hiding, totally ready for school, it would just make things worse. Samantha chose the least dangerous path and opened her bedroom door.

She heard the fight as soon as she was in the hallway. He was trying to be quiet. That was good. Promising. Samantha crept down the hall, waiting after each step to ensure she hadn't been heard. When she could make out their words, she paused.

"And you just let her take the car?" he asked.

"She's driven to school before. You've let her, too."

"Oh, so it's my fault?"

Her mom's placating tone made Samantha wince. "Heath, how could I have known? I didn't think—"

"No, you didn't. You never think," he interrupted. "Did you know our daughter was *friends* with that girl? Do you know what people are saying? Aren't things bad enough for us without her being involved? The fucking investors were already pulling out. Now they're *gone*. We're finished, and it's *your fault*."

Samantha reached the edge of the kitchen. If she turned back now, there was a chance her father's anger would burn itself out before it was time to leave. She could let her mother take the worst of it, like she'd always done.

Then she remembered Alex standing between Danica and the cliff and was halfway into the kitchen before she knew what she was doing.

"It wasn't her fault," Samantha said.

Her father turned. His face was red, his coffee mug raised like club. Samantha's mother stood behind him, shaking her head, warning Samantha off.

"What?" her father demanded.

Samantha pressed her feet into the ground. She wouldn't move. She wouldn't run. "It's not Mom's fault. She didn't know."

There was no warning. There never was any. Her

father thrust his arm forward and launched the coffee cup straight and fast at Samantha. The bottom edge caught her right above the hairline. She dropped to her knees, closed her eyes, and braced for what was coming. Her father would charge, arms swinging too fast and too hard for her to block, and wouldn't let her up until he'd had his fill. Samantha heard the pounding of his footsteps and raised her arms above her head.

Nothing happened. A door (to the garage?) opened and slammed shut. Then, silence. Samantha lowered her arms and opened her eyes. She and her mother were alone. She heard her father's car start, heard the wheels screech on the concrete.

He was gone.

Her mother grabbed a towel and brought it to Samantha. She dabbed at the spot on Samantha's head where the mug hit. It stung. Her mother said, "You're bleeding a little."

"I'm sorry." Samantha didn't know why she was apologizing. It was all she could think to say.

"It'll be okay. He's just upset. Things didn't go well in Charlotte," her mom said, trying to sound calm. There was something odd about her voice that Samantha couldn't place. "Don't worry about it, okay? It'll be fine. I promise. Okay?"

Samantha took the towel from her mom and held it against the wound while her mom filled a second one with ice. Samantha traded towels and stayed on the floor with the ice pressed against her forehead. Her hair would hide the cut and the bruise that was on its way. No one would know. Samantha thought of other wounds. The bruises on her mother's stomach, on her back, on her legs. The lines on Danica's thighs. Scars no one could see.

She pulled herself off the floor and set the towel full of ice in the sink. It was time to go to school. They wanted Samantha to speak, and she was finally ready.

~

Alex stayed with Danica all night. He never said a word, didn't look at her, never acknowledged the presence of anyone or anything in the room. He perched on the arm of the couch beside Danica, or on the edge of Fresh's desk, or on the floor. He vanished when she looked away only to appear somewhere else. Whether she was alone in Fresh's office or not, Alex was there, staring somewhere far away, his mouth slightly open. Danica wondered what would happen if she tried to touch him, but didn't have the nerve to try.

It wasn't heartbreak that drove her to the water. Nothing could go unseen and unheard for long in a village as small as Lenka's. The rumors and whispers started as soon as he returned to his father's manor with his betrothed. Lenka had shamed herself, they said. She'd allowed herself to be used and soiled. She'd tempted the firstborn son of their lord. If such news were to reach the manor before the wedding, the whole village would pay. They came to punish Lenka for her sins against them, and when she finally escaped, she knew the river's suffocating embrace would be a mercy.

Danica locked herself in Fresh's office after he left. Her hair was still wet from the rain and her skin clammy beneath the first dry clothes she'd worn in a day, when she remembered the notebook paper she'd shoved into her backpack. She retrieved it and limped to the couch. Though it was still water-logged, the paper wasn't weak or easy to tear. The ink hadn't run, either. She wondered again where it had come from. Had Lenka or one of her sisters given it to her? Had their touch protected it?

It was a letter, written in hurried, sloppy writing. Her

eyes drifted down the page without reading, searching for who had composed it. It was unsigned, though. The letter simply ended. She went back to the top, read it from the start. At the beginning of the second paragraph it mentioned a night with Samantha at her house, and Danica knew whose letter this was. She looked around the room, but she was alone. She wondered if Alex's absence was intentional. She returned to the letter. Read it twice before folding it carefully and returning it to her backpack. She understood, now, why he'd raced to stop her, and why he stood his ground when she fought to get past.

Too tired even to cry, Danica lay on the couch and closed her eyes.

Death was all she desired. There were stories of things in the water, terrible things, but Lenka never believed them. She'd gone swimming in the river as a child and had seen nothing in the depths but fish and rocks. She learned, then, that some things can only be found at the proper time, in the proper way.

The river was dangerous in the spring, flushed with snowmelt from the mountains and runoff from the rain. A tired, injured girl had no chance of swimming without being pulled under. That's why she'd come. For the current to be sweep her away. To be free. She expected to die alone, not for hands to close on her wrists and ankles and neck. They pulled her down and held her against against the rocky bottom. Water filled her lungs. A pale woman swam towards her, a golden pin held in her fingers. The last thing Lenka felt in life was the sting of it entering her heart.

She slept fitfully through the night. It was hard to tell if she'd drifted into Lenka's memories or her own dreams, or if there was a difference anymore. Alex was always there. He was there when Fresh came in to tell Danica he was leaving and that they'd figure out their next step in the morning. He was in the hallway when Danica shuffled through the darkness to the bathroom. He was there whether her eyes were closed or open. It took Danica until morning to understand and decide what she had to do. She sat at Fresh's desk, took one of his pens and a piece of printer paper, and wrote. The letter wasn't to him, but she needed him to find it.

In her anger she was not alone. It was rage that made them sisters. They became one through it, and through it were made whole. Together, they waited for Constantine. All things returned to the river in time. It was nearly fall when he arrived, bearing flowers and wearing black. The sisters waited for Lenka to act. The flowers gave her pause. Lenka assumed herself forgotten and cast aside. Not mourned. But her indecision was brief. The sisters were watching. Lenka rose out of the water and allowed Constantine to see what she had become.

Before she left, Danica knelt by the couch and closed her eyes. She prayed, though prayer felt as empty and lonely as it had for weeks. She didn't pray for forgiveness or release. She prayed for Alex, and for the strength to help him. To be taken by the Rusalka meant something worse than death. Alex would stay with them, trapped forever in the numbing grasp of the deep. It was a pain Danica knew too well. She wouldn't let that be Alex's reward for what he'd done.

Danica left her backpack on the floor. Alex sat beside it, staring in the direction of the door. It was as much of a sign as Danica could hope for. She placed the note she'd written for Fresh on the desk and walked out of the office. Everything felt heavy. Her head, her arms and legs, her clothes. She'd been hollowed out by Samantha and the memories of Lenka's fall. The only strength she had left was her obligation to the boy who'd saved her.

She held him on the ground without effort. She was strong now. She could have stolen his fear and replaced it with desire. That was in her power, but it would have blinded him to his fate. Lenka wanted Constantine to know. She wanted him to feel. She let him struggle beneath her and pulled forth the golden pin that bound her to her sisters.

"Begging won't save you," she said. "If I let you go, my sisters would come for you instead. You are marked by the water, and it will have you. There is only one way for you to survive. This pin is my bond to my sisters. There is only one thing that can break it. Do you know why I'm telling you this?"

His eyes closed, and his lips moved silently. Lenka took it for prayer, proof of his helplessness.

"I want you to know, through all the years that you are mine, that I could have freed you. But only if I forgave your crimes against me. Forgiveness would shatter this pin, and break the ties to my sisters. No one so absolved could be harmed by us ever again. You'd be free to live out your life. I want you to know that I could have spared you lifetimes of pain, and all it would have taken was my love. How sad that you cast it aside."

Constantine opened his eyes. He pressed the tip of his finger against Lenka's golden pin and pierced his flesh upon it. Blood dripped from the wound. Constantine smiled. Something moved through him and into the pin. Into her. Lenka knew then that he had not been praying, but drawing on a power of his own. The magic he had learned in his time with the smooth-faced man.

He said, "My soul is yours. So long as we are tied together, I am as unbreakable as your bond to the water. Only your forgiveness can release us." Constantine pushed Lenka off of him, back into the water, back to her sisters. "I wanted to stay with you forever, but I wasn't given a choice. Anyone would have done the same."

Lenka watched him escape — invulnerable to her and her sisters — as she would so many times in the long years to come.

Danica stepped back into the rain. She would have to return to the water. The reservoir was too far, but there was somewhere else she could go. A place where an unfamiliar hand had held hers and pulled her to the surface. It was close. She could force herself that far, and when she arrived, she'd offer Lenka anything for Alex's release. Maybe someone who deserved to take Alex's place. Someone who'd caused them pain. Constantine. Or Samantha. It didn't matter. Lenka's pin stirred within her breast and Danica lost herself in centuries of anger and pain.

~

They held the memorial in the school auditorium. Samantha waited backstage with three other speakers. One was Ms. Granger, Alex's homeroom teacher. She also taught Samantha's graphic arts class. There were few people Samantha wanted to be near less than Ms. Granger. She sat in a plastic folding chair ten feet from Samantha and, every few minutes, glanced up from her index cards. Samantha slunk into the backstage darkness, away from the teacher and whatever she was working up the nerve to say.

Samantha looked around and caught two sets of eyes staring from the far wall. She recognized both people. Leslie and Will, friends of Danica. They knew. They had to know. The rest of the school might have believed Danica killed Alex, but her friends knew things the others didn't. Samantha found strength in that. People knew the truth. It would come out no matter what Samantha did today.

"Samantha Rowland," the principal said, summoning her to the stage.

The auditorium was half-full. Most students sat toward the front, with scattered groups spread through the back rows. Krista, Ferris, Conn and a handful of others watched from the far corner. She remembered Conn's threat. Had never forgotten it. Samantha didn't know what her life would be when she walked back off this stage. It wasn't something she could allow herself to consider. All that mattered was this: Danica would be safe. She'd decided that on the floor of her kitchen, bleeding from where her father's coffee mug struck her.

The principal stepped aside. Samantha adjusted the microphone. There would be no running today.

"None of you knew Alex very well. I didn't, either. I knew he had a cute smile. I knew he was kind. One thing that I didn't learn until it was too late was how brave Alex was. The day he died, he saw me and my friends... bullying Danica Perlich, and he jumped in and broke it up. By himself. No one did that for Danica. No one. But he did. If you heard what people are saying about how Alex died, it probably doesn't make sense that Danica would do that to him after he helped her. It doesn't, because she wouldn't. She didn't. She only wanted to hurt herself. Alex went there to help her, and what happened to him was just an accident. It wasn't her fault."

Samantha paused, then forced herself to say the rest. "It was mine. The only reason they were on that cliff is me."

The audience reacted, but Samantha was too focused on what was left to say for her to care if it was disbelief or just surprise. The principal put a hand on Samantha's shoulder and said something she didn't really hear. Samantha shrugged out of the principal's grasp, put a hand on the microphone, and raised her voice.

"When Alex asked me out, I was already seeing someone. Danica." That caused another reaction from her classmates she had to ignore. "I used him. I let him take me out because I was afraid you'd find out who I am if I didn't. I hid behind him. Danica couldn't hide, though. She had to watch me pretend I didn't care about her while everyone made her life hell. We chased her out onto that cliff and I let it happen so you wouldn't chase me instead. Alex was brave and kind when I was weak and cruel, and that's why he's dead. Not Danica. The person you should hate is me."

She stepped back from the podium and walked off stage without another look at the audience. No one applauded. No one said anything. Principal Ross fumbled with the microphone and stammered out a stunned thank you for Samantha's honesty. Ms. Granger nodded at Samantha with a tired smile as she was called to the stage. Samantha hurried to the exit. She needed an empty hallway, somewhere she could be alone.

The hallway was not empty. Leslie and Will flanked the doorway. They were waiting for her.

Leslie and Will shared a look. It was Leslie that spoke. "I thought you'd be hiding with your friends."

"I doubt they're my friends anymore."

"They didn't know you were going to do that?" Leslie asked.

Samantha shook her head.

They shared another look. This time, it was Will who spoke. "Have you heard from her?"

Again, Samantha shook her head.

"Shit." Leslie picked at her fingernails as she spoke. " You don't think she… you know…?"

"No," Samantha replied. "She didn't."

Will started to say something, but Samantha's phone

rang and cut him off. She put up a finger to stop them from asking anything else and looked at the number on her phone. It wasn't one she recognized. "Hello?"

"Hey, uh, is this Samantha?" a man on the other end of the line asked.

"Yeah, I'm her."

"This is Fresh. I mean, Pastor McElfresh. I'm Danica's youth pastor."

"Oh, right. Fresh," Samantha said.

"I'm sorry to call like this, but I've got kind of a problem. Danica came to the church and—"

Samantha interrupted him. "What? She's there?"

"No, not anymore." Fresh sounded sheepish. "I caught her stealing food last night and I was worried about her, so I let her stay here for the night until we could figure out what to do. But when I got to the church this morning she was gone."

"Why call me?" Samantha asked, heart racing. She turned away from Will and Leslie, wanting what little privacy she could manage.

"She left a note. It said she wanted to talk to you somewhere and that you'd know the place. Hold on, let me read what she wrote. 'If you talk to Sam, tell her I want to see her again. Tell her I'll be waiting where we used to meet.' Do you know where she's talking about?"

Samantha closed her eyes and willed her heart to calm. "Sorry, no. I don't."

"Crap. If something comes to mind, will you please call me?"

"I will," Samantha said. "Thank you for letting me know."

She ended the call. Samantha knew she shouldn't have lied. She should have told Fresh and let him help. It was just too much of a risk. Telling him would get others involved, and that could draw Conn right to Danica.

Samantha had to be sure Danica was safe. Had to protect her from Conn, from anyone who wanted to hurt her. To do that, Samantha needed to get to Danica before anyone else found her.

Samantha felt a familiar cascade of fear, echoes of something that had already played out once and gone very wrong. A story that didn't conclude the way it was intended, trying to repeat itself one last time to get it right. Danica at the edge of the water, her friends racing to get there in time, those things, waiting, their moment about to arrive. They weren't the only players in this story, though. This wasn't a tale only they had the right to end.

She turned to Will and Leslie. "Please tell me one of you has a car. I think I know where Danny went, but we need to move fast."

Will, nodding emphatically, had a set of keys out of his pocket before Samantha could even finish her sentence.

Chapter Twenty-One

WATER RAINED DOWN from the broken faucet over Krista's hands, splashing off the discolored ceramic and onto her shirt. Her friends were waiting for her in the lobby, probably wondering what was taking so long. *I need to wash my hands*, she'd told them after the memorial ended. It was a terrible lie, but Krista wasn't exactly on her game. When Samantha walked off stage it felt like the whole school had turned, necks craned and eyes wide, to see Krista's reaction. She couldn't give them the chance to ask her how long *she* knew Samantha was gay (or bi, or whatever the hell she was) and why she hadn't told anyone.

And then there was the other thing. The thing Krista *didn't* know: Danica hadn't killed Alex, accidentally or on purpose. Nothing Conn had said to Krista and her friends had been true. Conn lied to her. But, why? After everything he'd told her, after every crazy thing she believed, why lie about what happened to Alex? Maybe he had to lie to keep her friends in line, but she deserved the truth. She was supposed to be more to him. Unless that was a lie, too.

Krista walked back into the lobby. Nick paced back and forth across the linoleum floor. Conn sat on a long bench attached to the wall with Ferris beside him. He had a hand over Ferris' and looked directly into her eyes as he spoke. Krista's guts twisted. The hand on Ferris, his voice low, their eyes locked on one anothers'; it was how he talked to Krista when she was stubborn.

"What the hell is going on?" Krista demanded.

Ferris and Conn looked up. Conn took his hand off of Ferris' and replied, "We were talking about our next move."

"What next move?"

"Danica, dumbass," Nick said.

Krista didn't like the look on Nick's face, or the way he was almost panting, like an animal ready for a fight. He wasn't alone. Ferris looked just as ready for blood. "What about Danica? She didn't even do anything. She's a sad little cutter who wanted to check out, that's all."

"You didn't believe any of that, did you?" Conn asked. The bastard was smirking. "She'd say anything to protect her girlfriend. That's all that was."

Before Krista could reply, Ferris cut in. "You're worse than Sam. You knew she was seeing that bitch the whole time and didn't say anything."

"Yeah, because you're a moron. I was handling it."

"Ladies, come on. Calm down," Conn interrupted. He stood up and walked toward Krista. "It doesn't matter what Sam said. You know we still need to find her."

Krista flinched away from him, afraid of what would happen if he touched her. Could he make her trust him? Could he force her to do whatever he wanted? The thing that scared her most was that she almost *wanted* him to. She wanted to believe, totally believe, because there was nowhere else for Krista to go. Samantha wouldn't want anything to do with her. Not anymore. Conn was all she had. Krista couldn't take another lie, but if she let him convince her, if she let him touch her, maybe it wouldn't feel like a lie anymore.

Logan charged into the lobby, red-faced. "Dudes! Hey! I saw her!"

Conn turned from Krista, breaking the pull she'd felt toward him. He asked, "Samantha?"

"Yeah. She was with what's-her-face. That girl Danica's always with."

"Leslie?" Ferris offered.

"Uh-huh. They were headed to the parking lot."

"Take Nick's car and follow her. All of you," Conn said, smiling. "I'll go with Krista."

Krista wanted to argue, but kept her mouth shut. Better to wait. See what happened. Before Conn could take her hand, Krista retrieved the keys from her purse and headed for her car.

~

Samantha sprinted across a field of soupy grass towards a lightning-scorched maple tree. She'd parted ways with Leslie and Will at the park's entrance, where a locked iron gate blocked the road to the lake. Danica's friends left the car to continue on foot while Samantha looked for another way down the hill. It was Samantha who suggested splitting up to cover more ground. She felt guilty lying to them, but Danica's letter was an invitation to her and her alone. The main road would lead Leslie and Will the long way around. If Samantha could find one of the trails Danica had shown her weeks ago, they'd have plenty of time to talk before they were found. Assuming talking was what Danica had planned.

It took Samantha a few minutes to locate the trailhead through the mass of overgrown weeds. Days of downpour had turned it into a slick of mud and rainwater. Samantha walked sideways in tiny steps, digging her foot into the mud to keep from toppling down the hill. As she descended, she caught sight of a decaying wall. The day she and Danica walked this path, they'd climbed over that wall and discovered the ruins of a house beyond. They'd found sunflowers growing in a circle around the house's well.

Samantha's foot lost its grip a few yards from the bottom of the hill. She slid through the mud on her butt and splashed into an enormous puddle. Swearing, Samantha stood and shook herself off. She was filthy — the back of her pants were covered in a thick layer of muck — but she hadn't twisted anything. The rain would wash most of the mud off, and there were worse things ahead. Samantha continued forward, weaving between empty pavilions and fire pits, until the lake came into view. It was so swollen from the storm that the pier was nearly submerged. A figure knelt at the end of the short, wooden dock, hands dangled over the edge and into the water.

Raindrops beat down on Samantha with so much force they stung her arms and face. The rain was unnatural, like the mist that had taken over the woods around the reservoir. She thought of the girl whose touch filled her lungs with water. That girl had nearly killed her there, in the woods, under that blanket of fog. There'd be nothing to stop her if they met again. Samantha put it out of mind (tried to, almost succeeded) and continued forward. The figure on the pier stood as she stepped onto the boards, and Danica and Samantha faced each other alone for the first time since it had all gone wrong.

"Hey, Danny," Samantha said, smiling unexpectedly at the sight of her.

"Sam," Danica replied. Though her voice was low, it cut through the rain as if she was shouting.

"I got your message."

"Where are your friends? Where's Conn? I didn't think you'd come without them."

"Conn isn't my friend. I just wanted to see you. I wanted to talk." Samantha took a tentative step towards Danica. "Why don't we get out of the rain? The benches in the pavilions are soaked, but at least there's a roof."

"No. We can talk here." Danica inched back to the very edge of the pier.

"Fine." The rain made it impossible to see below the surface of the muddy lake. She told herself the shadows moving at the edges of her vision were her imagination. Trying not to look at the water, Samantha asked, "They want to kill me, don't they?"

Danica nodded.

"If you'd jumped, if Alex hadn't..." Samantha couldn't finish the thought. She'd talked about it, about his death, too much already.

"I'd be one of them," Danica answered.

"And you'd have come for me."

Danica nodded again. Even though Samantha already knew, even though Conn had warned her, it burned her heart to hear Danica admit it.

"Is that still what you want?"

Danica hesitated. "I don't know."

Samantha wanted to be off the pier, away from the lake. The runoff from the rain flowed around her shoes with so much force it felt like it was trying to drag her along with it. Like the water itself wanted her dead.

She forced herself to take another step down the pier and said, "How could you want that? How could you want to kill *anyone*? That's not who you are."

"I don't know what's me and what's her, anymore. I hear her like she's me."

"I don't know what that means. Who is *her*?"

Danica looked down into the water, her hand over

her breast. "Lenka. She loved Constantine the same way I loved you. Now she hates him. They want *us* to hate each other, too. That's all they have left."

"That's all this is? Two pissed off lovers from whenever ago, using us to get back at each other? Screw them. Stop letting them play with us. Come with me, Danny. Please."

"I can't," Danica replied. "They keep them, Sam. Anyone they kill, they keep. That's why I came. They have Alex."

Samantha calmed. Understood. "Tell her I used him. Tell her this is all my fault."

"I did. She knows. She doesn't care. They want someone in his place."

"Me?"

"No."

"Conn. They want Conn," Samantha said as the pieces fell together.

"I thought... I thought he'd come if you did."

"I don't want his help. He wants you. Like they want me," Samantha said, gesturing at the lake. "I'm not going to let him hurt you."

"You can't stop him."

Samantha chanced another step closer and continued, "All we have to do is give them Conn, right? Then this is all over."

"Stay back!" Danica shouted.

"Danny..."

"It doesn't matter. He can't die. He can *never* die. There's nothing we can do," Danica said, angrier with every word. "You deserve what they'll do to you. You deserve to be their toy. That's all I was to you. *I hate you*!"

"I know. I know you do. I wasn't... I was so afraid, Danny. You don't know how afraid I am."

"You're a coward." There was something in Danica's voice that wasn't her, something harsh and pained.

"I know. I know." Samantha wished she'd told Danica about her father. Realized, now, she'd have understood.

Danica's eyes were fury itself. "I hate you."

"Danny, please. This isn't you, okay? Please, just talk to me."

Danica screamed and lunged. Samantha fell backwards, Danica on top of her. Her head hit the pier's wooden boards with a painful *thunk*. Her right arm was twisted behind her back, pinned. Danica grabbed Samantha's free wrist and forced it to the ground. Samantha saw something in Danica's eyes, something she recognized. Fear and anger together, one driving the other, leaving room for nothing else. Samantha had been the strong one, the one who told Danica what to do and when. Samantha had *made* Danica weak. She'd done it on purpose, to control her, to make Danica *hers*. It was instinct. It was the only way to survive. It was what her father had taught her to do.

How could Danica not have wanted this? If Lenka had called Samantha, if she'd been offered the strength to fight, to hurt her father the way he'd hurt her, she'd have thrown herself into the water without a thought.

Samantha found her words. The ones she should have said as soon as she stepped onto the pier.

"I'm sorry, Danica," Samantha said.

"What?"

"I'm sorry. I'm sorry for everything. This is my fault. Everything. All of it. It's my fault, and I'm so sorry."

Danica slowly released Samantha's wrist. "Sorry isn't enough."

"I know. I know you can't forgive me." Samantha wished she could touch Danica on the arm, on the hand, on the cheek. Wished she'd have the chance again, someday, but knew better. "I told them about us, Danny. Everyone. I told them everything. I know it's too late for me, but now everyone knows. For you."

Danica leaned back, which took enough pressure off of Samantha's body for her to free her pinned arm. The rain hammered down on Samantha's face, but she kept her eyes open and on Danica. Samantha wanted to keep apologizing, but she'd said all she could. What happened to her now was up to Danica.

Slowly, tentatively, Danica reached out a hand and pushed a wet strand of hair off of Samantha's face with her thumb. The corners of her lips twitched up. The slightest shadow of a smile.

The moment was shattered by a distant scream.

Danica turned in the sound's direction, to the woods behind the main cabin. "Was that Leslie?"

"She came here with me. Her and Will."

Danica rose and offered her hand to Samantha, pulling her to her feet. Leslie cried out a second time. Other voices followed, shouting, each closer than the last. One of the voices, louder than the others, Samantha recognized immediately. Danica did too. She growled his name.

"Constantine."

He'd found them. Had they followed her? Had she led them here, right to Danica? There wasn't much time before Conn reached the lake. Samantha could escape, but could Danica? No, not with her limp. They were trapped between the creatures that wanted Samantha dead and the man that was coming for Danica. Out of options, Samantha reached out and took Danica's hand.

They waited there together, on the pier, in the rain, with nowhere left to run.

~

Samantha's hand was the most important thing in the world. It held Danica where she was, reminded her *who* she was. She squeezed Sam's hand as hard as she could, afraid even a second apart would give Lenka a chance to overwhelm her again. Whatever was coming, Danica would face it as herself.

She'd known the mounting fury in her heart would take over when she saw Samantha. She was ready give into it so it could be responsible for what happened. She expected Samantha to blame her for Alex's death, to humiliate her like she'd done in front of her friends. She expected everything but an apology.

"Could Lenka protect us? Would she?" Samantha asked as Constantine ran out of the trees with and five others following him.

"She can't. Not from him."

Samantha pulled Danica a few steps back, toward the end of the pier. "What if we swam? Would they let us pass?"

"Me," Danica said. "Just me."

"But you'd be safe?"

"I'm not going to leave you here alone," Danica replied, her voice firm.

"Ladies! I thought we'd never find you!" Conn shouted, bounding down the flat, muddy field toward the pier. Trailing behind him were Krista, Ferris, Nick and Logan. Leslie was with them, Logan's fat hand on her arm, pulling her along. There was a bruise forming on her cheek. Her eyes were unfocused, her face slack. Lenka stared out through Danica's eyes and they saw the aura of Conn's sorcery surrounding Leslie, his magic keeping her docile.

"I'm really sorry, Danny," Samantha whispered.

Danica gave Samantha's hand another squeeze. "You said that already."

"Sammy, I have to be honest. You surprised me." Conn stopped at the end of the pier while his followers caught up. "I thought we had an understanding. I thought we could be *friends*, you know? Things were going great. All you had to do was sit back and watch the show."

"Yeah, I've been screwing things up for everyone lately. Sorry." Samantha sounded calm, almost cocky. If Danica didn't feel her hand shaking, she might have believed Samantha wasn't scared.

Krista and the others spread out along the shore. Samantha tried to pull Danica a step closer to the lake, but Danica yanked back. She didn't want Sam any nearer to the water than she already was.

Samantha looked at Ferris. "Megan told me what happened with Danica was an accident. You don't have any reason to hate her and you know it. None of you do."

"You talked to Megan?" Danica asked. Samantha spared her a glance and nodded.

Krista stepped forward. "Yeah, what about Alex?"

Danica replied before Samantha could. There was only one thing that mattered enough to say: "He saved my life."

There was a brief glance between Krista and Conn, a look Danica couldn't read. Whatever was being said by it, Conn lost his smile. He put an arm out and pushed Krista behind him. "Look, Sammy, you pissed me off, but that's okay. If anyone understands how stupid love can make you, it's me. Now's the time to be smart. We're going to take Danica. You can't stop us. Give her up and everything's cool. I really don't want to hurt you. It'd be like hurting myself, you know? Problem is, my friends don't have that problem. Do you, Nick?"

"Nope," Nick responded, like he was looking forward to the opportunity.

Danica leaned close to Samantha. "You don't have to do this for me, okay? You can let them have me."

"Hey Conn," Samantha yelled, ignoring Danica. "You were right about us. We are alike. We're both cowards."

Conn grinned. "Which is why you're going to give me Danica."

"No. It's why you won't follow me."

Samantha grabbed Danica around the waist with her free arm and fell backwards. Danica's feet left the wooden boards of the pier as Samantha lifted her up and back. There was a moment of weightlessness, her body suspended in the air before beginning its fall toward the lake. Danica cried out to Samantha to stop, but it was too late. Their momentum shifted, Danica's stomach lurched, and they both plunged into the lake. Samantha kicked, dragging Danica away from the pier before anyone could get to them. Something brushed Danica's bare leg, then her hips, then her face. They were not alone. Danica tried to warn Samantha, but the sound was lost under the muted roar of rain striking the lake's surface.

A hand closed on Danica's ankle and pulled, forcing both of them to a stop. Samantha spun to help free her, but the sisters had already surrounded them. A pale shadow appeared behind Samantha, arms outstretched. Danica screamed as the figure wrapped itself around Samantha. She panicked, kicking her feet against her attacker, fighting uselessly to escape its grasp. Her hold on Danica slipped, and Danica barely managed to catch Samantha's wrist before she was lost. They were caught between two of the sisters, one holding Danica back while the other pulled Samantha down. Even if Danica kept her grip on Samantha, it wouldn't matter. The sisters could simply trap them here until the water filled Samantha's lungs. Samantha thrashed against the thing that held her, nearly shaking off Danica's weakening grasp. Danica somehow screamed again, though she should've already been out of air. It was the touch of Lenka's sisters. They kept her alive, gave her air while denying Samantha the same. Danica cried out to anything that was listening, prayed in a panic — to God, to Lenka, to the lake — for the strength to save Samantha.

Something detached from Danica's heart. She reached for her breast, leaving only a single hand on Samantha's wrist. There was something cold and metallic there. The head of a pin. She gripped it between her fingers, pulled, and felt it slide out of her heart. The gold of the pin seemed to glow here under the water, in its home. Danica looked back to Samantha, and she remembered. Not her own memory, but Lenka's. There was only one thing that could break the pin. One thing that could save someone from the Rusalka.

Before they could be pulled apart, Danica kicked off of the woman holding her and stretched out the hand holding the pin. Its tip touched Samantha's forehead, pierced her skin and found the hard bone of her skull beneath. Danica closed her eyes.

I forgive you.

The pin snapped. Danica felt the hand on her ankle release. The sister holding Samantha lurched away. Danica wrapped a frantic arm under Samantha's and pulled her up and away. The two kicked desperately toward air. As they broke the surface, Danica heard the lake itself scream.

Chapter Twenty-Two

"Is THAT THEM? I think that's them!" Krista ran to the edge of the pier. Two figures had surfaced near the middle of the lake and were paddling hard for the opposite shore. She couldn't see them clearly enough to be sure, but it had to be Samantha and Danica.

"Krista!" Ferris shouted, panicked. "Oh my God, Krista!"

Krista almost ignored her. Ferris hadn't stopped screeching since Samantha dove off the pier. A few more minutes of it and Krista was going to throw Ferris into the lake herself. Still, she took a grudging look over her shoulder to see what had Ferris so scared.

Conn had fallen to his hands and knees, his body shaking like he was freezing to death. Krista approached slowly and crouched beside him. Was this some kind of seizure? She reached out, tried to put a hand on his shoulder, but he lurched away from her touch and started to laugh. The sound was manic, uncontrolled. It scared the shit out of her.

"What the hell is wrong with you?" Krista demanded.

"He's mortal."

Krista looked up. A woman stood at the end of the

pier. She wore a thin, filthy dress that stuck to her skin. Her brown hair hung over her face in clumps, hiding a pale, corpse's face. Conn's laugher trailed off. He pushed Krista away from him and stood.

"How does it feel?" the woman asked.

"I don't understand. You didn't... you never..."

"Forgave you? Of course I didn't."

"What's going on, Conn?" Krista asked, rising to her feet.

"Yeah, man, what the hell is this?" Nick sounded nervous. Krista wished she wasn't too afraid to enjoy it.

"Shut up. Adults are talking," Conn snapped.

Lenka continued, "You thought your trap was perfect. You thought we'd play this miserable game until I set you free. But you forgot the rules, Constantine. The ones *you* etched into my heart to save yourself."

"This isn't right. I'm getting out of here," Ferris said, backing toward the path that circled the lake. When no one tried to stop her, Ferris spun and ran towards the woods.

"Enough with the riddles, Lenka. What the hell happened?" Conn asked, impatient.

"I let Danica carry my pin, like the others you tormented. I marked Danica as my own. I made her mine. I let her carry a part of me within her, and in the end she did for Samantha what I could never do for you. The only thing that could shatter my — *our* — bond."

"She forgave her."

Lenka smiled, "The pin broke and freed your soul. It was Samantha who was forgiven, though. My sisters can never harm her again. Her, Constantine. Not you."

"Yo. I think there's something in the water," Logan said, dragging Leslie behind him.

"You're here to kill me." Conn walked backwards toward land. There was something in his eyes Krista had never seen before. Fear. Conn was *terrified*.

"No," Lenka said with a rage that made Krista tremble. "I don't have the right to hurt you. Danica cut my ties to the others forever."

"Well, at least one of us got what we wanted. Thanks for that." Conn smirked, but his arrogance was a mask.

Nick crept to the shoreline and gazed into the water. "Dude, there are ladies down there. And they're...really hot."

Lenka ignored Nick. Her mocking stare stayed fixed on Conn. "You were always a fool. Did you forget about my sisters? The ones you chased to their deaths as part of your game? I didn't come to say goodbye. I came to watch."

Hands reached out of the water, grabbed Nick by his arms and legs, and pulled him off the shore. He didn't cry out. In fact, as he disappeared into the lake, he looked happy. Logan did scream. He stumbled backwards and tripped over a rock, dragging Leslie to the ground with him. Krista took a step toward the shore and felt her foot splash, as if she was in a puddle. The lake was rising. An inch of water already covered the pier.

"Conn, what's going on?"

The last of Conn's confidence shattered. "We need to run."

"Nick's dead, isn't he? We're all going to die here, and it's your fault."

"Logan, get up and take the girl with us. Those things won't kill her to get to us. We have to get back to Krista's car."

"I'm not going anywhere with you!" Krista shouted.

"Then you'll die here with Nick. Is that what you want?"

Krista knew he was right. The pier had disappeared under the rising lake, and the shoreline receded as the water reached out into the grassy field. Conn shoved Logan hard in the back, turning him off the path and up the hill.

Krista didn't feel the hand on her ankle until she tried to walk. It yanked backwards when she moved and sent her face-first into the ground.

"Conn!" Krista shouted as a second hand grabbed her leg. "Conn, something has me!"

He didn't stop. Didn't even look back at her. Krista tried to scream again, but instead of sound, it was water that poured out of her mouth. There were more hands on her, pinning her to the ground as the lake rose around her. Krista fought for breath, but there was no room in her lungs. The last thing she saw was Conn's back vanishing into the rain.

~

They took turns dragging each other toward the shore, both so exhausted that they couldn't paddle for more than a minute or two without a break. Pain radiated out of Danica's knee and into her leg with every kick. Samantha would try to swim for both of them if she knew, so Danica forced herself through the agony and let the rain hide her tears. They'd turned toward the main cabin of the camp. It was closer to the pier than Danica wanted to come ashore, but they wouldn't manage a longer swim. She hoped the downpour would make it too hard for Conn and the others to see them. It was Samantha who carried the last leg with Danica half on her back. Ten feet out from the shore, the lake shallowed enough for Danica to touch the bottom and walk out of the water. She collapsed beside Samantha on the muddy ground.

"Danny?" Samantha asked, panting.

"Yeah?"

"What just happened?"

Overwhelmed, exhausted, with no idea where to start, Danica laughed. She touched Samantha on the hand. "You almost got yourself killed is what happened."

"I didn't know what else to do. I couldn't let him hurt you."

Danica didn't know how to reply. Samantha knew what was waiting for her in the lake and went in anyway. For her.

"So why am I *not* dead?" Samantha asked.

Danica replied, "I did something so they can't hurt you anymore. Not ever."

"You stabbed me with something, didn't you? What was that?" Samantha lifted a hand to her forehead and touched the spot where the pin had pierced her. There was a small red dot there, but it wasn't bleeding.

Danica swallowed. "It was a needle, sort of. It's what tied me to Lenka. When I forgave you, it broke. It's hard to explain, but now they can't hurt you. I promise."

"You forgave me?" Samantha asked, leaning up. Her eyes were full and clear, unguarded, like they were when they first met.

Before Danica could reply, someone yelled from beyond the cabin. It was Will. He shouted again, "Danica! Danica, you're okay!"

"Will!" Danica yelled back. She jumped up to wave, but collapsed when she put weight on her injured leg.

Samantha held up a hand. "Hey, quiet. We aren't safe."

Will dropped to his knees in front of Danica and wrapped his arms around her. Quieter, he said, "Have you seen Leslie? We split up to find you."

"Oh, God, they still have Leslie." Danica pulled away from Will and looked in the direction of the pier.

"What's going on? Who has her?" Will looked ashamed. "We shouldn't have split up."

"There were five of them," Samantha said. "It wouldn't have mattered."

Danica looked back at the shoreline. It was smaller than it had been a moment earlier. "The lake is rising."

"What?" Samantha asked, eyes focusing on the shoreline.

"He's mortal again. What I did... it means Conn can die. They're coming for him," Danica mumbled.

"I don't know what you're talking about, Danny," Samantha said.

Danica turned to her. "There was a spell on the pin that kept him alive. Now it's broken."

"Spell?" Will interrupted.

Danica continued. There was no way of making sense of this to Will in the time they had. "They can be anywhere there's water, but it hurts them to go too far from it. Sam, I think they're flooding the park to trap him. They'll do anything to keep him from escaping. We have to help her."

Samantha stood and leaned far to one side, stretching, then reversed the motion. "*We* aren't doing anything. I am. You're taking Will and getting out of here."

"I'm coming with you!" Danica demanded. She tried to rise, but another jolt of pain in her knee forced her to lean on Will's shoulder for support.

"The park's flooding and you can barely walk. You'll slow me down." Samantha continued to stretch as she spoke.

"Sam, there are *five* of them," Danica pleaded.

"Yeah, let me come at least," Will added.

"You're her crutch. Conn's between you and your car, so you have to find another way out. Danica can lead you."

Danica limped to Samantha and put her hand on Samantha's shoulder. "Conn is dangerous. You don't know what kind of power he has. He could kill you."

Samantha straightened from her stretch and smiled. Whether it was false confidence or not, Danica couldn't tell. "I'll be okay. Leslie will, too. Just be safe. Please."

The water was already up to their ankles. There wasn't much time, and Danica knew it. She put her arms around Samantha and squeezed her in a brief but strong hug. Then she limped to Will and put her arm over his shoulder.

"Sam?" Danica said.

Samantha dropped into a crouch and looked over her shoulder. "Yeah?"

"Thank you."

"Shut up. Thank *you*." Samantha launched herself into a sprint across the mud of the shore as if it were as solid as cement and disappeared into the rain.

"Danny, we should go," Will said.

Danica nodded. She took a long look around the park, mapping out the safest route. She pointed at a nearby trail that wound uphill, away from the rising water.

"There," she said, and spared one more glance in the direction of the pier before allowing Will to help her up the hill.

~

Samantha ran without the push for the first time in her life. She was the pursuer. She was the hunter. Samantha focused on her feet and the ground below them. Each and every step could twist or break her ankle, send her face first into the mud. Balance and form were instinct, but she'd never run on ground that *wanted* to hurt her. Danica may have saved her from Lenka and her sisters, but the water itself didn't care if she was forgiven.

Forgiven. She hadn't wanted that. Didn't deserve it. Couldn't understand why Danica believed she did. Samantha wouldn't let herself dwell on it. Not yet. The lake was rising unnaturally fast, and Danica's friend needed her. All she could do was move forward. All she could do was run.

The pier was underwater by the time Samantha passed it, visible only by the tall posts at what had once been the shore. She paused and looked for a sign of which direction Conn went. There was the shortcut that Samantha had taken, but if Conn knew about it he wouldn't have come in the long way. As she searched, she spotted something bright poking out of the water's surface. Something the color of Krista's jacket. Without a thought, Samantha waded in after it. The water closing in brought Samantha back to the moment of sinking into the lake, hands pulling her down, lungs burning. She reminded herself that she was protected now, that Danica had saved her, and found the strength to press forward. The water was up to her armpits when she reached the jacket and realized it wasn't empty. Samantha didn't have to feel for a pulse to know she was too late. The sight of Krista face down in the lake bent something inside of her to the point of snapping. It seemed stupid after everything that had happened, but Samantha still loved her. She couldn't leave Krista here. Tentatively, Samantha slipped her arms around Krista's lifeless chest and lifted. She dragged the body back to shore a step at a time, pulled it as far from the rising lake as she could, then fell on her knees beside it.

Though it sickened her, Samantha searched Krista's pockets and pulled out her keys. Once she'd found Leslie,

Krista's car might be their only hope of escape. Samantha put a hand on Krista's cheek and said goodbye.

She left the body where it lay and put distance between herself and the water. Her foot caught on a tree branch the length of her arm. Samantha bent down, picked it up, and gave it two swings to test its weight. A weapon wouldn't hurt. She shifted the branch to her left hand and slowly worked herself back into a run.

Samantha was a sprinter, not built for long distances. Her stomach cramped, her heart beat against her ribs, and her muscles burned, but there was a place beyond exhaustion if she could push herself through. Samantha allowed her to mind soften. Kept her eyes steady, straight ahead. The only thing that existed was the next step, the next breath.

They appeared suddenly, as if someone had drawn back the curtain of rain. There were only three of them: Logan and Leslie in front with Conn trailing behind. No Nick, no Ferris. Were they dead, too? More casualties of Conn and Lenka's war? Wherever they were, there was nothing Samantha could do to help them. Right now, it was Leslie that needed her. Samantha lifted the branch like a baseball bat. The motion made her think of Alex, and that chased away the last of her fear.

"Constantine!" she shouted.

He spun in time to see the branch coming, but not to get out of the way. It struck Conn in the jaw and whipped his head back. Blood sprayed from his mouth. He cried in pain and crumpled in a heap, hands over his face. Samantha ran past him and pointed the branch at Logan. He did exactly what someone with a weapon pointed at them was supposed to do. He raised his arms.

"The water's getting close. It's Conn they want, not you. Let her go and get out of here before you end up like your friends," Samantha said. She walked forward as she spoke, branch outstretched.

Samantha's suggestion was all Logan needed. He looked from Conn, to the lake, to the bludgeon in Samantha's hand, and bolted. Leslie stumbled to the ground, her eyes distant. It was doubtful she could run. Conn would have no trouble catching them. Samantha would have to deal with him first.

Conn was still on the ground with his head in his hands. She lifted the branch again. "Get up."

"Sorry, you caught me off guard. Kind of embarrassing to get laid out like that," Conn replied. Blood dripped from his mouth and onto his hands. "I mean, we're both used to taking a lot worse. Aren't we, Samantha?"

"What's that supposed to mean?"

"You think you're the first person to get smacked around by Dad?" Conn stood and lifted his shirt. On his chest were long, criss-crossing scars. "Mine liked to take a poker out of the fire when he was having a day. After what happened to me — you know, after I had to rip out my own soul to survive — I decided to return the favor. Between you and me, it wasn't as cathartic as I'd hoped. Revenge is sort of a let down. Lenka never got that."

"Can you please shut up?" Samantha tightened her grip on the branch.

"You should be happy we're talking. Anyone else who hit me would already be screaming. Now be nice or I'll track down your girlfriend and take it out on her."

Samantha stepped forward and swung the branch, aiming again for his head. It clipped him above the ear and he staggered to the side. She reversed the motion, caught him in the cheek with an upward blow. Twice more she hit him, first in the shoulder, then again in the face. She drew back the branch and waited for his head to come up. When it did, she twisted into the swing, aimed for his temple and a strike that would send him to the ground. This time Conn got his arm up. He hit the branch with an open palm. The wood exploded into a cloud of splinters and flame. The force rebounded into Samantha, knocking her off her feet. Samantha tried to push herself up, but the blast had left her too stunned to move.

"That never hurt before. This is going to take a while to get used to," Conn said, shaking embers off his hand with a grimace. He pointed a thumb at the still-dazed Leslie. "Did you really come back just for her?"

Samantha didn't answer. She clawed at the ground, looking for something to use as a weapon. All she found was mud and rocks too small to bother throwing.

"Because if that's the only reason we're fighting, I should get rid of her before you hit me again. Next time, I'll hit back." Conn retrieved what was left of Samantha's branch and stalked toward Leslie.

Samantha staggered up and lunged between them. She wouldn't let him past. She wouldn't.

"Come on," Conn said, sighing. He stopped where he was and dropped the remains of the branch. "Don't make me hurt you, Sam. I want you to get home safe and see what I did for you."

"What?" Samantha gasped.

"Well, after your little performance at the memorial — which, by the way, really pissed me off — I remembered I owed your dad a call." Samantha opened her mouth to protest, to beg him not to, but Conn cut her off. "Don't bother. I called him from the school. I know he was going to find out anyway, but I figured if he heard from me first, I could tell it my way. Get him in the right mood, you know? Let him know how you and your mom were about to blow town. How she's got a bag packed and everything."

"That's not true."

Conn laughed. "Shit, right, she didn't tell you yet, did she? Guess it doesn't matter now. If he hasn't found her bag yet, he will soon. I'm not *exactly* sure what he's got planned for Mom, but whatever it is, you only have yourself to blame."

She felt wobbly. Too weak to stand. If Conn charged, there was nothing she could do to stop him. But Conn didn't try to get past her. Something else had caught his attention.

"Shit. I guess I'll have to find another way out of here."

Samantha looked over her shoulder. An arm of water had reached down the beach and cut off the path to main road.

"Looks like it's time to get going. Say hi to Dad for me." Conn smiled, but Samantha could see the fear behind it. The steady flooding had shaken him. He took two steps back, then turned and fled up the hill and into the woods.

She'd won, but Samantha didn't feel safe. Would never feel safe again. She knew her speech at Alex's memorial would get back to her father, but she'd hoped there'd be time to prepare. Maybe even control what he heard, and from whom. What Conn had done was worse than anything she'd imagined. Her mom had no idea what was waiting for her, no way to guess how much danger she was in. There was no way to warn her, either. Samantha's phone (all of their phones, probably) had been ruined by the unrelenting rain. She could flee, could save herself, but not without leaving her mother to pay for Samantha's mistakes. That left only one option. She had the keys to Krista's car, and home was only a few minutes away. She could get there first, use the phone to warn her, or at least call the police. Unless her father was there. Unless he was waiting for her...

Leslie's eyes cleared. She looked up at Samantha, confused. Before Samantha could speak, she realized they weren't alone. A woman stood at the edge of the water, a woman very much like the girl who'd attacked Samantha in the mist. She said nothing, only watched with an expression Samantha couldn't read.

She blinked, and the woman was gone. Samantha shook off the vision and turned back to Leslie. There wasn't time to waste. "Please tell me you can run," she said.

Chapter Twenty-Three

THEY CIRCLED THE lake along a winding path, the ground beneath them uneven and slippery. Danica's knee twisted and strained no matter how hard she leaned on Will's shoulder. She held tears back with every step, refusing to cry while they were still in danger. Feeling anything, even the agony of her leg, was a blessing she didn't deserve. A blessing Alex had paid for with his life. He was still with her, waiting on a fallen log or in a tree branch. He'd vanish as she approached only to reappear again farther down the path.

Will never complained. He bore her weight through the woods and over hills without asking for a break or a rest. When she could spare a chance to look, Danica searched for Samantha amongst the half-submerged cabins and pavilions. There was nothing. No sign. Just the water claiming what was left of the park.

Danica was facing the lake when Will elbowed her gently and pointed ahead. The route through the trees Danica had chosen ended suddenly in a wide cleft in the earth. There were ditches like this throughout the woods, eroded paths that rain followed to the lake below. The downpour had widened and deepened them into small creek beds. This one was the worst they'd seen, five feet across and almost as deep. Danica looked up and down the hill for a narrowing point where they could cross.

"Are we in trouble, Danny?" Will asked.

If they were, Danica wasn't going to tell him. She gestured to a point above. "Let's go this way."

Will nodded and slid his arm back under hers. They'd made it halfway to where the ditch narrowed when Danica saw movement farther up the hill. She grabbed the sodden front of Will's shirt and pulled him into a crouch beside her.

"What is it?" Will whispered.

Danica shook her head. "I don't know. We should wait a minute. Just in case."

"Yeah," Will agreed. He kept quiet for a moment before speaking again. "How are you holding up?"

"My knee sucks, but I'm okay."

"I didn't mean your knee."

"Will," Danica sighed. She didn't look at him and didn't want to. "I don't want to talk about how I'm feeling right now."

"Do you want to talk after?"

Danica forced herself to turn to him. "I don't know. I'm not really sure how I feel, anyway. I'm better. I think. Maybe I'm just too scared to feel like crap."

"Scared about what?" Will asked.

"Scared of dying, dumbass. Aren't you?"

"Yeah," Will said, cracking a bit of a smile.

Danica realized what she'd said — what she was afraid of — and smiled as well. She was afraid of not making it to the next day. She'd been falling for so long that she'd given up on catching herself. Danica hadn't realized anything had changed until the words were out of her mouth. She prayed it wasn't a temporary reprieve, a response to danger, and that she'd still be herself when the rain stopped.

"You could have talked to me. Before now, I mean, " Will said.

"I couldn't. And anyway, I didn't think you'd want to hear about, you know, who I was seeing."

"Well, worry less about me next time and tell me what's going on." Will touched Danica on the shoulder and squeezed. "Maybe we should get moving again."

Danica nodded. "Yeah, okay."

"Wait!" Will whispered. He pointed up the hill. The first thing she saw was Alex leaning against the truck of a tree. For just a moment, Danica thought Will could see him, too. But that wasn't it. Beyond Alex, someone was making their way towards them. Conn. Danica crouched lower. She was certain they'd been heard until he turned and headed in the opposite direction. He was looking for a way out, not them.

Danica knew, immediately and without doubt, what she had to do. She whispered just loud enough for Will to hear her. "After you cross the ditch, keep walking with the lake on your left until you get to a trail. That will lead you to the road."

"Great, so let's get going," Will said, confused.

"You're going without me," Danica said. When Will tried to protest, she raised a hand to quiet him. "Don't make me explain. Just go. I'll keep him from seeing you."

"He's leaving. If we wait a minute we can get out without him seeing."

Danica didn't take her eyes off of Alex's pale, slack face as she spoke. "I'm doing this. Wait here a minute and then go."

"Danny!"

She ignored him. Will would argue as long as she let him, but he wouldn't do anything to stop her. Danica limped in Conn's direction as quietly as she could on her unsteady legs. When she was no longer directly between him and Will, Danica let her leg give out. She didn't have to fake the cry of pain when her kneecap landed on the rocky ground. Conn turned, startled, expecting an attack. Then he saw Danica. He smiled and stalked toward her. There were faded streaks of blood on his shirt. Danica closed her eyes, more afraid that Will would do something stupid than she was of what Conn would do to her.

Conn knelt when he reached Danica. He looked injured, with a swelling bruise on the side of his head and blood caking his hair, but his face was still plastered with a grin. "I didn't expect to see you out here. How's the knee?"

The tears in her eyes answered well enough, so Danica said nothing and let him talk.

"That's what I thought. You should really keep your weight off of an injury like that. What are you doing walking around, anyway? There's an army of angry mermaids down there that would love to take care of you. Coming up here was just begging to get caught. Though I guess you aren't really the self-preservation type, are you?" Conn snapped his fingers and his smile widened, a desperate thing meant to convince her he was just as in control as ever. "Oh, by the way! I saw your girlfriend! She says hi."

"Where is she? Is she okay?"

"I'd worry more about yourself if I were you. And thank God I'm not, because just *looking* at you is depressing."

Danica let her eyes close again. Conn was smart, but there was one card she had to play. He knew he was stronger than her. He wanted to enjoy it. She slid her hand to her right, into a large, muddy puddle. She let the agony in her knee and her heart find its way into her words and said, "Please don't hurt me. I just want to go home. I'll do anything if you let me go."

"Oh, Danny, you sad little thing." Conn's smile twisted as he continued, "I guess I owe you one for breaking that damn pin. I mean, your timing *really* could have been better, but still. Let's say I let you go. What's in it for me?"

Danica focused. Not on convincing Conn. She'd already done that when she begged. She pressed her hand into the bottom of the puddle, let the water touch as much of her skin as possible, and pictured a ruined cabin surrounded by a wall. She pictured an old well. She pictured sunflowers. Danica said, "You're lost and they're coming for you. I know all the trails here. I can lead you out before they trap you."

Conn didn't need to think the offer through. He just stood, offered her his hand, and pulled Danica effortlessly to her feet. Alex waited on the branch of a tree ahead. *Just hold on a little longer, Alex*, she thought, and led Conn through the trees.

~

Samantha pulled Krista's car into the driveway and turned off the engine. The lights in the house were off and the garage door was closed. There was no way for Samantha to know if her mom had beaten her home without going inside to check. Samantha turned to Leslie, who lay across the back seat, sleeping. She'd passed out when they reached the car, exhausted from whatever Conn had done to her. Samantha hated leaving her alone, but it was safer in the car than the house. She touched the door handle. It was time to go.

She closed the car door behind her as quietly as she could and dashed up the cement steps to her front porch. With trembling hands, Samantha found the house key and slid it into the lock. She pressed an ear against the door, straining to hear sounds of a fight, or footsteps approaching. When she heard nothing, Samantha turned the key. The lock disengaged with a click and the door swung open on well-oiled hinges. Samantha stared into the dark living room in shock. There was nothing that hadn't been thrown to the floor, broken, or ripped to pieces. Samantha crept in, her feet crunching on the broken pieces of Mom's crystal lamps. Samantha imagined her father tearing the room apart, pulling bookshelves over, ripping paintings off the wall, flipping over furniture.

The house was quiet, but silence was no relief. There were too many things silence could mean. Samantha thought she'd seen the peak of her father's rage, but this was something else. His house was a temple to the perfection he expected of himself and his family. Everything measured against his impossible standards and put in its place. To have done this...

She searched the floor for a sign of the phone, the one that once sat on the flipped-over end table. She tiptoed across the debris, each step a horrifying crunch, following the phone cord across the room. It ended not in a phone but a cracked plastic plug. Useless.

It took a few moments to convince her body forward. The closest phone was in the kitchen. She took the clearest path to open doorway and peeked cautiously around the corner. Like the living room, the kitchen was a disaster. Not as bad, maybe, but only because most of it was nailed to the walls. Two of the cabinet doors had been ripped off their hinges, and most of the others were cracked and splintered. Dented pots and pans lay on the floor, cast aside after being used as weapons in her father's attack on the room. The only light came from the stainless steel refrigerator, the door to which had been left ajar. Samantha shut the door, slipped around it, and breathed a sigh of relief. The phone had survived.

Samantha lifted the receiver and stopped. What was her mom's number? She hadn't *dialed* it years, not since she got her first phone. Panic scrambled and shifted the digits she managed to remember. She paced across the kitchen, hoping that movement would settle her enough to clear her mind. She stepped in front of the window, the one that looked out onto the deck, and froze. She saw his eyes first. Her father, standing in the pouring rain, hunched over, his hair matted over his ears and forehead. Had he been watching her the whole time?

He didn't have to call her out to the deck. She'd go. It was always worse if she made him chase her. She lowered the phone to her side and dialed three numbers before dropping the receiver to the ground. Then she walked to the sliding glass door. Her father watched without moving as she took a single step out of the house and into the rain.

She saw reflections of the neighbor's porch lights shimmering off something in her backyard. Water. The creek had flooded, same as the lake. Samantha had called this down on all of them, and now there was no escape.

"Dad. What are you doing out here?" she asked. It was a stupid question, but all she could find in herself was the instinct to be a good, polite, concerned daughter. Even now.

He responded in a deep, loud voice. "Is what they're saying true? Are you some kind of queer?"

"Dad…"

"Answer me."

Samantha nodded. "Yes."

"This is her fault," her father said. Samantha knew what this was. It was her out. Blame her mother, say she knew about it and encouraged it, let her get the worst of what was coming. Her father repeated, "This is her fault."

She'd been offered the out before, and always took it. Always.

It took what little strength she had to form a reply. One torturous word at a time, she said, "It wasn't her fault. Mom didn't know."

"I'll deal with your mother! You're talking to me. How could you do this to us?"

"I'm sorry." His sudden fury shattered her control, reduced her to what she really was. A coward. She pleaded, unable to stop herself, "Please don't be angry. I'm so sorry."

"You couldn't keep your fucking mouth shut?" he shouted. "You had to go in front of your *school* and embarrass us?"

"Dad, I'm sorry." Samantha hated herself for apologizing. She said it again, though. And again.

"What do you think my partners are going to think about us when they find out my daughter's *girlfriend* is a murderer? When they hear your mom thinks she can *leave this family*. You ruined us. You ruined *me*."

"But—"

"Shut your mouth! You think sorry means anything after we lose the house? I bet everything for *you*, so I could leave *you* something. But you're just a stupid, selfish slut like your mother, aren't you? Now come out here and sit down."

Her father pointed at a chair, and Samantha saw black metal in his hand. Her heart stopped. She croaked out, "Dad, why do you have your gun?"

"Sit your ass down and wait for your mother. I'm not going to tell you again." He kept the gun up, but angled away. Not aimed at her. The threat implied, not explicit. Not yet.

Samantha knew, then, what was coming. He'd have never torn apart the house if he thought there would be a tomorrow. He loved it more than he ever loved her. His plan was set. They'd wait until Mom got home and her father would finish what he'd started with the house. No, what he'd started years ago, the first time he'd curled his hand into a fist and showed her what fear was. What he'd nearly done the last time the creek overflowed and he took that black, awful thing out of his safe. Maybe the call she'd made would be enough. Maybe the police would arrive before her mother, but Samantha saw the rage in her father's eyes and knew he'd never let them have his daughter. If Samantha sat down she was surrendering, finally and completely. Surrendering not just herself, but her mother.

The word Samantha had never been able to say became her one and only thought.

No.

Her father was too large, too strong to fight. Even without the gun. Samantha could never match his strength. Except.

Samantha wasn't strong. She was fast. Faster than anyone she knew. Faster than the push.

If she was fast enough to outrun the push, then maybe.

Maybe she was fast enough.

Samantha slid a foot back against the lip of the doorjamb. Not a starting block, but close. Her father had seen her brace for a sprint a thousand times, but in the rain and the dark he didn't realize what Samantha was doing until she'd already sprung. After all, what did he have to fear? How could someone he'd broken so long ago fight back now?

She took three hard steps forward, keeping her body low and centered. The gun in her father's hand shifted, the black barrel aligning just right. Samantha kept her eyes off of the weapon and on her father's chest. Looking into the void of that bore would take something from her. Samantha needed everything.

It all seemed to happen at once. A noise like thunder, a punch to her stomach harder than a thousand of his beatings, the shock of her arms on her father's muscular chest, the same weightless nausea she'd felt when she fell into the lake with Danica. *Into the water again*, she thought, and knew it was right that it should end like this. The world tilted. Her father was below her. His arms reached out for something, anything, to catch himself. She continued forward, past him, until all that was below was the endless dark sea, waiting to claim her at last.

~

They trudged ahead for at least twenty minutes with Conn grudgingly allowing Danica to lean against him. Though it still pained her to put weight on the knee, everything below it had gone numb. It scared her, but she never asked to slow down. It was time to be strong. They were almost to their destination. *Her* destination. Conn wasn't headed where he thought.

"Satisfy my curiosity. Are you and Sam back together, or what?" Conn asked, his forced grin returning.

"No," Danica replied.

"Huh. You seemed so close on the dock. You were holding hands and everything. You're really not a thing again?"

"She hit me." Danica couldn't afford to lie any more than she had to, and silence might make Conn angry.

Conn nodded. "Oh, that. Right. Following in her old man's footsteps, there, wasn't she?"

"What does that mean?"

"She didn't tell you?"

"Tell me *what*?" Danica asked, hating how easily he baited her.

"Cut her some slack. It's hard to admit your dad kicks the shit out of you. I should know."

Danica didn't have a response. Was he telling the truth? Why would he lie about *this*?

Conn went on, "The truth is, it's not the getting hit that breaks you. It's what it teaches you: *you're weak*. Doesn't matter how tough you are otherwise. You believe it because they don't give you a choice. And after a while, after you get hit enough by someone you can't hit back, you look for someone else to take it out on. And let's face it, Danny: you're an easy target."

"Was Lenka an easy target, too?"

Conn lost his smile. "We're not talking about Lenka."

"Then we're not talking about Sam."

Their path sloped gently upward. They were getting close. Danica had chosen this route carefully. They wouldn't have a clear a sight line to their destination until they were on top of it. She couldn't give Conn a chance to guess what she was doing. Surprise was all she had left.

"I wasn't really talking about Sam, anyway," Conn said. "This is about you. I've been through this game a lot, and I still can't figure it out. It's like you all *want* this to happen. I mean, yeah, Samantha treated you like shit, but all you had to do was tell her to screw off. But no, you keep suffering silently until you can't take it anymore, and then you want to blame us for it."

The only way to distract him was to keep him talking. So Danica talked. "You think you and Sam are the same, but you're not. I know what you did to Lenka. She didn't have the chance to leave you. Do you know what they did to her after you got married?"

Conn waved the question off. "At least I was honest with her. How'd you find out about Alex, again?"

"I know what she did to me," Danica said without a trace of anger. The image of Samantha hiding bruises the way Danica covered her scars was clear in her thoughts. "I never knew why, though. Thank you for telling me."

The rotting roof of an abandoned shack rose into sight, followed by its collapsing frame. They crested the hill, and the ground before them sloped gently down before flattening out into a wide field. In the center of the field was a stone well surrounded by four tall sunflowers. The broken ring of a stone wall blocked their path. Conn climbed over it, then helped Danica, annoyed that he had to lift her.

Danica kept talking, eyes on the well. Had the sisters heard her call? Were they still listening now that she was free? She prayed that their hatred of Conn would be enough reason to listen. "I guess I hurt myself worse than Sam ever could have. I did it all the time, even when I thought I was better. There's this voice, you know? It keeps telling you that the *end* is all you deserve. And you know it's lying, but you believe it anyway. I don't want to listen anymore. I know that's what Alex was trying to tell me to do, because no one deserves it."

Conn never had to fear Lenka's sisters before. He didn't understand them half as well as he thought. When the well suddenly overflowed, a thick sheet of water pouring over its sides and across the ground, he didn't seem concerned. He kept his eyes on Danica as it lapped around their feet. A bit of water was no threat. It never had been. He saw the sisters as they had been: patient, cautious, careful. Despite all his talk about being powerless and how it changed people, he still didn't understand. It was harder for them in shallow water. It hurt. But pain could be endured. Danica slipped her arm out from under Conn's and pushed him off of her. She staggered backwards, knee screaming at her for her to stop, refusing to fall until she was safely away. Pain could be endured.

The water rose over their ankles, and Conn finally saw it for what it was.

"They didn't deserve it, either," Danica said, and pointed to the center of the field.

Twelve women blocked his path. All pallid, all with hair and clothes that drifted and floated through the air. He backpedaled, but in the blink of an eye there were three more behind him.

"Weren't you just saying no one deserves to die?" Conn asked. He tried to sound in control, but Danica knew terror when she heard it. "Maybe you could tell them that."

"It doesn't matter what I think. I'm the one that lived. It's up to them to decide what you deserve." Danica limped backwards towards an opening in the wall.

"Where's Lenka?" Conn demanded, spinning, looking each of the women in the eyes. "She said she'd be here. Where is she? I want to see Lenka! I want to say goodbye!"

Danica had expected Lenka to be here as well. "Maybe you aren't as important to her as you thought."

Conn's expression was one of impotent fury, a look of someone who'd forgotten what it was to be helpless. He twisted away and tried to run through an open space between the women, but was tripped by something below the surface of the water. Danica moved as quickly as she could, hurrying out of sight of what was about to happen. She didn't want to watch. She couldn't.

Danica picked up a branch on her way down the hill and used it as a crutch. She tried not to hear the sounds that followed, but she was too close and moved too slowly. When it ended — and it took much less time than she feared — she felt the tears come. Conn was gone. It was over.

Danica didn't see Alex once on her long, painful walk out of the woods.

~

Lips pressed against Samantha's and held back the flood. She couldn't see or hear or move, only feel a mouth against her own. It was Danica's, she thought — when she could manage thought at all. Danica's lips and Danica's kiss, holding her there, keeping her whole until she slipped away for good. She didn't welcome the darkness. She didn't want to go away. But Danica was there, and it was more than she deserved, and she'd live in the kiss for as long as she was allowed.

Then her eyes opened, and she could see.

Samantha floated in a dark and murky cloud. Her eyes burned and her skin was cool. Sound was deep, muted, distant. This wasn't a cloud, but water. She was facedown in it. She was drowning. She was dying. Alone.

Except she wasn't drowning. Nor was she alone.

She hadn't imagined the kiss. A pale face floated before her, eyes locked on Samantha's. She'd seen those eyes before, on the shore of the lake where she'd faced Conn. Panic filled her and she thrashed, tried to escape the thing that wanted her dead, but movement sent flame through her chest. The woman's hands rose up through the water and held Samantha by her cheeks, kept Samantha's mouth pressed against hers.

Samantha felt air enter her lungs. Felt it through the woman's lips and hands. The woman pulled her face away, but kept her hands where they were.

She smiled. Her mouth moved and sound emerged

without air. Her voice echoed around Samantha, the words perfectly clear. She said, "I was afraid you were gone."

"You saved me?" Samantha asked tentatively, unsure at first if she could also speak.

"I kept the water from claiming you. I can't help more than that. I'm sorry."

The pain in her gut. The sound of thunder before she fell. Her father's gun.

"I'm dying," Samantha said.

"You're bleeding. You may die. All I can do is hold the water back. And wait with you." The woman's thumb stroked Samantha's chin as she spoke.

"What about *him*?"

The woman replied, "He is in no position to hurt you anymore."

Samantha knew by the coldness in her voice what she meant. There'd been no one in the water to keep him alive. Samantha asked, "Are you Lenka?"

The woman nodded.

"Why are you helping me?" Samantha asked.

"Because I wanted to."

"I thought you wanted to kill me." The wound in her side throbbed when she said *kill*, reminding her of the darkness that waited for her.

"I thought I did, too. I thought I had to. Just like you. None of us thought we had a choice. Danica gave that back to me. I chose to be here with you, so you might have that same chance."

"If I live," Samantha said. She'd thought the murkiness was dirt suspended in the water, but now she feared it was her. Her blood flowing out with every heartbeat.

"Yes, if you live."

A warbling whine built from somewhere far away.

She was fading. It wouldn't be long. While she still could, Samantha asked, "Is Alex...?"

"Yes," Lenka responded. "My sisters freed him."

"Where does he go? Where will I go?"

"There is a place beyond death. That much I can promise." Lenka smiled, and stroked Samantha's cheek again.

Something grabbed Samantha from behind and pulled. Hands, reaching into the water, grasping her ankles and arms. She came out of the water and gasped for air. Her first inhale left her as a pained groan. She was flipped onto something hard and flat. She saw flashes of red and blue in the distance and silhouetted forms hovering over her. A blinding point of light moved from eye to eye.

"She's breathing," a voice said.

Another voice broke in, asking, "Can you hear me? Can you tell me your name?"

"Samantha," she mumbled.

The questions kept coming. Have you been shot? Are you in pain? Can you move your feet and hands? Can you tell us what happened? She answered them mechanically, her mind elsewhere. On Alex. On Danica. On the woman in the water. She heard their feet splashing as they carried her, the water shallow enough to be waded through. It had seemed endlessly deep when Lenka was with her.

They placed her in the back of a vehicle. Her eyes focused. There was a man and a woman, the ones asking questions, and someone else. Her mother, face torn between relief and worry. Samantha opened her mouth to speak, but even that was too much. She let her eyes close. Felt a hand touch hers. Her thoughts softened and dissolved, the world faded into darkness, but she wasn't afraid. She wasn't afraid.

Chapter Twenty-Four

DANICA SAT ON the lid of the toilet, one hand holding a wad of crumpled up toilet paper, the other over her eyes, as if it could do anything to stop the tears. Her mother had walked up to the door, stopped, and padded away three times. When she did, Danica made herself cry louder. Silence might scare Mom enough for her to burst in. That was how things were going to be, at least for a while.

There'd been a brief, merciful window of hope in the days after the storm when it seemed she was free of it. That hope ended with Danica on the floor of her bathtub, sobbing uncontrollably under a shower that had gone cold a half hour before. Her mom had charged into the bathroom that time, and Danica's screams of protest had been enough cause for Mom to drag Danica out of the tub, dress her, and drive her to her new therapist. Danica hated to admit that her mother was right, but admitting things was the therapist's first demand.

Now, a week later, Danica could feel the cloud passing. Passing, but not yet gone. It came in waves, the peaks of which Danica rode out in the bathroom or on her bed. When the tide receded, the numb fatigue that followed was a relief. Bit by bit, though, she was finding herself amidst the wreckage. Bit by bit, she was becoming Danica again.

She blew her nose into the wadded toilet paper and washed her hands and face. She was careful not to look at herself in the mirror. Danica hated how she looked after crying. After a moment of collecting herself, she opened the door and returned to the kitchen and her now-cold breakfast. Her brothers had moved into the living room, leaving Danica alone with her mom. She didn't mind. Danica had learned not to resent the concerned looks and probing questions. She was tired of facing things alone.

"Anything you want to talk about?" Mom asked.

Danica shook her head.

"Do you need to call Becky?"

"No, I'm okay. I'm sure," Danica replied. Becky, the new therapist, had given Danica a card with her number and written **DON'T THINK, JUST CALL** in Sharpie on the back.

Mom sat in the chair across from Danica and said, "You know tomorrow's Monday, right?"

"I know what day it is, Mom."

"You're sure you're ready to go back?"

Sick of days trapped in the house, Danica had begged her mother to allow her to go back to school. It had taken a long talk with Becky to convince Mom that the best thing for Danica was to get back to a routine. Agreement came with a condition. Her mother gave her a phone — a cheap, tiny rectangle without even a brand printed on it — and explained that she expected regular texts to check in.

"I'm ready," Danica said. She itched her knee, digging fingers under the tight elastic straps of the brace they'd given her at the emergency room. There'd been a lot of x-rays, plus an MRI, all of which proved that Danica hadn't done any lasting damage to herself. A few weeks of healing was all she needed.

"Okay," said Mom, standing. "Do you want me to heat that up?"

"I'm not hungry." That got another look of concern from Mom. Danica's appetite was one of the many things on the watch list. Afraid Mom would press the issue, Danica quickly added, "I have to go soon."

Mom frowned and went back to the dishes, a silent protest over Danica's plans. The argument over returning to school was nothing compared to the fight to see Samantha. Mom would have nothing to do with it, even as Samantha spent days in the hospital recovering from the gunshot wound. Just the thought of the word — *gunshot* — made Danica ill. She'd pieced together part of what happened. What little she'd learned made Danica even more desperate to see her. She had no idea what Becky had said to Mom to get her to give in, but she was deeply grateful.

Jake ran in and jumped onto Danica's lap. His butt landed directly on her injured knee. "Jake!" she shouted. Danica grabbed him around the waist and moved him to her other leg.

"Your eyes are funny," he said.

"Your whole face is funny, munchkin." Danica poked him in the side. Jake giggled.

"Are you sick?"

Danica paused, then nodded. "A little."

Jake pulled himself up by Danica's shoulders and kissed her on the cheek. She smiled and kissed him back. He asked, "Want to watch TV?"

"I can't. I have something I have to do, okay?"

"What?"

Danica set Jake on the floor, then stood. "I have to send a letter before I go see a friend."

Jake nodded. He turned on his heels and ran to the

couch, threw himself onto the cushions, and went back to his cartoons. Pete and Steve were somewhere in the living room as well, out of sight. Ian had gone on a weekend fishing trip with friends, giving the family a rare opportunity to spread out through the home. Danica scraped the remains of her breakfast into the garbage, handed her mother the plate, and walked to her bedroom. She left the door open. After spending most of the morning in the bathroom, it was better not to give Mom a reason to worry.

The room was clean for the first time in months. Mom's doing, though Danica had helped when she was able. A tall glass vase (discovered, stuffed with cleaning supplies, under the sink) sat on the nightstand, holding a bouquet of tulips. A card rested against the vase, angled so Danica could read it from the bed.

Get well. Talk soon. Love, Megan.

Danica wondered if Megan's family knew she'd sent the flowers. If they'd tried to stop her. Maybe not. They had enough to worry about. Danica heard they'd hired a lawyer for Ferris. The police were desperate for answers. Three kids dead, all by drowning, and no one's story made sense. Of the students that attacked Danica at the lake, only Ferris and Logan had survived. If the police needed someone to blame, that's where they'd start.

The detectives got only a vague outline of what had happened from Danica. She'd gone to the lake to hide, Conn and the others found her and chased her, and her friends — including Samantha — helped her escape the flood. She blamed shock for the haziness of her memory, and the detectives didn't press for details. Samantha's speech at the school, and whatever she'd told the police, had been enough. Alex's death was ruled accidental, and the police's concern shifted to the deaths of Conn, Krista and Nick. Despite everything they'd done, their passing ate into Danica. Their faces, even Conn's, rose up through the blurred memory of dream every night.

Danica sat on her bed and opened her backpack. A relieved and apologetic Pastor Fresh returned it to her the day before with a message from the church that they hoped to see her back at youth group. She'd hugged him. Not just for the invitation to return, but for what he'd done for her. For believing her.

She found the yellow notebook paper in the backpack's front pocket, right where she left it. Alex's letter to his father. Though it should have dried, it still felt damp. As if it had been left out on a humid day. Danica wondered if it would ever fully dry.

She refolded the paper and set it on the nightstand next to another letter, one she'd written herself. Danica placed both letters, his and hers, into an envelope addressed to Alex's father and sealed it. Maybe it would help to know why his son had stood on a cliff and held back a girl who thought she wanted to die. She'd tried to explain how much it meant to her. Told him she could never do enough to be worth it. Promised him she'd still try.

Her phone buzzed. A text from Leslie. **good luck girl**, it said. Leslie knew where Danica was headed next. She was the only one who hadn't tried to convince her not to go. "She was awesome," Leslie had replied when Danica asked what happened at the lake.

Danica turned to the card on her nightstand, to the vase and the flowers it held. She felt the weight of the letter on her lap, heard the clamor of her mom washing dishes. She closed her eyes and told herself to remember. This moment, these things, these people. To hold onto them, to never forget (not again, not if she could help it) that she was never as alone as she feared.

~

"Mom, you're in the way!" Samantha craned her neck to the left to get a clear look at the television, but it was no use. She could slide to the other side of the bed, but even on the painkillers that much jostling *hurt*.

Her mom finished folding the last shirt in the laundry basket without responding. Finally she looked up, then over her shoulder, then back to Samantha.

"Sorry, honey," she said. "You ready for lunch?"

Eating was a trial, but Samantha was constantly hungry. She nodded, and Mom left to get food ready. It had been like this since they'd discharged Samantha from the hospital with orders to stay in bed for at least a week. Her mother checked in on Samantha every thirty minutes, brought food half the time, and asked if Samantha *wanted* food the other half. Samantha did her best not to complain. Mom was barely coping. Neither of them were. It was hard to feel safe here, in the house. In *his* house. Samantha still heard him in every slam of a door, every creak of the stairs, every footstep in the hall. Silence wasn't a relief, either. It was easier when there were distractions. Without the TV and food and Mom's nagging, the memories returned. Krista's pale, drowned face, and the black metal of her father's gun, and the hands holding her below the lake's surface.

Mom came through the door with the tray of food. She set it on the overbed table they'd bought, then reached behind Samantha to adjust her pillows. "I'm not sure how hungry you are. If you want another bowl of soup, just ask. I made pudding, too, so when you're done, have some of that."

"Stop it! I'm fine!" She shouldn't have shouted. Shouting was as bad as moving and eating. The pills didn't stop the pain so much as distance and dull it, as if she were feeling it through someone else's body. That wasn't the worst part, anyway. It was the unceasing itch of the sutures in her back. There was a large, ragged hole in her where the bullet passed through. Having failed to bleed her to death, it was trying to drive her insane.

Mom held up her hands in surrender and sat down in the chair beside the bed. She fidgeted with the buttons on her shirt for a moment before speaking. "The police were wondering if you were up to some more questions. I told them you're still recovering, so…"

"Which ones?" Samantha asked. Between the detectives investigating the deaths at the park and the officers who'd taken away her father's body, Samantha was very popular with the police.

"It's about your dad." Mom never met Samantha's eyes when she mentioned him. They still couldn't talk about him without shrinking away from each other.

"Okay. Sure. Yeah."

The doorbell rang. Samantha's mother shot up out of the chair and ran to answer it. If those were the cops she'd mentioned, Samantha was going to have a long talk with her about advance interrogation notice. She shifted herself up and brought a spoonful of soup to her mouth. Another round of questions didn't mean she had to let her lunch get cold.

Mom knocked on the wall beside the door when she returned. "Hey, there's a friend here to see you. I hope you're up to a visit."

Samantha sighed. Mom hadn't let anyone in to see her in days, and Samantha was really, truly not up for it. At least, she wasn't until the visitor stepped into the room with a nervous smile on her face.

"Danny?"

"I'll leave you girls alone. Eat your soup." With that, Mom was gone.

Danica walked into the room cautiously. She paused halfway to the bed. "Hey."

"Just come here already." Samantha put her arms out as Danica approached. The hug was the most welcome pain Samantha had felt in days.

"I'm sorry it took so long for me to come. I called, but…"

"Yeah, Mom's got me in lockdown. How'd you get her to let you in?"

"I sort of begged."

Samantha smiled, and Danica smiled back. She wanted to hold Danica's hand (had been imagining it since she first woke in the hospital) but fought back the urge. Danica was here as a friend, she told herself. That was all.

"How are you?" Danica's eyes drifted to Samantha's midsection.

"It hurts, but I'll be fine. The bullet went straight through. It didn't do any real damage, I guess, other than the bleeding."

Danica nodded. Her mouth moved a little, like she was trying to find the right words and failing. Finally, she said, "Sam, I didn't know. I wish I'd known."

"No one did." Samantha gave in and allowed her fingertips to settle on Danica's hand. She repeated, "No one did."

"Why didn't you tell me?"

Samantha moved her hand to Danica's thigh, near where she'd once felt raised, white scars. "You didn't tell me, either."

"Oh. You know about that?"

"From Megan."

Danica looked away. Chewed on her lip. They sat in silence. Samantha realized her hand was still on Danica's leg and pulled it away. The movement caught Danica's attention, shook her out of whatever thoughts she was lost in.

"I'm not doing it anymore," Danica said. "I still want to, sometimes. It's kind of hard right now. I can't sleep, and even when I do, my dreams are awful. I think about Alex all the time, you know?"

"Yeah. Me too."

"Sorry, I'm guilting all over you." Danica forced a smile.

"It's cool." Samantha took the moment to bring something up she couldn't admit to anyone else. "Did they tell you I fell off the deck? Jumped off, I guess."

Danica winced. "Yeah, it was on the news."

"The backyard was flooded. I don't know how long I was out, and I was facedown in water the whole time. I should have drowned."

"Then how…?"

"Lenka was there, Danny," Samantha said. "She kept me alive until the ambulance came."

"She did?"

Samantha nodded.

This time, Danica's smile wasn't forced. It was small, barely there, but real.

"What is it?"

Danica explained what had happened with Conn. How she'd led him to the house with the wall and the well and the sunflowers. Her voice quieted near the end, as she told Samantha about the women who'd surrounded Conn, about Lenka's absence, and about what followed.

"I thought she wanted to kill him. I thought that was all she wanted," Samantha said when Danica finished. Her memory of that night was hazy. Lenka had spoken to her, that much Samantha remembered. But she'd dreamed the conversation so many times since, with different words each time, that she was no longer sure what was real.

Danica said, "For a while, it was like I *was* Lenka. All of her memories and thoughts and everything were mixed up with mine, you know? I think it was the same for her. If I loved someone, she would have, too."

Danica stopped to give Samantha time to understand what she was saying.

Samantha caught herself fidgeting with her shirt, just like her mom had done. "They have me talking to this counselor. To see how I'm 'coping,' you know? She comes by, like, every day. She's all right. But there are all these questions I don't want to answer, and she just keeps asking them. Like if I'm afraid to trust people, or if it's hard for me to feel things. Love. Whatever."

"What did you say?"

"What do you think I said?"

Danica took one of Samantha's hands between both of hers.

"I wish you hated me," Samantha said.

"Stop it," Danica replied. "I'm sick of people treating me like a victim, okay? Alex is dead, and it's my fault, not yours. If I hate you, then you have to hate me back."

"That's not what I want."

Danica shook her head. "Me either."

"So," Samantha asked, "what do you want?"

"I want to give you another chance."

Samantha's heart pounded madly. She said, "I don't deserve that."

"I know."

"Then, why?"

Danica squeezed Samantha's hand between hers. "Because I want to be better than the things we did."

"Danny, you can't take me back." She didn't want to say that. She wanted to say yes, now, please. But she couldn't. Couldn't trust herself, couldn't let Danica trust her.

"Stop telling me what to do." Danica's voice was firm. Strong. Not asking, not begging, not desperate. If she was, Samantha could have pushed her away. Would've had to.

Instead, she nodded. "Okay."

"Do *you* want to try again?" Danica asked.

Samantha couldn't bring herself to say yes. She did manage to nod. "I'm just afraid... I don't want to be *him*, you know?"

Danica smiled. She let go of Samantha's hand, leaned over, and kissed Samantha on each cheek, then on the lips. "Then you aren't."

"What if you're wrong?"

"I'll dump your ass like I should have last time." Danica, still smiling, stood and walked to the door. She stopped there, turned, and said, "But the next time you kiss me, we'd better get caught."

Danica was gone before Samantha could reply. It was for the best. There was no way to hold the tears back any longer. Samantha wept for all the years she wouldn't allow herself to. All the years it hadn't been safe. She cried until the tears turned to laughter, until the laughter turned back to tears. She cried until she had nothing left and finally passed into sleep.

When she slept, she dreamed of Danica.

She dreamed of kissing her and not caring who saw.

She dreamed of deserving it.

Afterword

In 2013, I received an answer to a question I hadn't known how to ask. Though I'd struggled most of my life with confusing and inexplicable mood changes, I'd written it off as just the way emotions worked. Yeah, sure, I could go from a week of feeling unstoppable, straight into unmanageable anxiety and self-loathing even though nothing in my life had changed, but that was simply, I dunno, *not ideal*. It wasn't a crisis.

And then, one day, as things do, it became a

crisis.

It started with insomnia, days of not being able to fall asleep, to the point of crying helplessly in bed because I couldn't make myself do this very normal and expected thing. Then there was the day, during a mildly stressful conversation with my boss, when I broke down in tears and couldn't explain why.

Finally, driving home from my writers group on a winter evening, I was struck by a sadness so strong I had to pull over to let it pass. That was the one, that night in the car, that scared me. A few hours earlier I'd felt *totally fine*. I'd been happy, even. There was no reason — zero, zilch, nil — to crash like that. Before I could talk myself into brushing it under the rug with all the other bad days, I sent an email to a friend asking for a referral to her therapist.

There was a lot that happened after that, many steps toward understanding what was going on, but eventually (two therapists and a psychiatrist later) I got that answer that I mentioned. Though I suppose it actually came in the form of question: *What is cyclothymia, Alex?*

(The answer can be found under Mental Illness for $500: *This form of bipolar is marked by milder but more rapid swings between depression and hypomania.*)

I was thirty-four. I'd gone three decades before I learned that my struggle had a name, and that name wasn't *Eric Is Weak*. There was a reason some things were hard, and it was something I could learn to manage now that I knew what I was fighting.

Also, more importantly, I finally believed I wasn't alone.

~

That was my life while writing *Mimesis*. The story was never meant to be dive into the dark waters of depression, but as my brain was coming to understand itself, those questions found their way into my work. As Danica learned that she didn't deserve the pain her brain was inflicting, so was I. As Alex struggled to understand how he'd missed so many signs that his mother needed help, I was asking how I'd missed those same signs in myself. As Samantha fought to chase down her fears instead of running from them, I was also finding my feet. *Mimesis* isn't the story of what I was going through, but it reflected it, and in its own way, it held my hand and led me through the fog.

As every afterword on the planet notes, a novel is not the product of a single human on an island. It's built up and supported by the people who surround us. *Mimesis* is no exception, but in this case, my thanks go beyond help with the book itself. In fact, I owe so much to so many people, in so many ways, I'd end up listing everyone in my life.

I will simply say this: if you know me, and you're reading this, I owe you more gratitude and love than I can express. This book exists because you didn't give up on me. Because you were kind. Because you were fantastic.

Thank you.

Software engineer by day, writer by evening, Eric Sipple also makes a pretty killer pizza when they're in the mood. If you enjoyed this book, you should also check out their first novel, *Broken Magic*, and *The Deli Counter of Justice*, a superhero anthology they co-edited with Paul Smith and Arlo J. Wiley. You can find them on the digital plane at http://ericsipple.com.

www.ingramcontent.com/pod-product-compliance
Lightning Source LLC
Chambersburg PA
CBHW030321200626
46816CB00006BA/1877